THE DIONYSIAN PUBLIC LIBRARY PRESENTS
SPECTACULAR SPECTACULAR
AN ANTHOLOGY OF CIRCENSIAN HORROR
I0840357

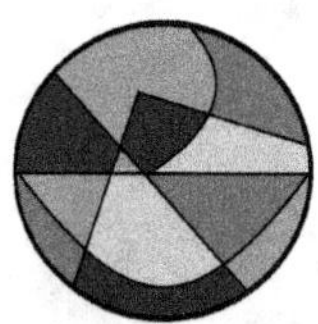

For Karrie Waarala, who dreams in ink, and for Rand Johnson, who knows about the gods and their grisly dances.

"That is your world!
That is a world indeed!"

—Goethe,
via Friedrich Nietzsche,
The Birth of Tragedy

TABLE OF CONTENTS

Preface:
Ring Around the Rosie

by v.f. thompson

So, you thought you'd like to go to the show, and here you are. We're thrilled you're joining us for tonight's presentation, the second in The Dionysian Public Library's annual series of themed Halloween horror anthologies, and the second book in our 2024 publishing season.

As signified by the name, DPL as an entity is constructed largely in the interest of bridging the gap between the oral tradition embodied by the performing arts and the written word as spat out upon the printed page. The little volume of tricks and treats you're holding in your hand is an exercise and experiment in the embodiment of that duality, a dirty little dance with the theatre of the mind. In selecting a theme for this year's collection, i considered several possibilities, but the cards were already on the table—i knew what i felt qualified to speak on and hold space for.

i feel, as many in the arts do, wildly *un*qualified for most of the positions i find myself in—but when you have thrown yourself into the air, have let go of the trapeze and are trusting that the momentum of the swing and the sheer chutzpah involved in the leap of faith will bring you back to solid ground, you really gotta find a way to flush that shit out. Self-deprecation has no place in the toolbox of the dedicated artist—self criticism, go all out, but flagellation? Save it for the judge. Don't kill the cop in your head, but keep a flower full of water at the ready for when he gets a bit too frisky with that billy club.

That's what i'm telling myself, anyway, as i look at the ground far below this little platform and ask myself—who the fuck do you think you are, little girl, to talk big about the big top?

Well, i have been a practicing semiprofessional clown for the better part of seven years, a card-carrying member of the World Clown Association for two, and a practicing idiot since i was switched with a fairy in the cradle. My background is in theatre and in burning out of creative arts programs at multiple academic institutions and in the scrappy world of d.i.y. publishing, and this little press and its little projects are the desperate juggling act that's come from all that jazz thrown into a wine barrel and left to rot. My academic background is a patchwork quilt of half-sampled disciplines and exploratory paths, my professional life a series of gigs ranging from hosting pride parades and fundraisers to playing the evil clown oil CEO in a protest theatre piece to commemorate the Kalamazoo River Oil spill.

All that's to say, i'm a spectator and spectacle all in one, like the rest of us, and for the last decade or so, i've been trying to report back what i see in the world in print and in various dabblings in event production. i am a camera, and life is a cabaret, and good googly moogly, it really is great to see you tonight. You turned off your phone and opened an honest-to-god book, unless you're reading this on your phone, in which case, hello from the past, we hope that in your technologically advanced future you are living long and prospering.

In preparation for curating this anthology, i spent over a year and a half doing ethnographic research into circus-related activities in the interest of better understanding my own craft and the cultural landscape it exists within. Though i've been slapping on the greasepaint and rouging my lips for the better part of a decade, i have no formal ties to the circus. i'm part of what circus anthropologist Paul Bouissac would call *the gentrification of clowning...* "It is a fact there now exists in the Western world a large population of semiprofessional and amateur clowns... But they are drastically limited in their antics by the rules of proper social behavior, which they can transgress only to some extent." (197)

Horror, meanwhile, possesses no such boundaries. It's probably worth mentioning that the title of this volume is a malapropism—"circensian" as an adjective specifically refers to the circus in ancient Rome, where the citizens would go watch sporting events. And that's what horror stories are, eh? Little shooting galleries of the mind—will the paper dolls survive the most dangerous game?

As i write this little precontextualization, i consider what exactly the fuck i am doing when i send this book to the printer. i have been scraping by on elbow grease and the grace of the good earth as i write and juggle and edit and try to worm my way through the miserable task of trying to start a publishing house-cum-traveling theatre troupe while the end of the world is on the telly. As i scribble this, i do so at the tail end of a summer where i have had to recontextualize my entire relationship to fiction as i reckon with the revelation that my favorite childhood author had quite a lot in common with his fictional monsters. As i receive these stories into my inbox, read through them, decide to print them, who am i being? What am i doing with the power in my hands?

Fiction is a knife, and a helluva sharp one. Odds are, if you're reading a collection of circus horror stories, you're looking to get gutted to some capacity—or at least the air let out of your lungs once or twice. i hope you find something in this collection that elicits that little gasp. But i hope you also take a moment to breathe—take a moment to laugh. Take a moment to remember it's all just a show. Educator Christopher Bayes writes in *Discovering the Clown* "... Slapstick is one off-balance disaster after another. 'Comedy is dangerous'... 'It's more funny when it hurts." (12)

Here's the funny thing—i'm not a scary clown. Or, i don't *want* to be a scary clown. To some regard, my interest in editing this collection is an interest in reconciling that. Bouissac goes on in his discourse on my sort of tomfoolery as a crass democratization of the circus tradition: "Party clowns... lend an air of exceptionality and freedom to family and social celebrations because they evoke the festive atmosphere of the circus... We cannot forget, however, that some individuals have a kind of psychological allergy to clowns, whose persona and behavior they resent and fear." (197) i'm a horror writer, and i'm a clown, and as much as i want those things to be entirely separate, when i show up to a mic to do a set or am hanging out at a house show in my facepaint, i have to face the unfortunate reality: as much as i want people to look at me and see the makeup as something that makes me approachable, appreciable, for some people i'm never going to be Loonette on her *Big Comfy Couch*, but Tim Curry in his whiteface popping up from a shower drain to scare the hell out of Eddie Kaspbrak. Some people see all clowns as haunt clowns—so i guess, at some point, i became interested in that phenomenon, and i guess, at some point, i decided i was going to process those complicated feelings by putting together this book.

The other funny thing is, at first, i only planned on including one clown story: i was more interested in other takes on the circus theme. Clowns felt played out and obvious—but as the stories tumbled in, i realized i had been hopelessly naive to resist the clown car. The more you try to smack us down with a mallet, the more we pop up somewhere else. We *are* played out and obvious, and editing this collection became an odd sort of Jungian house of mirrors for me. That the subject would inevitably end up inviting a litany of painted fools worth admitting to the show should have been evident. To have thought otherwise was an exercise in self-denial. When i chose my discipline, i could have been a magician, or a hula-hooper, but no, i settled for the basest of vanity acts, the pompous bumpkin donning the lead-laden white makeup of the preening aristocrat. We're vermin, and it turns out we're irresistible. So, send the clowns on in, but fear not—this book is far more than a Festival of Fools.

One of the bits of research i conducted in this book's production was attending two circuses, the Paranormal Cirque August, 2023 on tour from Italy in a mall parking lot in Kalamazoo and the Garden Bros Nuclear Circus on tour from Canada in a mall parking lot in Lansing. The latter was a traditional circus show, charming in its archaic straight-faced presentation of its acts. The former, though, was a horrorshow—demons leaping through the air on spinning wheels, an aerial silk dance with a chainsaw wielding maniac, fire-dancing succubae, and a wonderful comic interlude with dancing nuns.

Each show had a framing narrative, and each framing narrative shared the same basic musculature: both followed a recurring clown character who inhabits the loose path of a story between the acts, connecting them as destinations along a Fool's journey. One traveled country to country, one tried to collect three souls to save his own, both interacting with the audience along the way. While each show presented incredible feats, it was undeniable that the dark carnival presented by Cirque Italia was unlike any live experience i have ever witnessed. i saw a nightmare ballet, the human form pushed to its limits—the whole time, as the extreme athletics on display left us on the edge of our seats, i saw artists who bore none of the scars of forced happiness that the traditional show leaked between the seams. By scrubbing away the false joy, by examining the brutality of the body in the potential for its destruction, the primal circus was evoked.

The hope is to here do something similar, taking advantage of the extra dimension of plasticity allowed by the mind's eye as opposed to her naked cousin. In putting out the call for submissions on the theme, i was inviting in people's dreams and associations with the term "circus", hoping to see what stripping away the artifice of delight to reveal the darkness beneath would inspire in the auditionees. It was a study in combining my disciplines in a way i had resisted up until this point, an examination in questioning and querying the collective consciousness as to what it thinks of when it thinks of the circles of the circus. It is an anthropological project insofar as it is a catalog of what some people imagined about circuses and about violence at a point in history where less and less seems funny at all. These fine folks answered my question "Tell me about what you're afraid of," and they did it with a depth and breadth of death-defying bravery that i am tickled pink to present to you tonight as ringmaster. The submissions we received truly ran the gamut in interpreting the theme, anatomizing the various limbs that spiral off from the root concept in a squamous ice cream swirl with a bloody strawberry topping.

The violence of the ring goes deeper than slapstick—that's where the horror kicks in. Clowns absorb most of the blows, but the big top is as brutal as the open-air predecessors where splintered chariots tore riders to shreds. In print, we had the freedom to explore that association in its extremity. The malapropism was not misplaced at all, but a mask. The concentric nature of the project came full circle when i encountered a story about a Saturnalia celebration and the grave terror it engenders when the boundaries of performance are tested and the diegesis breaks free. Whatever lingering misgivings about borrowing a word no one was using but the classicists turned into something sweet when i realized that it was all knitted together like candyfloss. In his investigative text *Bad Clowns*, journalist Benjamin Radford quotes Enid Welsford "... In her classic study, *The Fool: His Social and Literary History*... '[in] ancient Greece... we discover him... parodying the wanton orgies of Dionysus.'" (5) What is the dismemberment of Pentheus but a slapstick clown show? Blood and wine are never so very far apart, and here we engage in the reversal of power embodied by misrule: as phantasy writers, we are juggling knives. When we throw them, we must throw them wisely, and with wonder, and with care. i feel confident in saying the fine cast of tonight's show has done nothing less in the work herein. As you catch them, audience, i pray you catch them with your heart. Feel the fear *and* the delight. It's what we're here for. It reminds us that we're what paper dolls, even the ones who inspire us the most, are not—alive. As Stephen King, that rat bastard who has damned me and my ilk to a lifetime of associations with eating children, reminds us: "Life isn't a support system for art. It's the other way around."

i may blush a little under the greasepaint, never feeling quite comfortable under the spotlight as i see the fight-or-flight that always shows up in some spectators' eyes, but as i stand here center-stage tonight, i am proud to introduce *Spectacular, Spectacular: An Anthology of Circensian Horror*, a bloody nightmare of shock and awe. Find a little joy here, or a little fear, or a little death, or a little cheer.

Thank you for playing along.

v.f. thompson
dpl librarian
10/08/24

BIBLIOGRAPHY

- *The Semiotics of Clowns and Clowning: Rituals of Transgression and the Theory of Laughter*. Paul Boussaic. Bloomsbury. 2015.
- *Discovering the Clown: The Funny Book of Good Acting*. Christopher Bayes. Theatre Communications Group. 2019.
- *Bad Clowns*. Benjamin Radford. University of New Mexico Press. 2016
- *On Writing: A Memoir of the Craft*. Stephen King. Simon & Schuster. 2000.

TICKETS, PLEASE

'*The warning is an invitation*'.

It's the only text on the flier, in block print below below the black-and-white image of a sprawling tent. Not even a name or an address, though the latter would have been superfluous: everyone has by now seen the canvas spires out on the edge of town, arriving in the night and hidden throughout the morning by thick fog.

"I guess it's some sort of festival," says your friend, taking back the flier and shrugging. "I found this on a telephone pole. I don't really know. I think it's a juggalo thing, maybe. Wanna check it out?"

So here you are, checking it out, in line with a jumble of other curious gawkers and thrillseekers looking for something novel to do with their Devil's Night. No one seems to know where the wrought-iron fences and the tents beyond them had come from, but this only adds to the buzz—surely someone organized this thing, as you can see a few entertainment journalists with orange press passes around their necks smoking by the parking lot.

"By the parking lot"; ain't that a laugh? Prior to the pandemic, the tarmac where the structures are set up had been a Sears across from a strip mall, and then that had been gutted and, during lockdown, converted into a drive-up testing center. Two years after that it had been knocked down entirely, and now it's all parking lot, and now you're almost at the gate, and now you're handing over your money to the ticket teller, whose painted-doll makeup includes a spiderweb crack that compliments her white face and painted lips. The chemical-tinged city air is ruptured by the aroma of hot oil, bubbling dough dusted with hot cinnamon sugar and crisp turkey flesh clinging to jumbo size bones.

"The event is free-roaming and all-inclusive," the doll says, blinking through colored contacts as she hands back your stub. "As long as you have your ticket, nothing inside can harm you, and anything you wish to partake of is

yours." Pocketing the paper, you rejoin your friend as the teller calls "Next!", moving with the rest of the line through the black velvet curtains that cover the gate.

It is clear from one look at the courtyard beyond that this production, whatever it is, is not, in fact, a juggalo thing. Though you spot a few of them in the crowd, mingling between the punks and the goths and the normies, many of whom are hard to tell apart through the cacophony of costumes, the presentation is clearly something far slicker and shinier. "Wizard," breathes your friend as you both look around. There are a litany of smaller tents, arranged here and there at odd angles that produce looming shadows, a Dr. Caligari *presentation of black and white punctuated by explosions of color. Food vendors and face-painters line the courtyard, and a few buskers work the open air, a fire eater and a contortionist moving through a metal hoop, each attracting their own circle of spectators.*

You flash your ticket at a lion-faced boy at a keg, who pours you a stream of sweet, cold lemonade into a swirly paper cup. He smiles silently as he hands you your drink, and as you turn around to look for your friend, you see that they have already scampered off into the village of curiosities, leaving you to your own devices. Putting your lips to the straw, you watch the half-naked showman spit an arc of lighter fluid into the air and ignite it before wandering off down one of the spiraling paths.

There's a big top at the center, spiraling up above everything else, but for some reason you find yourself drawn along the alleys, towards the nooks and crannies; at one point you slip through an opening between two tents so narrow that you're at first not sure if you're really supposed to go this way until you open into a wide midway lined with people playing carnival games, ring toss and water gun races and balloon darts. Somewhere else off in the distance you can hear the telltale clickity-clack and screams of rides, and you're sure that's where your pal has wandered to.

As you pass by their doorways, you see a sign above each one: "FORTUNES & FUTURES", *reads one.* "PICKLED ODDITIES & MEDICAL ABERRATIONS" *reads another.* "THE CAROUSEL OF DREAMS", *promises a third. You pass by canvas apertures offering magicians and acrobats, hypnotists and tattooed ladies. Several of them almost draw you inside, but you carry on, not knowing what you're looking for until you've found it.*

"HOUSE OF MIRRORS", the banner declares, and you push inside.

Where you expected a hallway lined with reflective glass, you instead find yourself surrounded by more of the black velvet, dotted with diamond stars as you shoulder through what feels like several layers of curtain before emerging into a circular chamber lit by racks of standing candles. Instead of a maze, you see a spiral of standing mirrors holding vigil around the room, and reflected at their center, a slender figure in top hat and tails, seated at a table set upon the sawdust floor. Above them, a bulb-studded sign flickers to life: "LYSISTRATA WOODROSE", it proclaims, and below that: "STORYTELLER". Xe lifts the brim as you approach, revealing a pair of sharp, shining eyes. "Good evening, seeker," xe says in a voice like dark caramel. "Join us." As xe gestures to a single stool across from xem, you feel a tickle at your ankles and look down to see a hairless cat nuzzling against your feet.

"Feel free to give him a scratch," xe says. "He loves the spotlight."

As you take your seat at the table, there seems to be nothing between you but blank cloth covering the wood, and you wonder what this odd exhibit has in store.

"You came seeking reflections," says the host with a flourish, gesturing to the mirrors around the room. "Around these grounds, you'll find a feast for the material senses. Here, you'll find only food for thought. You are here because you seek to indulge your mind's eye, and so: Eighteen glasses, eighteen dreamscapes waiting to be exhumed. Until you have tasted each, there is no escape." Xe smiles. "Unless, of course, you'd prefer to back up and back out, pursue some more physical pleasure. I promise I won't be offended."

You shake your head, and xe grins, xer black lips revealing ivory white teeth. "Your ticket then," xe asks, and you pull it from your pocket and show it off.

With a nod and a wink, the host throws back xer head with an intoxicating toss of xer hair as xe plucks off xer hat, reaching inside and plucking out a ragged clown doll, setting it on the table between you. It smiles at you through button eyes, red nose trailing a bit of stuffing like snot, and the host stands, circling the table as the cat leaps up on top of it. "With that, our dark ride into the imagination begins," xe says, moving behind you, whispering into your ear, hands on your shoulders. "Our first story, then, comes in the form of a question… a nightmarish query, a horrible inquiry… As we begin our journey, we ask…"

I. What's In a Clown Name?

performed by Sam Logan

I earn my clown name tonight. It has been a long journey, called to serve God through clowning after a motorcycle accident. Pain led to cruelty and alcohol (a family tradition), then to an Alcoholics Anonymous offshoot that taught a dittology of the Good Book. Our troupe bears witness to the twelve steps, a zealous community to the Old ways. It took several months to reach step nine; make amends to people I've harmed. I managed to track down the people I hurt most, wrote them letters to express my regret. Stark white envelopes marked with black pen, licked to seal my absolution from past deeds. I managed through the remaining steps, the work never complete but I have found my purpose, my brethren, my rescue.

The crumbling brick building that contains my studio apartment rests at the corner of a busy intersection, the occasional honking car horn and constant glow from stoplights and streetlamps penetrating slits of drawn shades. I am fortunate to live only a few blocks from the church where our clan gathers to practice our performances and hold meetings.

Sparsely furnished, a deadened mattress squatted on the scratched hardwood floor in the corner, lumpish and covered with congealed stains of bodily fluids from its many owners.

"It's morning again in America…" crackles from tinny speakers of a shortwave radio that rests on the primrose Formica countertop in the kitchen. Perched atop a tall barstool, I consume the same breakfast I've had every day for the past several years—a grapefruit with white sugar sprinkled on top. On this overcast, humid morning in Alabama, the sour-sweet flavor elicits an event laid dormant for years, a psychological defense despite the memory's significance.

My childhood was less than pleasant, an amalgam of unpredictable calm and chaos. This pattern culminated in a fit of fury and destruction. My mom in the kitchen making a fruit salad, the citrus aroma bleeding into the living room. An invisible but palpable layer of cigarette smoke entombed the space, perpetual ash swirled about from the constant motion of the ceiling fan. The paper-thin, dusty beige carpet underneath me as I lay at the foot of the television, hands interlocked behind my head. *The Wizard of Oz* plays and Judy Garland's dreamy voice is on the last note of "Over the Rainbow" as gravel crunches beneath my father's cobalt blue pickup truck. He tears the screen door off its hinges, like a wing plucked off a butterfly. He is sweating, slurring words as he yells at my mom for some perceived transgression from the morning. She's used to fending off attacks, but something is different about tonight. I hunker down, small enough to make myself nearly invisible behind the brown leather armchair. Insults hurled, plates and furniture thrown, then a brief silence. My father spent the next several minutes spewing, spitting, and sputtering into the porcelain toilet emptying all stomach contents. The foul stink invades the whole house. He calmly splashes water on his face, gaining composure and begs my mom for forgiveness. It is clear he has crossed a red line as she does not budge in her defiance. Furious again, he wrecks what little dinnerware remained and storms out. My mom follows and throws a rolled-up newspaper at his truck as it peels out. The flash of red from tail lights visible in between the broken blind slats of the living room window. Glancing at the television, Dorothy opens the door and enters the technicolor land of Oz, wonder flashing across her face as she realizes nothing will ever be the same.

A crack of thunder from the impending storm shakes me from the reverie. My dry, calloused hand riddled with hangnails wipes away salty tears.

My grandmother's cherry oak desk with vanity mirror is where I spend most of my time, perfecting the craft of toggling between overexaggerated and subtle facial expressions. Despite the three generations of use, the desk still emits a thin scent of arboreous sweetness from its worn surface. An experimental lab of sorts, half-empty and dried-up makeup cases of white foundation and vibrant colors strewn about. Black, aged moleskin notebooks filled front to back with notes on skits to share God's message, the scratching of pencil to paper often bloating the stale air. Clowning is hard work. It takes a certain kind of creative mind to write and perform a sermon with passion, humor, and intensity, evoking emotion from the congregation. I am almost always out of scarlet red lipstick, my favorite shade that layers on thick and smooth, filling every pore with color. After taking a bitter-tart sip from a rocks glass filled with ice, soda water, and lime juice, I glance at the ticking owl clock as it moves its eyes back and forth above the copper brown stove covered in weeks-old pizza boxes. It is time to get ready.

Gray, empty eyes stare into the mirror, my face plastered with a representation of my inner self. A classic bright white foundation. Midnight black star-shaped eyes, royal blue arched eyebrows, a ghoulish green nose, rose-red cheeks, and a naked mouth with three-day old stubble breaking through like early Spring flowers on a grave site. A painted mask that reveals and hides, ebbs and flows between who I am in this moment and who I will become. At last, I engulf my bald head with a curly, traffic cone orange wig. Elastic stretching, the wig's edges scrape along my scalp until it finds its perfect fit. Taking a slow deep breath, I sheath my cleaver under my ruffled rainbow blouse and leave for the church where it all began. One more sacrifice to collect and fulfill my troth, redemption gained. Make a name.

HA
HA HA
HA
HA
HA
WHEEE!
HA
HA HA HA
H H H

The last three clowns-in-training failed to earn their name, disappearing from our community without a trace except their props left behind in a haste to flee. A dark haze of shame in their wake, like a radiant slug trail on dry pavement. My own guilt looms from before I got clean and joined the ensemble. I put a guy in the hospital for some perceived slight at the bar, knuckles ripped to stringy shreds from his yellow, pointed teeth. A brief stint in jail had no effect. The traditional twelve steps bore no fruit. Only the unique doctrine of sacrifice and chance fueled my ambition to serve and follow the yellow-brick road. The final sacrifice is the hardest to collect, an element of chance involved. There must be a first timer at the AA meeting, not a willing martyr like the others. The twelfth sacrifice must be taken with force and without hesitation, a commitment to seize someone else's flesh to pay for your past wrongs. Many turn back at the precipice, unable to cross the Rubicon. I will succeed where others have faltered.

Our troupe runs AA meetings in the basement of the oldest Methodist church in the city. It is a mostly closed community. We can only have twelve named clown elders to guide our work, a nod to the disciples and the steps that enlighten our way. I will be the final elder, fulfilling the prophecy that has taken years to achieve. Beyond the elders, our flock includes a dedicated handful of devotees who have found their own solace in our message, serve as voluntary sacrifices, and invite new members. My surmounting depends on a newcomer showing up tonight. I must not fail.

The walk to the church takes several minutes, it should only take a few. A staggering gait, a hitch in my step because of a lopped off big toe, my own sacrifice as a first timer. I can mostly stay under the shadows of moderate-sized buildings and alleyways. I am not trying to stay hidden, per se, but the cops have been called twice before, a clown walking by unsettling at least one neighbor. I turn down the last alleyway before reaching my destination. Dimly lit, buildings on either side block most of the remaining daylight as sunset looms. An open dumpster steams with stench from wet trash, drenched from the day's earlier rain. A lingering humidity permeates the late summer evening, saturating my skin, drooping and blurring the edges of my decorated face.

I enter the church through a side door. Bright fluorescent lights pierce my eyes, a stark contrast to the pale pink dusk from outside. The hallway is lined with a large bulletin board filled with children's drawings from Sunday School. They must have read the story of Noah's Ark this past week. About thirty variations of the same coloring page forms a collage, a giant boat with zoo animals peeking out of windows, a rainbow across the sky. A kaleidoscope of colors swim past me as I reach the stairs that lead to the basement.

Pushing through a set of double doors, I emerge into the basement. The last rays of sunlight filter through frosted glass of the few small windows that rest near the ceiling. Elders in full regalia and attendees mill about, mostly huddled around a folding table where refreshments are laid out. Coffee offering a warm and cozy aroma in stark contrast to the planned ritual. I am a bit early, anxious for the potential of my performance tonight. Scanning the small crowd further, I do not see a newcomer. I immediately break out into a slick sweat, droplets running down the back of my neck. Deodorant no longer masking my natural, tangy body odor of vomit and cotton candy. I practice breathing exercises to regain control, remind myself there is still time.

A makeshift stage is set up in the back corner—a homemade black curtain stretching across the fifteen feet length of the stage. Drawn to a close, it hides our props trunk filled to the brim with objects for juggling, costume accessories, and a set of sunshine-yellow rubber chickens. Yours truly will give a solo performance tonight, accompanied by the wheel for an encore.

The Wheel of Sacrifice is our Star of Bethlehem, a carnival game of chance that guides our actions toward serving God. The wheel is never wrong, it dictates exactly what needs to be done. It is fastened to an easel, upright and ready to spin. Its rough, plywood surface painted in a pinwheel of bold primary colors, sectioned into twelve parts. *Left leg, left foot, right leg, right foot, toes, left arm, left hand, right arm, right hand, fingers, torso, head.* Where the wheel lands, a sacrifice must be collected.

Two minutes until show time. Tall candles in stout crystal glass holders line the perimeter of the basement, flickering as the light streaming in from the windows dwindles to nothingness. I peek out from behind the curtain, scanning the crowd as everyone files into metal folding chairs arranged in neat rows. Familiar faces stare back at me. Panic creeps up from the back of my skull, threatening to cocoon any clarity and conviction I had on the walk over. Finally, in the last row of chairs I notice an unknown face, my sacrificial lamb. I open the curtains wide in a theatrical move, a dramatic flair. A spotlight from overhead blinks on. It is my time to shine, earn my name.

Flawless. I captivated the audience with a performance infused with drama and humor, assailing their senses with almost every prop in the trunk. Commanded their attention with my projected voice, held their gaze with a flurry of juggling and pranks, all while teaching the story of a shepherd who loses a sheep and rejoices in its finding, a metaphor for saving lost souls. Once lost, now found. Once a wretch, now saved. Following a standing ovation, I ask if there are any newcomers to our meeting, but of course, I already know there is one. He meekly raises his hand. I invite him to the stage and after some convincing, he acquiesces.

I bring the wheel of sacrifice to center stage and with a sweeping gesture, it is revealed in all its glory. Confusion flashes across the newcomer's face, an audible huff escapes his thin lips. He is paralyzed with terror. With all my might, I spin the wheel in a swirl of colors as it ticks around the possibilities.

tick tick tick tick tick tick tick tick   tick   tick   tick   tick
    tick   tick   tick
   tick   fingers

In an instant, my brethren grab the newcomer's arms and throw him down. He is spread eagled on his stomach, hands splayed out on the stage, like a pair of starfish. Only his ragged breaths fill the dead air. I reach beneath my ruffled rainbow blouse without hesitation and unsheathe the cleaver, its handle-heft in my palm, gripped with white knuckles. Bursts of motion pump my hand up, then down, crashing through flesh and bone with precise, devastating blows. The cleaver hacks off each finger at the base of their stalk, each bone snapping in turn. Pinkish sinewy strands slink from the disconnected digits. Blood spills from each gaping wound, a tributary of deep red rivulets. The orchestra of noises repeated like an echo until the deed is complete, all ten collected. Lifting his chin slightly, I stare into his hollow eyes and whisper…*thank you.*

Shallow breaths come and go, panting from spent effort. Nostrils ballooning with the sharp metallic scent of blood spilt on the stage, slick with splatter. A glint of dim light reflects off the scarlet-spattered cleaver blade. My prey lies whimpering in a crumpled heap, all ten appendages from both hands cleaved clean at the joints and placed in the ceremonial urn. Ascension across the rainbow bridge between Earth and Heaven, redeemed for past sins. Relief ripples through my entire body, vibrating with jubilation. My remaining time in the physical realm will be spent sharing The Message through the art of clowning, shepherding others to salvation.

My name is *Fingers.*

— FIN —

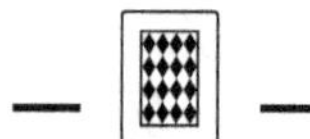

*... **A**nd you think that you feel xer nails brush your cheeks until you realize that xe has resumed xer spot at the head of the table across from you. Your eyes have been fixed on those of the stuffed doll as your host's voice wove its chrysalis around you, drawing you into the mind of a painted killer. You can still smell the fresh iron in the air mixed with stale coffee, and are startled out of your reverie when the mirror directly across from you suddenly shatters and falls to the floor in a flurry of shards.*

"The first seal is broken," xe says, taking the doll, setting it aside. "One tale told, one lock on your coffin popped. One step closer to reentering the world you know, and a long, long walk still ahead." They again doff their hat, and from it they draw out a single tarot card: The Tower, portrayed here as a cycloning panopticon where an ogling audience gazes back upon itself from the cage at the center while a column of lightning descends from above.

As you take in the artwork, a splitting whip crack of thunder rends the air and the sudden thrum of pouring rain begins drumming on the roof of the tent, even though the dusky sky had been clear and cloudless when you arrived. "We leave behind one temple to enter another perilous chapel, a canvas sanctuary offering itself as a safe space for the weird and the wild and folding in on itself when all is not what it appears," the host says. "In this strife we find the subject of our next tale, a story of deception and Depression called..."

II. The Lake Michigan Mermaid,
& Other Freaks of Nature

performed by Kathryn Healy

On the fifth night of June, 1934, a circle of wagons sat a few miles outside of Carlinville, Illinois. Rain battered their roofs, and darkness obscured the brightly colored murals painted on their sides. The only movement came from the beasts pacing in their cages, the only light was a warm glow coming from inside one of the wagons. The night was silent, until a woman shrieked.

"You're a cheater, Corrine!" yelled Anita, throwing her deck of playing cards at the woman sitting opposite her.

"I'm not a cheater, you just don't know how to play," Corrine said, dragging her winnings—three wooden drink tokens and a single pearl earring—across the table and into her lap.

"You were making up rules!"

"If you're not happy with my version, go play with Madame Ciuperca."

"She's no fun either… she always predicts all my moves."

Corrine Corcoran, the Ringmistress of the Dime-A-Dazzle Circus, gave her lovely opponent a fond smile. "Come on, Anita. You were doing much better that round. Let's go for one more—at least so I can have a matching set of those earrings."

Anita Avalon, the circus's trapeze artist, gave Corrine a glare as she collected her scattered cards. With a sigh, she unhooked her one remaining earring, set it on the table, and examined the cards fanned out before her. After a few brow-furrowed moments, she said, "Got any threes?"

Before Corrine could respond, three sharp knocks pounded against the wagon's door. The women frowned at each other, and Anita mouthed, "Who's that?" Corrine shrugged and bent down to pull a small switchblade out of her boot. Anyone associated with the circus would announce themselves, and any stranger in their right mind wouldn't be wandering around so late, especially not in this weather.

"Who's there?" Corrine called, standing up and approaching the door.

"My name's Ben," said a voice from the other side of the wall. "I'm looking for work."

Corrine rolled her eyes. Everyone and their dog was looking for work these days. "Out in a storm in the middle of the night?"

"I had to wait until my brother was asleep. I would have come tomorrow, but I wasn't sure how long you'd be in town." There was a heavy silence on the other side of the door, and then Ben's voice again. "Can I come in, please? It's really wet out here."

Corrine looked at Anita. "Maybe we can rob him," mouthed Anita.

Corrine scoffed. If he was looking for work, he probably didn't have any money on him. More likely, *he* was trying to rob *them*. "Are you armed?" Corrine asked the man outside.

"No," was the reply. "Are you?"

"Yes. Have you ever fought a carnie?"

"No."

"You don't want to. If I let you in, there better not be any funny business. The next wagon over has three strongmen who owe me life debts. Get me?"

"Yes, ma'am."

"Good boy," Corrine said, and threw the door open. The man who stood in the mud below her couldn't have been older than twenty. Though he wasn't small by any means, Corrine figured she could hold her own against him if it came down to it.

"My name's Ben, ma'am," he said, extending a hand.

She took it and helped him step up into the shelter of the wagon. "You mentioned that. I'm Corrine Corcoran. I run this show, and the woman behind me is one of my performers, Anita." Corrine could hear the jangle of Anita's bracelets as she gave Ben a wave. "You said you were looking for work?" Corrine asked. "Our only opening right now is in the Freakshow, and you don't strike me as particularly freakish."

Ben blinked. "Thank you. Look, I'm not asking to be a performer, I'm just offering to help out. I have electrician experience, but I'm happy do any random odd jobs." He was speaking quickly, desperation edging into his voice. "My brother's not well, and I can't afford medicine right now. My parents are dead, so it's up to me to provide for the both of us."

Corrine raised her chin at the man. "Your brother—what's wrong with him?"

Ben gave a nervous sort of laugh. "He was born wrong, I guess? He's fifteen years old but all he does is sit there and drool on himself and stare at you. He can't talk at all, and his legs are stuck together so he can't move, either. Recently he's been coughing a lot, so I'm trying to get some money together to take him to see a doctor."

"Sirenomelia," said Corrine.

"I'm sorry?"

"The birth defect that your brother has—it's called 'Sirenomelia.' Most cases result in stilllborns, so it's a wonder your brother's made it to fifteen." Ben just stared at Corrine, silently digesting this information. She smiled at him. "How much do you want for him?"

"What?" Ben asked. "Like, how much medicine?"

"No, silly! How much money? I'm offering to take your brother off your hands."

Ben took a step away from Corrine. "I'm not going to sell you my brother!"

"Why not?" Corrine asked. "I thought you needed money?"

"Yeah, to take my brother to a doctor! Selling him to you would defeat the purpose, not to mention the ethical dilemma."

"Ethics, schmethics," Anita offered, and Corrine nodded.

"I'm not selling you my brother," Ben said again.

"Fine," Corrine shrugged. "We don't have a lot of money ourselves right now, so we couldn't afford to pay you even if we did have you scoop elephant shit for a few hours. So, how about this instead: as a traveling circus we have a doctor on staff. We could take your brother into our employ without any money changing hands, and then he can be seen by our doctor free of charge. We use him to round out our Freakshow, and then we send you a cut of the profits every month. How's that?"

Ben was silent for a long time. "I don't know," he said. "It feels wrong."

"Well, Ben, the way I see it, this may be the only way you can get your brother medical attention without having to pay for it yourself. Plus, your brother will have a job—something he'd likely never be able to have otherwise—and you'll make a passive income off of him while you sort out your own employment. It's a win-win."

Anita piped up again from her perch at the card table. "It's real nice here, Ben. I'm sure your brother would be happy and feel right at home with us. And you can come visit him whenever we're in town!"

Corrine gave the young man a bright smile, which he eventually returned. He once again held out a hand to her, and she pumped it heartily. "It's a deal," Ben said. "As long as you promise to treat him well, and to let me know if anything goes sideways."

"Of course, of course," Corrine said, patting Ben on the arm as she ushered him back towards the door. "Go fetch your brother while we get a contract written up, and then Anita and I will get him all settled in."

Ben tipped his soggy hat to the ladies as he exited the wagon, and Corrine latched the door behind him. She turned to Anita, her grin triumphant.

"Corrine Corcoran, you are a gifted businesswoman," Anita said, turning in her chair so that her knees faced the other woman.

"Why, thank you, darling," Corrine said as she approached Anita and dropped into her lap. She placed a gentle hand on the back of Anita's neck and pulled her into a kiss, wrapping her other arm around the woman's waist. She felt Anita's fingernails drag loosely along her spine, sending a shiver down the length of her body.

Corrine cocked her head to the side and planted a kiss right underneath Anita's jaw, planning to travel downwards, but Anita put up a hand to stop her.

"There's just one thing: we don't have a doctor on staff," Anita said.

"I know," said Corrine. She wasn't in the mood to talk right now.

"So what are you going to do about the sick kid?"

"I dunno, give him to Anderson to look after? How different can being a doctor be from being a cook? They both use big knives."

Anita laughed and Corrine resumed her southern migration. She nipped at Anita's skin, and she gasped, clenching some of Corrine's hair in her fist. "Close the window," Corrine ordered. "Who knows how long it'll be before Ben gets back."

On the tenth evening of June, 1934, a large crowd had gathered in Chicago's Grant Park, outside the gates of a traveling circus that had appeared at some point during the early morning. Beyond the gates sat an array of tents, wagons, animal pens and food stalls. The air smelled of candy and popcorn and gunpowder, and children and parents alike waited impatiently for the opening of the Dime-A-Dazzle Circus. According to the flyers, the newest member of the carnival's Freakshow—The Lake Michigan Mermaid—was to be revealed that evening as part of the trapeze act. At only ten cents admission, it had drawn quite a crowd.

Inside the gates, Corrine was in her wagon putting the final touches on her Ringmistress uniform. She had been working on a few more acts over the off-season that required wardrobe adjustments, such as boots that could slip into stilts, and rubber gloves for pulling outlandish objects out of the lion's mouth. The gloves matched a set of rubber undergarments fashioned for use during a particularly daring trick involving a decommissioned electric chair, but only Anita got to see that bit of her wardrobe. Just as she was wrestling on the gloves, there was a light knock at the door and Anita let herself into the room.

"Hey, doll," said Corrine with a smile. "Nervous?"

"Me? No how." Anita said, giving Corrine a peck on the cheek. "Why, do I look nervous?"

"You look beautiful," Corrine said. She spat into her cake of mascara and began mixing it with her brush, giving Anita a long once-over. The tall blonde woman was sporting a low-cut powder blue leotard with pink tights, little silver slippers, and dainty white butterfly wings. A gauzy parasol shed glitter all over the wagon's floor. "How's your new act coming along? The one with the sea of fire, or whatever."

Anita shrugged. "It's not quite ready yet. We're having trouble figuring out the water to gasoline ratio."

"Well, no rush. I'm sure it'll be wonderful," said Corrine. "How's the Mermaid? Does he seem ready to go on the trapeze with you tonight?"

"He seems okay. Same as usual. He's still coughing a little bit, but Anderson gave him another lozenge, so hopefully he'll be fine."

"Creepy little thing, isn't he?" Corrine asked, shuddering slightly and cursing as she messed up her lipstick.

"I think it's sad," said Anita. "He's a sweet kid. The clowns have gotten him to smile a few times, and he likes listening to the calliope. He also seems to get a kick out of watching me practice."

"Well, he better not get any funny ideas about you. I don't like to share," Corrine said, and she shot a smile at Anita, expecting to see it returned. It was not. Anita was staring at the floor, her mouth a hard line.

"Do you think he's conscious in there?" she asked suddenly. "Like, do you suppose he can think like the rest of us, he's just trapped in that body?"

"I don't want to think about it," said Corrine. "A freak is a freak is a freak."

Anita was silent before she spoke again, very quietly. "Lots of people would consider you and I to be freaks."

Corrine met Anita's gaze in the mirror. "Let them think that. If anything, doesn't that make it all the more poetic? Freaks looking after freaks?"

Anita frowned. "I guess."

Corrine pulled her pocket watch out of her waistcoat and flipped it open. A quarter to eight. She would have to open the gates soon. She turned to Anita. "I'll see you after the show," she said, giving her a tight hug. "Break a leg, love." With that, she hurried out of the wagon, leaving Anita standing alone, her butterfly wings drooping.

On the tenth night of June, 1934, Corrine and Anita stood on a deserted strip of Lake Michigan shoreline. Despite it being the height of summer, the wind whipping off the lake chilled Corrine to her core. Anita let out a shuddering breath and wrapped her arms tightly around herself, which prompted Corrine to take off her uniform jacket and drape it over Anita's shoulders. "You cold in that little outfit?" Corrine teased.

"I think I'm going into shock." Anita said.

Corrine frowned. "Probably. I'm just embarrassed, myself."

Anita glared at her companion. "You are so selfish."

"What? How am I selfish?"

"You couldn't spare ten bucks to get that kid to a doctor, and look what happened!"

"I didn't know it was that serious! Everyone kept telling me he seemed fine!"

"He was never fine to begin with!"

"Exactly! Nobody could have done anything for him. Besides, you're the one who dropped him from thirty feet in the air."

"I didn't realize he had died until after the stunt started! Maybe I shouldn't have screamed and dropped him, sure, but you can't expect me to just take a dead body on the trapeze with me like it's nothing. I'd like to see you nonchalantly toss a corpse around."

Corrine stared at Anita. "Oh, yeah? Watch." In one smooth movement, Corrine bent down and picked up a burlap-swaddled bundle at her feet, then launched it into the lake. It landed with a loud splash, and sunk beneath the waves. "How was that?"

The light from the moon caught the tear tracks traveling down Anita's cheeks as she gazed coldly at Corrine. "You are a monster," she said.

Corrine's pride was wounded, but she wouldn't let it show. "Maybe so," she said softly, arms crossed. "But you've been pretty damn complicit, Miss 'Ethics, Schmethics.'"

Anita blinked, and a few more tears slid down her pale face. "I didn't know…" she began to protest, but she cut herself off with a shake of her head. She fixed Corrine with another dead-eyed stare. "I'll travel with you back home to St Louis, but after that I'm out of the production. I don't ever want to hear from you again, either. We're through." With that, she turned and walked away down the shoreline, her little silver heels wobbling on the sand.

"Anita! You don't mean that, come on!" Corrine called, only to be met with Anita's perfectly manicured middle finger. Corrine bristled and turned back to the lake, watching the reflection of the moon ripple on the waves. Once she was sure that she was alone, she buried her face in her hands and screamed. She sank to the ground, her sobs sending violent tremors through her body. Every bone in her body ached to run after Anita, but her pride held her back. She'd rather die than give Anita the satisfaction of seeing her beg. For a moment, she considered falling headfirst into the water and allowing herself to join the Mermaid at the bottom of the lake. Her eyes drifted along the horizon, wondering how long it would take for someone to notice she was gone, and what Anita would say when she was questioned. Anita, who chose some crippled sideshow freak over her. Anita, who had called Corrine the monster when that malformed little creep had been doing nothing but drooling all over himself for the past five days.

Well, fine. If Anita wanted a monster, Corrine would give her one. Corrine Corcoran was not the type of woman to let someone else have the last laugh. She'd give Anita a humiliating sendoff worthy of the weak-minded traitor she was. Corrine pawed at her tears with her gloved hands and stood up. First, she would have to keep her word and send a telegram to Ben to let him know that his brother was dead. She should probably omit the details, but there had been so much press at the show tonight that the news would probably travel to him on its own. Maybe it would be better if he got it from the horse's mouth? In that case, she'd send Ben a descriptive telegram and a formal apology and a coupon to one free show, and that would hopefully be that. Corrine set her mouth in a determined line as she marched back towards the circle of tents in Grant Park. Swallowing her heartbreak, she let spite fill the void as she fixed her gaze forward, brushing past Anita's wagon as the light within clicked off.

On the fifteenth night of June, 1934, a circus had set up camp on the outskirts of Carlinville, Illinois. There were less people milling about the cluster of tents and wagons than there had been in Chicago—partially due to the population difference and the gathering storm clouds, but also because of the unsavory press that the circus had recently received. Many of the attendees were there due to morbid curiosity, some even driven by the grim hope of seeing a tragedy for themselves. The performers, however, didn't seem affected by their newfound reputation at all. In fact, Corrine was more manic than ever, her plan to humiliate Anita finally kicking into gear.

Corrine waved at the audience from atop her star-spangled pedestal, her grin plastered on as she scanned the audience for Ben's face. She didn't see him anywhere, which was a relief. "Ladies and gentlemen," Corrine called to the audience as a trio of strongmen moved the electric chair from her previous performance out of the ring. "If you would be so kind as to give me and my friends just a few more moments of your time, we have one final jaw-dropping performance for you."

Corrine motioned upwards as Anita stepped out onto one of the high-wire platforms, giving an elegant wave in every direction but Corrine's. "This is the lovely Anita Avalon, who usually performs a trapeze act, but tonight she has one new trick up her sleeve that she's excited to debut for you." For the first time in days, Anita looked at Corrine. Her face was stricken, and she gave a quick shake of her head. There was a low rumble that sounded like more thunder, but then a large tank of water and gasoline was rolled out into the center of the arena by the strongmen. They positioned it directly underneath Anita's high wire, and then one of them lit a match and tossed it into the water, where it caught on the floating layer of gasoline. In moments, the surface of the water was engulfed in flames.

"This is Anita's last performance with us, unfortunately," said Corrine with a pout. "So we wanted to make sure she went out gloriously. Isn't that right, Anita?"

"What are you doing?" Anita called down from her platform. "I told you the trick wasn't ready yet!"

Corrine smiled. "It's okay, Anita, you don't have to be scared!" Ignoring Anita's shouts of protest, Corrine turned back to the crowd. "Anita may need a bit of encouragement. Ladies and gentlemen, please join me in a round of applause for Anita Avalon and the Lake of Fire!"

Anita glared daggers at Corrine as the entire tent chanted her name, drowning out the thunderclaps from the storm outside. Corrine smiled up at her, waiting for her to surrender and climb back down the ladder in defeat. The seconds stretched on, but Anita just looked down at her from the platform. Corrine was about to call up to her again when Anita leapt forward. She sprang off the edge of the platform and flipped into the air, grabbing onto the high wire and holding herself up in a perfect handstand. Corrine gasped. Anita had never mentioned this part of the trick.

Quickly and confidently, Anita made her way across the high wire, her hands carrying her across the line as smoothly as a set of legs across solid ground. Once she reached the other platform, she turned around and went back the other way. Corrine respected a show-off. She gave Anita an approving nod, and Anita's eyes sparkled, the barest hint of a smile on her painted lips.

There was a clap of thunder outside the tent, and everything went dark. The only light in the big top came from the inferno in the water tank at the center of the ring. There were a few screams—likely from surprised audience members—and Corrine had to shout to regain control of the room. "There's nothing to worry about, everyone! All of our tents are equipped with lightning rods, so we are perfectly safe from any lightning strikes in here. Once the lights come back on, we'll continue the show."

As if on cue, the bulbs strung across the roof of the tent flickered back on, and Corrine had to blink a few times in the sudden brightness. There was another scream, and Corrine's eyes snapped to the high wire. Anita was hanging from the line, her legs flailing as she tried to get enough momentum to flip herself back on top, but she was having trouble. She was tired, Corrine realized. Anita had overexerted herself with the impromptu handstand and couldn't pull herself back up.

Corrine leapt from her pedestal and hurried towards the ladder, yelling at the strongmen to evacuate everyone into another tent. She called to Anita to hold on, and scrambled up towards the platform as quickly as she could. "Corrine!" shouted a man's voice from below. She looked down and nearly lost her grip on the ladder. Ben stood below her, feet planted as the panicked audience swarmed around him, rushing to escape the tent. His hands were clasped behind his back, and he was dripping with rainwater and caked in mud. "Thanks for the free admission," he called. "It really helped to soften the blow." The man lunged towards the ladder and Corrine gave a little shriek as she scrambled upwards towards the platform, the young man close at her heels.

Another crack of thunder shook the ground, and Corrine had to cling to the ladder so she wouldn't lose her footing. Just as she was pulling herself onto the platform, she felt a hand grasp her ankle. She yelped, but Ben just tossed her foot aside and climbed up beside her. Corrine backed up towards the edge of the platform as Ben advanced towards her. "I'm so sorry about your brother," she said to Ben. "It was a tragedy, but we did everything we could—" Ben thrust out an arm, and Corrine flinched back, expecting a slap across the face, but was met instead with a searing pain in her left shoulder. Her hands flew to the wound, where a long spike of metal protruded from her flesh. The lightning rod from on top of the tent—Ben must have climbed the service ladder and detached it.

"I believe I mentioned I had electrician experience," Ben said as another rumble of thunder shook the platform. "And you should really tighten security." He wrenched the lightning rod out of Corrine's flesh and she fell to her knees with a moan, clutching her bloodied shoulder. Behind her, Anita shrieked as her grip on the wire began to slacken.

The sound of Anita's terror snapped Corrine out of her shock, and she kicked out with both feet as she threw herself towards the high wire. One of her legs connected with Ben's knees and sent him tumbling over the edge of the platform. He fell for a long time, and then there was a snap, and a single shrill scream. Corrine focused on dragging herself along the high wire towards Anita. The pain in her shoulder was unbearable, but she kept inching closer until she was near enough to grab Anita's hand. "I'll pull you up," she said.

"You can't," said Anita, looking at Corrine's shoulder.

"Oh, yeah? Watch." Corrine threaded her legs around the wire and wrapped her good arm around Anita's waist, fighting through the agony in her shoulder to haul the other woman back onto the tightrope.

Just as Anita was cresting the tightrope, Corrine's vision went yellow. She screamed. The unprotected center pole of the circus tent had been struck by lightning, sending a bolt of untethered electricity shooting along the high wire and across both women's bodies. There was a sharp prickling just under Corrine's skin, the brunt of it concentrated around the wound in her shoulder. Her ears rang, and her hold on Anita released before Corrine could stop it. When her vision cleared, she saw Anita—eyes wide and skin a smattering of charred black and raw pink—drop from the electrified wire. Anita was dead before she hit the burning water.

Corrine didn't have time to register the horror of what had happened before lightning struck again, sending a current of electricity skirting across her body and scattering her thoughts. Corrine realized in a brief moment of clarity that her rubber gloves and undergarments were protecting her from the worst of the electricity. Though it wasn't killing her, she almost wished it would. This was worse than the dull buzz of the electric chair—this was soul-shredding agony.

There was the sound of fabric ripping and wood splitting as the roof of the tent tore open, flames from the lightning strikes consuming the structure. Strings of support wire, also electrified from the lightning, dropped from the ceiling as the roof fell away. Corrine screamed as a tangle of live wires fell onto her, their momentum from the fall wrapping them around her legs and sending electricity coursing through her. She convulsed, but her legs were held together by the wires. Her hands wouldn't let go of the tightrope. She was stuck. There was too much current for her suit to handle, and it was beginning to melt and fuse with her skin. Corrine longed to die like Anita had, like the Mermaid had, but she stayed horribly, excruciatingly alive. She couldn't scream anymore, but her mouth wouldn't close. She couldn't see. Her face was warm and sticky. Her cognitive function nearly depleted, all Corrine could think was a single phrase over and over again: *A freak is a freak is a freak is a freak is a...*

On the fifteenth night of June, 1934, a circus tent on the outskirts of Carlinville, Illinois, was burning to the ground. Ben, his left leg broken, dragged himself out of the tent. One of the strongmen ran towards him, helping him towards the safety of the wagons. In the distance, Ben could hear the sirens of approaching fire engines, but he knew it was too late for the women who had killed his brother. He turned back to the tent as the strongman led him away, but there wasn't much left to see. Only a burning tank of water with a charred corpse floating on the surface, along with another body hanging above, its legs fused together.

— FIN —

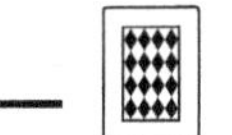

The thunder booms and crackles again as you blink yourself back to the here and now, and as if on cue, the second mirror falls to pieces. You see the card on the table ignite in a burst of flame, and xe scoops it up with xer fishnet-gloved hand before tossing it next to the clown doll, where the flame spreads to the fabric and sends one eye drooping before burning itself out trying to eat through the mildewy stuffing. Again the top hat is removed, and again the painted nails dip into its mouth.

Xe smiles as xe reaches inside, nothing like the sharp and cunning grin xe wore before, and pulls out what appears to be a folded orange flower until xe turns the key and the petals unfold to reveal the stripes of a mechanical monarch butterfly. It rattles to life, sputters turning to flutters as it jumps from xer palm and into the air. You watch as the automaton circles above the table, spinning in a hypnotic arc above as the cat tries to jump up and paw at it in vain.

"From bodies in free fall to bodies in flight," xe says, the candlelight turning the butterfly's movements into flickering calligraphy across the attending mirrors. "Watch as our next story stretches out and soars, as we leap into the air and catch ourselves..."

III. ON GOSSAMER WINGS

performed by Toshiya Kamei

When your green eyes travel across the barbed cage and meet mine, sympathy, or at least concern, flashes across your face and kindles the dying flame of hope in my chest.

Funny; you look so familiar, but I can't quite place you. I search my past in despair. Alas, my transformation has distorted my memory. The days I spent in the open air, fluttering among the flowers, have taken flight, condemning me to solitude.

My circus travels from city to city by train, and there's no way to tell how long I've been held captive. The only constants in my life are the scenery speeding outside my window, the leering stares accosting my seminude body, and the occasional smattering of applause mixed with jeers.

The red-nosed clown steps into my cage, brandishing his long-handled butterfly net, and the audience bursts into cheers. I flicker through the air in my skimpy Tinker Bell outfit, trying to evade capture. My heart pounds, and my head spins. The clown narrows the distance with each step, his hot breath palpable. He scoops me up after several attempts, wearing a triumphant sneer. I struggle inside the net, flapping my gossamer wings in vain. Help! Get me out of here! My mute plea echoes in my head until I pass out.

When I wake, the crowd is gone. The clown pulls me to my feet, chains my wrists together, and shoves me. We start off toward my train car.

Underneath his jester makeup is a prematurely bald man with a trimmed goatee. According to gossip, he used to work night shifts at a cannabis dispensary to supplement his meager teacher's salary. As we pass several cars that cage exotic animals, the chain connecting the shackles rattles between my wrists. An elephant lets out a mournful shriek. A black tiger drools in her fitful slumber.

As soon as the clown pushes me inside my car, the stale stink of animal urine pricks my nose. With my tired wings weighing heavy and leaden, I unroll my straw-like tongue and sip nectar from deep inside the wilting flowers scattered across my cold floor. The bittersweet flavor swirls in my mouth before I swallow.

It's dark, and the whole circus sinks into a deep sleep. There's no noise except for the occasional footsteps of the guards.

Trapped in my solitude, I feel the sudden urge to explore your body—to search for your nectar. I will my imagination, my only escape, to soar high.

With my hunger half-sated, some long-forgotten summer floods back. That summer, I was still free. Riding a green-scented breeze, soft and warm, I spotted a young girl in a park named after a once-renowned figure who had fallen from grace over a sex scandal. Shaded by a canopy of trees, she sat alone on the lawn, engrossed in a picture book open on her lap. Colorful drawings depicted a famished caterpillar who changed into a chrysalis and emerged as a butterfly by the end. I was still a butterfly-sized fairy, most often mistaken for a tiger swallowtail with yellow and black stripes.

Drawn to her smell—floral shampoo mixed with healthy sweat—I perched on her shoulder without being noticed. I observed the girl up close. Her ivory skin was translucent in the sun's rays. Fiery red hair, reminiscent of Tori Amos, framed her freckled face. Her pink summer dress barely covered her legs.

I saw the girl every day, and I basked in the sun-kissed park with her for hours on end. When the summer ended, she left. Afterwards, she occupied my thoughts, even my dreams, and my persistent longing for the human world prompted me to seek the witch's counsel in the dark forest. It dawns on me that you look like the girl of that summer.

Sharp taps on the window jolt me out of my reverie, and I gasp at the grotesque Halloween mask pressed against the pane. A closer look reveals a dead president, a third-rate actor turned politician. Familiar green eyes stare into mine. It's you. You unmask, and loosened ginger hair falls over your freckled face. A frown mars your otherwise sunny features.

You take a glass cutter from your satchel and press it against the lower part of the frame, the blade noiselessly digging into the pane. You remove a large strip of glass and signal for me to crawl through to you. I do so, my heart pounding, afraid of making noise. The glass grazes my face, and I flinch, but the adrenaline rushing through me numbs the pain. I land on rough gravel, which crunches beneath my bare feet.

"You're bleeding!" you say, the alarm in your voice palpable. I touch my cheek, and my fingers come away wet. You step closer to get a better look. "The cut isn't very deep, thank goodness. You don't need stitches, but let me clean it for you." You open your satchel, take out a little can of disinfectant, and spray some on the wound. It stings enough for me to grimace.

"Hold on," you say, grabbling the chain between my shackled wrists.

You insert a bobby pin into the lock and wiggle it to the right, then to the left, but nothing happens. The frown deepens across your brow. You then wiggle the pin up, and the lock clicks open. My shackles thud to the ground, and the cold air stings my chapped wrists. I tremble and hug myself.

"You poor thing, you're freezing!" You remove your jacket and place it around my shoulders.

"I'm a moderator on an animal rights activism forum," you say as we start away from the train. "Mind you, violence isn't my scene." Animal howls nearby obscure your voice, and the guards noisily scramble in the opposite direction, yelling about the animals getting loose. I'm certain it's your doing. "Arson, property destruction and vandalism. That's not me."

Your hand on the small of my back eases my fears. "Don't worry. The authorities will seize the animals and turn them over to shelters." You almost have me convinced everything may turn out alright. After all, the black cloak of night surely provides the perfect cover for our getaway.

"Where do you think you're going?" A familiar man's voice thunders, and I freeze. It's the clown. He walks up to me, grabs my arm, and twists it behind my back. He gives my arm a violent jerk, and a sharp pain pierces my shoulder.

"Let go of her!" You lunge at the clown, but he twists and dodges you. His grip on my arm loosens as he shoves you down.

I spin, pick up a large stone off the ground, and smash it against his head. He groans and falls to his knees. I straddle him and bash his head over and over until he stops moving.

"Let's go!" You pull me, and I stagger to my feet, my hands smeared with blood. I run after you like nothing else in the world matters. I run until my lungs are ablaze, and my heart threatens to burst.

"I think we're safe now," you say, panting. The night air feels good against my sweat-slicked skin. You're slightly bent, your hands on your knees as you catch your breath.

"A few days ago," you continue, "an anonymous tipster alerted us to animal cruelty at your circus." You pause, trying to catch my gaze. "Admittedly, I do this often enough despite having a day job; I work from home as a web designer. I've never been caught so far. Knock on wood."

We hurry in silence along the moonlit path on the outskirts of the city. The gravel bites into my feet, and I wince with each step. The darkness assumes peculiar shapes, vaguely human. The silent shapes slip between the trees and watch me with dark eyes. Startled, I grasp your hand and hold it tight. You squeeze my hand to comfort me.

After a few minutes, we reach a wide road, and I see a white Honda Civic parked behind a fence.

"I'm Ronnie," you say as you walk to the front of the car and open the door. "Actually, it's *not* short for Veronica," you continue as you fasten your seat belt. I try to follow suit, but mine refuses to budge. "There you go." You help me retract it across my chest and click it into place, and we roll forward.

"I'm named after Ronnie Lee, the leader of the Animal Liberation Front. My parents met at an ALF meeting. As far as I know, they never became members, but they were always big on animal rights. Some of that rubbed off on me, I'm afraid."

We enter the highway and join the flow of traffic.

"I was raised as a strict vegan, but I lapsed when I left home for college. Sorry, I know I'm talking your ear off."

I shake my head. I touch your shoulder to reassure you.

"Sleeps with Butterflies" comes on the radio. Piano riffs tickle my ears and float alongside Amos's ethereal voice. The song slips through my consciousness like grains of sand; those poetic lyrics about letting go make me feel melancholy, and the chorus sends tingles down my spine.

"Do you know Tori Amos?"

I nod.

"Great," you say with a smile. "You're an Ears with Feet like me. That's what Tori calls us." She pauses, considering. "What should I call you?" you ask. "Butterfly is a lovely name, but maybe it's too literal. What do you think? How about… Vanessa? It comes from the goddesses Phanessa and Venus, but it also means 'butterfly'."

I nod again. Tears burn hot in my eyes. Frustrated with my inability to speak, I grimace, trying to keep the tears from falling. I miss my voice so much. Perhaps I can teach myself to write or sign.

"It's alright." You place your hand on mine and give it a gentle squeeze.

A single tear runs down my cheek as I recall how I gave up my voice.

"You don't have to tell me why you're here," the witch said, seated on a chair made of human bones. Smoke wafted from incense censers, filling the air with an earthy smell. *"I already know what you want,"* she continued. Dressed in black, she had ink-black hair, dark-brown skin, and six fingers on each hand. Her youthful features gleamed with a splendor that defied time, but I was positive it was all veneer, a result of her witchcraft.

"You want to take a human form and live among humans," the witch continued. *"It's a silly thing, but you envy them."*

The forest was pitch-dark except for the fire burning beneath a bubbling cauldron. The flames flickered across the witch's face, illuminating her delicate features and deepening the shadows below her brow. I hesitated to go near the fire, afraid of getting singed.

"You have the most enchanting voice of anyone in the forest," she said, stirring her cauldron filled with dead animal parts. *"You must give me the most precious thing you possess in exchange."*

"But what would I have left if you took away my voice?"

The cauldron spit and bubbled. I teared up as the rancid odor that smacked of blood and gristle assaulted my senses.

"Vanessa." Your voice brings me back to present reality. I watch the flat landscape outside the window for a while—the fields of wilted corn stretching toward the horizon—but eventually I doze off.

"My offer is more than generous," the witch told me, her voice echoing through my head. *"Remember what happened to the little mermaid? You're better off than that poor creature."*

"Alright," I said, without fully understanding what the witch implied. I was desperate.

"There you are." The witch passed me a cup containing a clear, sparkling liquid.

The drink burned my mouth as I sipped it, and soon my limbs felt warm before a pain pierced my shoulders, sliced through me like a sword. A beastly howl escaped my lips. My body swirled and stretched like dough as the potion changed me…

The car door opens, and the chilly claw of night air startles me. I open my eyes and see you waiting outside.

"Vanessa, we're here." You take my hand and guide me into what must be your apartment. The scent of carpet-cleaning shampoo seizes my nostrils as we walk down the dimly lit hallway.

You usher me into your bedroom. Magazines lie scattered about, along with a few books, and clothes pile in heaps on the floor.

"Excuse the mess," you say. "You can borrow my clothes until we can get you your own." You pick up pink pajamas from the bed and smell them. "They're clean." You hand me the sleepwear. "Change in the bathroom if you want privacy." You open the bathroom door a crack. "Adam's away on a business trip, so you can sleep in my bed tonight if you want. Don't worry. I won't bite."

The ceiling fan hums above my head as I slip into the pajamas. I gaze at my reflection in the vanity mirror. What stares back is a plain-looking girl with a shaggy mop of sandy hair. I'm a mess. I try to scrub away the blood caked on my face, but when that doesn't work, I open a cabinet and rifle through the contents to look for something to clean my wound. I find some estrogen pills, and I wonder why you need them.

I leave the bathroom and collapse on your bed, exhausted. Your lips move, but I drift into sleep before your words reach my ear.

I wake to find you asleep beside me. There's a gray tabby curled up in a ball between us. I brush a few stray strands of hair off your cheek, and you stir. I stare until you open your eyes.

"Hey, good morning." You stretch your arms above your head, yawning. "Did you sleep well?"

I nod.

"We had quite an adventure last night."

I smile, and you smile back. "I'm glad to see you smile."

I climb out of bed and walk through the morning sunlight to a half-empty bookcase, half-filled with cheap-looking paperbacks. It saddens me that I can't read any of them.

Browsing through the shelves, I spot a battered picture book with a fat wiggling caterpillar on its cover. I pull the volume from the shelf and perch on the edge of the bed. The familiar illustrations chronicle a caterpillar's metamorphosis; this is the same book the girl read in the park that summer. I wonder if you're that girl. The pages of the book crease beneath my touch, and I force myself to let go. Even if you are her, what does it mean? Maybe we were meant to find each other—or maybe not. It's too much of a coincidence. I shake off the foolish notion as I smooth the new wrinkles that marr the page. Life isn't a fairytale, no matter how much we wish it could be. I flip through the pages, and you sit next to me, close enough that your body heat warms my arm.

"Growing up, I loved this book." You drag out each word for emphasis. You rest your chin on my shoulder so that our cheeks touch, and the floral fragrance of your shampoo tickles my nose. "To me, it's about the beauty of transformation. It was the first book that taught me there's nothing wrong with being transgender."

The revelation comes as a surprise, but it delights me that you trust me enough to confide in me. Tears cloud my vision. Like butterflies, we both have gone through transformations. I hum the melody of the Tori song we heard on the car radio, and you join me for the chorus. I wish I could tell you how much we have in common.

"My parents have always been supportive." You smile. "I told them I was a girl when I was three." Before the urge to pull you toward me and kiss you overwhelms me, I take your hand and squeeze it.

"Do you have family?"

I shake my head, my gaze downcast. Climate change forced us to abandon our forest, our home, but even if that wasn't the case, my desire to become human bewildered my kind and alienated me from friends and family whose faces now blur in my memory.

"I know we've just met, but I feel I can talk to you about anything. You're like the sister I never had but always wanted! I love having you here, and I know Adam won't mind. You're welcome to stay as long as you like."

I smile again, but despite your words, I dread Adam's return.

In the afternoon, you draw a bath and insist on bathing me.

"Let me help you wash the places you can't reach." I must look filthy to you or smell bad; personal hygiene was never a priority during my captivity. Even so, undressing in front of you embarrasses me to death, but as luck would have it, the bubbles cover my naked body.

"Don't worry," you say. "We sometimes revert to infancy to cope with trauma. It'll take time to recover from what you've been through. All the more reason you should let me take care of you."

You trace a line with your index finger around the scar near my wings.

"That must've hurt you real bad." You sigh and sit on the closed toilet seat. "Let's lighten the mood." You turn up the music on your phone. Songs about girl crushes fill the bathroom, and we let the afternoon drift away. When you're done scrubbing, my skin feels raw. I step out of the tub, dry myself off, and wrap a towel around myself.

"Come with me." You take my hand, walk me into the closet, and pass me a pink dress with a backless design that will accommodate my wings.

"Put this on." I let the towel drop to my feet and slip into the dress. "Look how pretty you are." You point to my reflection on the mirrored door, and I blush. "Do you want me to braid your hair?"

Before I can answer, you sit me on the bed, grab a brush from the bedside table, and begin to detangle the knots I've gained over my time in captivity. With each stroke of your brush, I relax a little more. The tabby peeks his head out from between his paws and watches us.

The following morning, Adam returns. A cross between a high school teacher and a marijuana store clerk, he pulls off his black beanie to reveal a gleaming head. Ignoring me, he kisses you—hard—as if marking his territory. Jealousy raises its ugly head, but before I can say anything, Adam catches me looking at you, and he frowns.

He shoos me away, and while he spends alone time with you in the bedroom, I loiter in the living room. When the tabby joins me, I play with him, throwing a bell ball at a wall and letting him fetch it.

Eventually, we all sit down for breakfast at the dining table. You pour soy milk on your bowl of cereal, and I warm my hands on a cup of ginger tea.

"Vanessa," Adam says, running a thumb over his goatee, "how long are you going to stay with us?" His hostility sticks in the air like a knife.

"Adam, cut it out!" you say, face darkening.

I stand and put my cup in the sink.

"May we talk in private?" He grabs your arm and drags you toward the bedroom. As he passes, he bashes his shoulder against mine, but you don't notice.

"Adam!" you protest in vain.

He pulls you into the room, and he slams the door shut.

When I hear your muffled shouting, I can't help thinking of the clown. His cruelty. I grip the edge of the counter until my knuckles pale.

Once Adam storms from the room and out of the apartment—never sparing me another look—I run in to find you seated on the bed. I take your hand in mine, and you flinch at the contact. I glance at your wrist and see the finger-shaped bruises encircling your skin.

"Don't worry," you say, "I'm alright. I'm sorry you had to see him acting like a dick, but you won't see him again. We broke up." I hold you close, close enough to feel your heartbeat. Our hug turns into a prolonged embrace. Something—the same urge from before—makes me want to kiss you, and before I can figure out how, you kiss me.

That night, I fall asleep cuddled up against you. In my dreams, I wander around the forest. The trees stretch out their eager branches after me. The white skeletons of travelers who have gotten lost in these woods lie scattered along my path. The witch's hut looms in the dark. When I step inside, that familiar earthy incense wafts through the air.

"Take this with you," the witch draws a dagger from her bosom—its gilded hilt flashes as she lifts it. *"You must plunge the blade into the man's heart, drink his blood, and then you'll get your voice back. You'll finally have everything you want."* Her silken words soothe me, but when I try to look at her, I see only darkness.

I wake, my heart throbbing. Golden rays of morning sun seep into the bedroom, and they warm my body. To my surprise, I find old the weapon in my hand, the blade sparkling with an insidious light. I fight to tear my gaze away, and then I stash it under a pillow.

The bedroom door bangs open, and Adam steps over the threshold. The tabby jumps off the bed and scurries beneath it. "Why is she still here?" he shouts, jabbing an accusatory finger at me. His nose turns red from anger, and I can't help remembering the clown and how he hurt me.

"What are you doing here, Adam?" You sit up. "Give me your keys and get out!"

"Are you sleeping with her?" His words whip out like a viper's strike, and I freeze in fear.

The next thing I know, you and Adam are struggling and rolling on the floor. He pins you and sits astride you, hands tightening around your throat, the light dimming in your eyes. Before I can stop myself, I pull out the dagger and stab him in the neck. The blade severs his carotid arteries, and his blood spews forth and paints you with crimson streaks. Without thinking, I do as instructed in the dream and lick the warm splatter that has sprayed my cheeks. It tastes sour and salty.

Even after silence returns, I can't stop shivering. I drop the blade and collapse beside you in a heap. You wipe the blood off my face, and we sit together, locked in a tight embrace.

I try to say your name, but the word gets stuck in my throat. You hold my gaze, urging me to try again.

"Ronnie…" A soft whisper escapes my lips before it peters out in horror, for it is not my voice that rises from my throat, but Adam's.

— FIN —

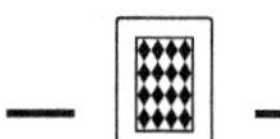

You feel her slip away, reach out a hand to catch hers, and realize that the mechanical monarch has wound down, perched on the back of your hand. The host scoops it up, folding it back into a flower, setting it next to the blackened doll and crisped card. The now-familiar chime of the next mirror letting go tinkles around the room, hanging on the air for a moment like the beating of a thousand tiny wings.

"Three down on your journey," xe says, running their dancing fingers along the spine of the cat, who arches his back and digs his claws into the tablecloth. "Your mind… It really is a fountain of possibility. Everything you see, everything you feel here tonight, everything you taste and touch and smell, is a creation of your own perceptions. I'm only feeding your senses a script, and you conjure up the texture. That's the difference between this tent and all the others—here, you make the show. No one is going to feed you from a silver spoon. Just you and what you make possible."

Into the hat xe dips again, and out this time comes what first appears to be a swatch of red fabric, but with a flick of xer wrist, turns in an instant to a pop-up puppet theatre, a tiny stage surrounded by a crimson curtain and a four-panel mirrored vanity at its center. You look at your face duplicated in miniature by the panes, falling under the spell of the thrumming rain, imagining the bruised tenor of the sky above. "Watch as the tendrils of the mind become pure image," xe purrs, "as the logic of narrative is abandoned, as bloody pulp gives way to the sweetly chiming bells of…"

IV. A Poetic Suite

A Clown Act

performed by John Grey

The ghosts come fully garbed,
skin-tight for aerial stunts,
frilly and flared
for trick-riding,
or cracking whips
or bearing swords for swallowing,
or conjuring up fire enough
for three meals a day.

My night
is three rings:
balancing acts,
bicycle-riding chimpanzees
and, of course, clowns,
the dreaded inhuman creatures
in polka-dotted pantaloons,
their faces daubed in greasepaint colors
of blood and fear.

I could cheer
for all the others
but I to fearfully know what's coming.

The most obscene,
Gwynplaine-grinning of them
will press his terrible face against mine,
skin touching skin,
the black of his eyes,
the white of his cheeks,
staining my nose and ears and mouth.
.

When I was a boy,
he'd have tried to make me laugh.
Now,
his otherworld assignment
is to make my skin crawl,
my stomach rise and drop.

For all his menace,
a half-hearted chuckle
escapes my lips.
It does not speak
for the other half.

NIGHT

performed by Diane Funston

Night
black as crow feather
shape-shifts daylight
hovers leaching darkness
over a small-town autumn
When did the tents rise
like sheets on a wash line
hung billowing to the ground
captured with a stake
like ancient stories of the undead
Slowly lights come up
vagabond voices rise

hurriedly shouting
of all the work to prepare
for this evening's deceit
A menagerie begins to
Shriek
Snort
Scream
it's way into the arena
snaps of whip
of sharpened metal hook
harsh dangerous words
wound furred backs
men with axes to grind
grueling long hours
with scant pay
and no respect
traveling circus
dime a dozen
roustabouts
working for a few scraps more
than the animals they beat
Step right up, brother,
step right up
See the fat lady dance
Hear unnatural tales of
two-headed babies
swarthy sword swallowers
a sexy lady with a tail
behind the silky curtain
The ferris wheel turns
horse-drawn hayrides
go around certain paths
Then the merry-go-round
that benign carousel
of all innocence
begins
to turn
Backwards

to dream the
impossible dream

slowly
faster
hats fly
skirts raise
the whole thing
spins like a string top
almost off it's post and rail
then slowly
slower
slowed
it stops
The carousel horses
camels and jungle animals
are empty of riders
Wood-carved serene faces
now sneer and smile
baring painted teeth
stained dark scarlet
a few still dripping
with stripes
of drying blood
Scraps of fabric scatter
over the floorboards
the fur-collared coat
one woman wore
t-shirt remnants
of entitled youngsters
who acted as if
the world bowed to them
corporate men and
women who
erased the progress
of animal protection laws
to keep circuses running—
veal factories going—
hunting safaris
to put heads on walls
as trophies

their guns against unarmed
sentient creatures—
the dolphins
and the dogs
armies use as artillery—
all rise
octopus with all
those thinking brains
and feeling hearts
all rise
what's next to do
what's next
in this cotton candy
sweet revenge

THE CURTAIN

performed by Cathy Joyce Lee

The curtain opens admission is free
Spinning rotation space odyssey
Flying floating lost in a show
Where is the audience
Why did they go
My life's now on stage
Where dark foam clouds spin
Impressionist forms
Dreams from within
A constellation coming to me
Invitation from heaven or hell
Possibly
Angels or devils
In costumed disguise
Who do I worship or pray
Or despise
Navigational tools I do not understand
Rotate in the ocean

Fly above land
fibril visions
hallucinate
sounds in my head
reverberate
Misplaced and lost
The moon, shadowed crescent
Sent from the past
But the futures not present
Frightening dystopic animal heads
Are hybrid creations
Of fear and of dread
Chariots driven on clouds
Or rogue waves
Horses are running
While harnessed enslaved
Rejected stars
Fall to the sea
Feel the wheel turning
Forms floating free
Jelly fish saucers
Gain lift in the air
Ancient words I can't read
Carve thoughts everywhere
Mercurial borders
Of heaven and earth
Pulsating blending
Dying and birth
Molding and melding a
Show for the gods whose
Desires and whimsies and
Plans are at odds
For what mortal ideas can
Construct and imply
Can't separate truth from
The maps sacred lie
For eons all travelers
Have walked through this curtain

We make our own hell which is
One thing I'm
certain

LAST NIGHT AT THE CIRCUS

performed by Fritz Dries

We found your face at the circus
where the nuns jumped rope
and the juggler carried coffins.
I watched you watch the
<u>show</u> and the <u>crowd</u> and
know there's not a damned
difference between the two.
3 souls is too many.
The audience laughs and
the show must go on.
Remember to interfere
Die with me.
Be a part of something.
The warning is an invitation.
Play with me.
The stage is where you are.
So sing.

— FIN —

It's as if with the opening of your eyes your feet land back on solid air, as if you have not been merely somewhere else but anywhere else, everywhere else, tossed through the space between worlds by phantom hands that hang from a heavenly firmament of trapeze wire. You touch your feet against the sawdust just to be sure that your body is still around you, still your own, and this time the mirror's destruction is itself mirrored by the panes of the vanity on the puppet stage, splinters of glass falling to the balsa wood slats. With another flourish of the host's hand, the stage again collapses into its own curtains, and the coiled bundle of cloth lands on the table next to the other curiosities.

"Welcome back to waking life," xe teases, the cat now lounging on xer shoulder and pawing at one of the epaulets sewn into the jacket. "If you can call it that, in a place like this." You expect xem to reach again for their hat, but this time, it stays firmly in place as xe reaches under the table and produces an ornate box, setting it on the cloth. It unlatches, and with ginger hands xe lifts from the box a twisted mass of meteoric matter, a shining chimera of rock and metal gleaming in the candle light. The space rock almost seems to take the shape of a skull, and as xer hands set it at the center of the table gaze into two dimples that look suspiciously like eye sockets. "For our next act, we present a story which is truly out of this world, a bone-chilling dispatch from the dark forest of the night sky...." You see something like liquid mercury flash in the dark crevices of the stone, glistering in the shadows of its twin pits. "We take you now to a tale of terror from the stars, hurtling towards the earth in the form of streaming..."

V. QUIKSILVER

performed by Danielle Davis

Ethan absently rubbed the backs of his knuckles, relishing the burn as his fingers scraped over the torn and bloody skin. He'd done too much on the elm tree in his backyard, using the trunk as a punching bag much the same as his father had used him. It helped, feeling the rough bark split his skin as he tried to exorcize his demons in a way he was never able to in real life.

His tongue once again slid over the cut on his lower lip. He'd been able to use his mother's makeup to cover the bruises on his cheekbone, but there was nothing he could do to hide the split lip.

He saw his friend, Brian, eyeing his cheek doubtfully. Brian was the only one in their circle of friends that knew what went on at home; the others believed Ethan when he blamed his injuries on fights at school. Though the four of them—Ethan, Brian, Freddy L., and Simon—had been friends since elementary school, Ethan's parents had transferred him to a prep school one county over for his sophomore year of high school. The boys still hung out after school when they could, but some distance had developed between them that had nothing to do with geography.

Tonight's visit to the Annual Turner County Carnival was an unspoken attempt to bridge that, since they'd gone every year since they were all nine years old.

"You know, Ethan," Brian began, "my mom wouldn't mind if you wanted to crash at—"

"I don't need your charity!" Ethan growled. "Now, c'mon, let's go."

Without waiting for a response, he stalked forward with Brian falling in line behind him.

They weaved their way through the noisy crowd, passing the fire-filled lanterns that cast dancing shadows along the dark walkways, the sideshow tents with their unwinnable games, and the House of Mirrors that Simon had once gotten lost in as a kid and had gotten so scared he wet himself—they never let him live it down. At the Ferris Wheel they turned left and headed for the tall, spired purple tent at the heart of the carnival.

The smell of sugared churros mixed with the lingering scent of cooking funnel cake, making Ethan's stomach twist with hunger. But he pushed the feeling aside. He'd been in such a rush after the fight with his father—over a stupid detention, the second one this week—that he'd forgotten to lift a few bucks from his mom's purse before he left.

Maybe he could borrow a few from Brian, he thought. Just enough to get a hot dog or candied apple. But that would have to wait until after the dare was done. He'd have all night then.

Freddy L. and Simon were waiting outside the purple tent's entrance. The thick fabric was closed, like a curtain, hiding what was within, but they all had read the sign outside advertising the tent's attraction: "The famous Quiksilver, proof of alein life!"

Freddy L. grinned as he caught sight of Ethan and Brian, elbowing Simon's lanky frame from where the taller boy had been leaning against a tall, wooden podium to one side of the tent's opening.

"Lookit who decided to show!" Simon crowed, as if there had been any question that they would.

From behind Ethan, Brian snorted. "Of course! Like we'd miss the fun. Besides," he glanced sidelong at Ethan, "we never choke on a dare."

Ethan scuffed his shoes in the sawdust that lined the walkways throughout the carnival. As high schoolers, all of them were too old to believe in dares but were all—though none would admit it—interested in what lay beyond the curtain. Rumor had it that there was a real, live alien inside, though nobody who'd claimed to have seen it were willing to describe the encounter in detail.

For Ethan, it was more an opportunity to escape his home than anything else—but he was a *little* interested in all the hype surrounding this particular exhibit. Those who'd been coming to the carnival for years all agreed that the alien display hadn't been there before. So, as such, it was the talk of the town.

Now Freddy L. pushed his hands in his jean pockets and looked around. "Where do we buy the tickets?" He stepped close to the podium and peered around the back. He straightened with a frown. "Were we supposed to buy them at the front gate?"

Ethan felt a sinking sensation in his stomach. He'd had to borrow entry money from Brian to get into the carnival and didn't want to do it again in front of his other friends—he knew they all assumed his father had earned enough as a lawyer to pay for the prep school, but only Brian knew how his family had had to take out a second mortgage and scrape their lean finances to pay for tuition.

Never let them see you weak, his father always said. Ethan hated the way his father's voice always seemed to be in his head and shook the sensation away. "Maybe we just go in? I mean, it's pretty sketchy looking to me." He pointed to the plastic sign next to the tent entrance, with the kind of crooked, two-inch vinyl letters one might put on a homemade garage sale sign. "'Quiksilver?' with no 'c'? And they misspelled 'alien!'"

The boys snickered.

"Did they teach you that in prep school, brainiac?" Simon snorted. "Who cares how they spell it? I wanna know who wants to go first?" He looked around at each of them, grinning that foolish grin that made Ethan want to punch it off him. Thinking about his father always made him feel like punching something.

"I'll go first," he said, surprising even himself. He hadn't known the words were coming out until they'd left his lips. Then he recovered, adding a smirk: "If only to show you pussies there's nothing to be scared of." He flashed a sidelong look at Simon, and couldn't resist adding, "Not like Simon in the House of Mirrors."

Freddy L. cheered his approval as Simon scowled and flipped up his middle finger. "Seriously? Give it a rest! *I was nine!*"

But Brian put a hand on Ethan's shoulder and stepped close. "You know we don't have to do this, right? We can just enjoy the rest of the carnival."

Ethan frowned at him. "Are you scared?"

"Screw being scared!" Brian hissed, flashing a distrustful glare at the tent. "I just have a weird feeling about all this."

"Then don't go in," Ethan hissed back, wrenching his shoulder loose.

But when he stepped forward towards the tent entrance, he registered a looming figure leaning over the top of the podium.

"Gentlemen!" the man exclaimed. He lifted one white-gloved hand to doff the brim of his top hat at them. Ethan dimly noticed it was made from the same heavy brocade material as the tent.

"Holy shit!" Simon whispered behind him.

The strange man grinned. "Holy shit indeed, my friend."

As Ethan stepped closer, he saw the man's face was sweating heavily, creating jagged cracks in the white pancake makeup covering his skin. His pancaked nose was oddly textured, like a cauliflower floret, and when he smiled down at them, he revealed a set of crooked teeth.

"You are about to enter the great unknown. A place where the extraterrestrial meets the mundane." His voice, at odds with his bizarre appearance, was a pleasant southern drawl.

Ethan looked up at him and realized the man's eyes were completely silver, with no pupils or irises or even whites, just a metallic shine like they were filled with mercury. He blinked quickly, in amazement, but when he looked again, the silver was gone. The man looked down on him with a sly smile but with normal eyes that danced from the light of the nearby lanterns.

Ethan shook his head. What was wrong with him? It had to be a trick of the light.

"Where did you come from?" Freddy L. demanded, stepping up so he was shoulder-to-shoulder with Ethan.

"Why, I've been here all along!" the man said in a surprised voice. But his eyes shifted towards Ethan.

He's lying, Ethan thought suddenly. *But why?* If he'd been there, he and Brian would have seen him as they approached. Or when Freddy L. had looked behind the podium.

But as Ethan opened his mouth to say so, the man reached up a long, gloved finger and touched his own white-painted lips with a smiling *ssh*. Without looking away from them, he reached one hand behind the podium and when it reappeared, four small purple rectangles lay in his hand. He held them out to the boys.

Hesitantly, Ethan reached up and carefully took the tickets. He turned, passing them out to the others and exchanging wary glances as each boy took one. As Ethan's fingers brushed the tickets, he noticed they felt different. He examined his own, rubbing his thumb along it like it was a worry stone, and realized it was made of fabric.

The same fabric as the tent and the strange barker's top hat, he thought, though he had no idea how he knew that with such certainty.

"How much?" he asked, fighting the sinking feeling in his stomach at the thought of having to borrow more money in front of the others.

The man waved the words away with a frown. "On the house."

A small voice at the back of Ethan's mind whispered one word: *pity*. As soon as he had the thought, a breeze kicked up, skirting down the walkways through the tents, kicking up clouds of trash, paper, and wood shavings. As it hissed past, he could hear the whisper again calling *pity pity pity*.

With a scowl, Ethan thrust the ticket back at the man. "We don't need your handouts!" He could barely hear his own voice over the whispering breeze.

The barker cocked his head, frowning for the first time. "It's no handout, boy. The exhibit pays for itself. And it's free for kids who are under the age of..." He paused. "How old are all of y'all?"

"Fifteen," Freddy L. offered in a hopeful voice. It made Ethan want to hit him again. Couldn't he see he was being pandered to? He contented himself with shooting Freddy L. a savage glare over his shoulder. His friend looked surprised at the look and shrugged, mouthing *what?*

The barker slapped both hands on the podium with a loud bang that made all the boys jump. "Fifteen! Fine age, fine age. As I was saying, this exhibit is free for kids," he paused to flash a conspiratorial wink "—excuse me, *young men*—younger than sixteen. But you can only go in one at a time." He turned and disappeared behind the podium, then reappeared on the ground in front of them.

Ethan was shocked to see the man was short, about three feet shorter than he was. A dwarf, or little person, if he remembered the appropriate social lingo. The man waddled to the entrance of the tent, moving almost painfully slow on severely bowed legs. He lifted back one lip of the tent flap and smiled.

"So, who's first?" His voice was sly and soft enough Ethan was surprised they could hear it over the noise of the carnival behind them. At some point, the blustery wind had died down—some small part of him noticed this, but he was too entranced to give it any attention.

"Me." He stepped forward.

The man bowed as he flashed a toothy grin. "You." His voice was a salacious hiss.

With a throat that was suddenly dry, he looked back at his friends. Their gazes darted from the barker to him, excitement plain on their faces—except for Brian, who Ethan thought looked a little queasy.

But this was the whole reason they'd come. And if they left now and just enjoyed the rest of the carnival, he'd know it had been because he'd been too scared, like Simon in the House of Mirrors. The boys would never let him live it down. The breeze would hiss *pitiful* at him. It would sound like his father's voice.

It always did.

He squared his shoulders—*like a man,* his father's voice said in approval—and he stepped into the tent.

The flap fell shut behind him, shutting away the busy sounds of the carnival and plunging him into a darkness so thick it pressed against his eyes like fabric. He closed his eyes and focused on calming his quick, nervous breaths. He wasn't scared of the dark, never had been, because the dark has always been his friend. The dark was where he was alone, where he was safe. His father never followed him into the dark.

After a few moments, after his breathing slowed, he opened his eyes. Ahead of him was a dark, barely visible pathway. Reaching to one side, he held out his hand until it hit a wall. Beneath his fingers

was a heavy fabric, which didn't really surprise him at all. He pulled out his battered cell phone and turned on the flashlight. As he suspected, the wall fabric was the same purple patterned cloth as the exterior of the tent and the barker's hat. And the entry ticket.

A shiver danced across his shoulders as he started forward, holding the light in front of him like a shield. He walked down the hall, turning when it turned, and feeling like he was a piece of food being passed through a fabric-lined digestive tract.

Finally, just when he'd begun to wonder if he was better off turning around and steeling himself for the ribbing he'd get from his friends, he noticed the hall was marginally brighter. His steps increased as a curious eagerness rose in him. He wanted to find out what the big deal was, why the air of mystery and hype from the barker when the tent's own sign was made with crooked vinyl letters.

A green glow emanated from around a corner ahead of him, bright enough that he turned off and stowed away his phone. When he rounded the bend, he was surprised to see a small, round room with a glowing green container in the center, about waist-high and as wide around as his torso.

To his surprise, the top of the container had no lid, nothing to keep someone from reaching into the tank or from dropping in trash or a discarded cigarette butt, like his father probably would have.

Inside the container was a body.

He stepped forward cautiously, his wide eyes crawling over the form floating vertically in the green liquid. This close, he could make out a humanoid frame covered in wrinkled, gray skin that reminded him of a hairless cat. He wondered if the wrinkles were from being immersed in liquid for a long time, the way his fingers would get pruney in the bath.

The figure had an oblong head and two arms and legs, but that was where the human resemblance ended. The arms had an extra elbow joint and the hands on the ends had three thick fingers with long, horney nails like talons. The legs were shaped like a dog's, with long femurs and hocks instead of knees. There were no feet, only three longer, thicker versions of the fingers—three curved "toes" ending in more ridged talons that looked as sharp as scythes.

The head was the strangest part: U-shaped at the sides and bottom with a softly curving expanse at the top. It reminded him of a flower planter with a cloth over the opening. The concave dip rippled slightly, like water gently boiling in a pot. Ethan wondered if that was from a current in the green water or if that indicated that its brain was working. But surely this thing couldn't be alive. The water had to be filtered and moving in some way so as not to become stagnant... right?

He noticed a small protrusion where a human's nose would be, but with no holes for nostrils, and below that, an expanse of wrinkled, gray skin lacking a mouth.

He found himself leaning close to the glass, kneeling down in front so that he was on the same level as the... creature? Alien? Did he really believe that nonsense?

The eyes, dark ovals above the nose protrusion, were closed—as best as he could tell, that is—and set in front.

Indicates a predator, he realized, remembering learning about evolutionary eye-placement in Biology. Eyes on the side of the head indicated prey animals, while predators had eyes in front.

The creature was disgusting, revolting to him in a way that made his skin crawl with unease, but he was strangely compelled to look at it.

Probably some custom taxidermied project made to look *like an alien,* he thought. Obviously, such a thing couldn't be real.

A sudden burning on the back of his hand broke the spell and he looked down. He'd been clenching his fist so hard the scabs on the backs of his knuckles had split open again.

He cursed softly. This was a huge waste of time, coming to see the stupid exhibit. At least he hadn't actually paid money for it, his or Brian's. He placed a hand on the glass of the container to steady himself as he stood.

The eyes suddenly flared to life, the wrinkled lids pulling back to reveal silver, mercury-filled orbs.

With a cry, he pulled back, landing hard on his butt so that a shooting pain lanced through his tailbone.

Touch the glass.

The words were a faint echo in his brain, like he was underwater and hearing someone speak from above.

Touch. The. Glass.

A gentle but firm request.

Without realizing he was doing so, he leaned forward until his palm lay flat against the outside of the container.

Hello, Ethan. The voice was stronger now, and he wondered if it had to do with his skin contacting the glass enclosure.

It does. He jerked his hands back instinctively, then forced himself to touch the glass again.

What are you? he thought, trying very hard to calm the thundering of his heartbeat echoing through his ears.

A friend.

Are you a... a...? He couldn't quiet his mind enough to focus on any one thought.

Immediately his brain went silent, like someone had turned down the volume on a radio station of static. Or like the purple tent curtain had sealed him away from the outside noise when he'd walked inside.

Yes. He didn't know which question the voice was answering, but he found he didn't care.

How are we talking? he thought with amazement. It was impossible to believe there was anything other than the creature communicating with him. The words weren't heard by his ears, they were in his head, as close as his own thoughts.

This is how my kind speaks.

And what is your kind?

A small burst of amusement went off in his mind like a firework. It took Ethan a moment to realize it was the creature's emotion he felt.

I think you know. There was definitely a sly tone to the voice.

Is this real? Ethan thought, both wanting this encounter to be real and not real in equal measure.

Do you believe it to be so?

Helplessly he nodded and felt an answering surge of approval. The creature liked that answer. *How do I know this isn't some trick?*

For a moment, there was no response, and Ethan had the panicked thought that he'd made it angry. That it wouldn't respond anymore. And that made him feel strangely scared.

Then he felt it. *Like this.*

The backs of his hands began to tingle, like ants crawling over his skin, and he looked at the hand splayed against the glass container. The skin on his knuckles was changing, creeping like something moving below the surface, as the bloody scabs dried up and flaked off, leaving fresh, pink circles underneath.

"Holy shit," he breathed. He checked his other hand and saw the same. He looked with wide eyes as the creature. *What do you want?*

Control.

Ethan thought he knew that desire well. He, too, wanted control—control over his life, control over his future, control over his well-being.

Who controls you? The question was gentle against the walls of his mind.

Unbidden, thoughts swirled in his head, images like an uncontrollable slideshow: large hands on his shoulders shoving him backwards into a wall so hard his head dented the drywall; his father, a dark god looming over him, daring him to get back up; an angry voice shouting so loud his ears ached, *wasting your potential, wasting your life hanging out with those loser friends, wasting my goddammed hard-earned money at that ridiculous school, pitiful, embarrassing, pathetic.*

Ethan reeled backwards, ripping his hand from the glass. His heart galloped in his chest and his lungs felt like they couldn't get enough air. He gasped, open-mouthed, like a fish and felt sweat dripping down his cheeks. But when he went to wipe it away, he realized it was tears, not sweat.

Touch the glass. The voice was faint, as if coming from some distance away. He clenched his eyes shut and shook his head vehemently.

Touch the glass. Please.

It took a few breaths before Ethan felt like he had enough control to touch the glass again. He did so and glared at the creature.

I'm sorry, it thought at him. The sensation had felt like fingers shuffling through his memories like a deck of cards and he thought he could still feel the mental fingerprints on his brain.

I can help, it offered.

Ethan cocked his head and risked a suspicious look at the creature. *How?*

I can remove... his... control.

Sitting up straighter, Ethan found himself curious despite his misgivings. *How?*

I can... change you... Give you back control.

Ethan removed his hand from the glass. Unconsciously one hand rubbed the back of his knuckles, remembering how the sensation of healing felt, how clean and unblemished the skin looked afterwards.

Really, it wasn't a hard decision at all.

He put his hand back on the glass and sat back on his heels. *What do I have to do?*

An image flashed into his mind: a small glass vial lying on its side next to the base of the creature's container. He leaned over, peering around the base until he saw it, exactly as it had appeared in his mind. It gave him a strange sense of *déjà vu*.

He picked up the vial, aware of the intent stare from those mercury-colored eyes, and turned it over in his hand, inspecting it. The vial was the length of his middle finger and scuffed on the sides, as if it had been dropped on rough surfaces before. He did not see a stopper anywhere on the ground.

Now what? he thought.

Drink. An image of the vial dipping into the green liquid the creature floated in.

Ethan's stomach twisted with disgust. *I don't think—*

DRINK. The voice was urgent, demanding, and before Ethan could process the sudden change in demeanor, his legs were lifting him, standing so that he could dip the vial into the open top of the glass container. The green liquid lapped at his fingertips, freezing cold, colder even than he thought it would feel. But when he removed the filled vial, the glass was warm against his skin. None of the coolness of the liquid seeped through.

Ethan closed his eyes, readying himself, then, before he could lose his nerve, tipped the vial to his lips and swallowed. The liquid burned on the way down, feeling as if it were freezing his esophagus as it made its way down into his stomach. The burn intensified, and he groaned as he dropped the vial and wrapped his hands around his gut, trying to soothe the smoldering pain inside him.

He had to let the others know. The thought blazed through his brain, urgent and loud. *They have to stay away. I have to tell them!*

But he lost all control of his body as he fell to his knees, still hugging his middle, then tipped over on his side. He lay in the fetal position on the sawdust-covered ground, tears streaming down his face as the cold fire consumed him.

Sometime later—time had lost all meaning—he rolled onto his knees, then stood. He took a moment to collect himself, brushing the sawdust off his clothes and feeling as if there was something he was forgetting. Cocking his head, he tried to recollect what it was that had been so important. There had been something, hadn't there? Before the... before the... the what?

He couldn't recall. Couldn't, in fact, remember what he was doing in this tent. He looked around, hoping something would jog his memory. He saw the large container with some wrinkled creature inside, its face strangely blank. Its eyes—or what he *assumed* were its eyes—were closed. Other than that, he was alone in the room.

Something was different, he could tell. He cocked his head, listening. From somewhere ahead of him, he heard the dull clamor of a crowd. A carnival. *That* was why he'd come! And there had been his friends, three of them, daring him to go into... a tent. And then...

...there was nothing.

He walked to the other side of the room and saw a slit in the fabric covering the walls. Pushing it aside, he saw a hallway and a dim light emanating from beyond. He didn't need to pull out his phone's flashlight—he could see better in the dark than before.

Before?

Before what?

A flash of bright light in his peripheral vision caught his eye before he walked through the curtains into the hallway. Turning his head, he saw a small mirror atop a wooden post. He walked over to it and peered in.

He saw his face, his expression strangely blank, like the way he felt inside. Empty. Hollow. Waiting to be filled. The bruise on his cheekbone was gone, but that didn't surprise him. He blinked and his eyes flashed silver, the pupils and irises of his eyes completely shining with mercury as he stared at himself. Then he blinked again, and it was gone.

A bone-deep satisfaction filled him, though it felt strange inside his empty body. The emotion didn't feel innate—it felt like something filling him from an external source.

He had to let the others know. He had to tell them... tell them... what?

That they can get control, just like you. The thought came to him again from a distance, like a mental whisper rather than a real thought. *They should drink, and then they'll feel it. Control like they've never known.*

"Control." The word hissed past his lips. He thought of his father and what might await him when he got home. Probably angry that Ethan had spent time going out with his worthless friends to a carnival when he should have been home studying for his Calculus quiz.

Control. Ethan would show him control. Triumph flooded him, filling him with a sense of euphoria. He looked down at his knuckles, noting the pink circles of freshly healed skin. He felt stronger than ever. He couldn't wait to show his father who had the control now.

We'll do it together, the internal voice whispered. But first... his friends. They had to see. They had to know. To drink. To get control for themselves.

Grinning, he went to the exit and pushed aside the curtain. He couldn't wait to see their faces when they got out of the exhibit. One after the other, they would all come out better than they'd started. Like him. He'd also show his father, even if he had to drag him to the carnival himself. And together they'd show everybody in the town... eventually.

Eventually they'd *all* have control.

— FIN —

The silver dims from your eyes as the sense of control ebbs away, and as you look at the rock it's just a rock, and you wonder how you ever could have mistaken its craggy surface for a face. Xer hands move the meteorite towards the growing collection as the fifth mirror loses cohesion, this shatter somehow sharper and higher than the rest, sending the cat scampering under the table. "For a moment, you held the stars in your hand," xe says, "and luckily for you, it was only for a moment. Looking up can be dangerous, you know."

The edge of danger in xer voice is mocking, playful, but also seems gilded with just the slightest edge of grief. "There are consequences to knowing, you know."

You nod. You know.

This time, the hat is launched into the air, and out of it tumble one, two, three glass juggling balls which xe catches with the other hand, sending them back up as the hat lands carelessly back upon xer head. You watch their arc as xer arms carry out the loop, keeping the orbs aloft. These too catch the light of the candles, making it appear as if there are flames within the arcing spheres. "To teach, some say, is divine, but some lessons are infernal," xe remarks, the balls getting faster, flying higher. "Our next such tale offers just such forbidden knowledge, a freefall of fancy for those who dare to step into the..."

VI. HOUSE OF THE DANCING SHADOW

performed by Segio "ente per ente" Palumbo

"Dlouhý jak písnička"

—Czech Proverb
(Translation/equivalent:
"As long as a song")

Walking the dusty path among the gilded and vividly-painted wagons, the black-haired man of thirty-five looked attentively at the members of the circus company—some of them attired in ring costume and mounted on piebald horses. He followed the quick pace of his new boss, who was leading him to his lodgings for the night. It didn't take very long to get there: that far from the big top, the only attractions were dark rides or mechanized thrill machines, a few fun houses and wooden bumper boats floating on small ponds. There were also booths on the fairway where men could flaunt their expertise at tournament skills such as running, throwing knives, or the likes.

The house on the circus grounds that Bořivoj settled into after being hired on as a new employee wasn't big—not that he expected something luxurious or expensive, as he only needed a place where he could sleep when he wasn't busy attending to the circus's nightly shows. Actually, more than a real house, it looked like a sort of enlarged shed with four wooden walls and some worn-out furniture—but it was big enough to let him sleep at night after he got off his job and to store his bags and all his personal belongings.

"You'll start tomorrow; have a good sleep." his new boss, a tall man with a peculiar, chestnut-colored beard and long hair had told Bořivoj in a low tone before leaving him alone. So he had placed his things inside a cabinet in a corner and then began to clean the area as best he could, as the floor seemed to be in bad condition. It was also obvious that his single bed had seen better days in times gone by, sure thing. The small space was clear, but vaguely shadowy and dim, for the lights were out and there was nothing really there to see anyway.

Viewegh Circus was considered a first-class show in those days, and its managers had a good reputation. It had only one single round big top for shows, and a smaller tent that provided dressing rooms for the company and temporary quarters for the horses, which were generally put up in some livery stable. A long stand for musicians stood next to his sleeping quarters, about 60 yards away, so Bořivoj noticed as he went outside after putting on a short jacket. He headed for the cafeteria, feeling in definite need of something to drink.

As he went inside, his eyes saw a slim blonde woman with vivid chestnut eyes, sitting at a small table sipping a cup of tea, or so he thought. The young man inadvertently smiled at her, just to show his good predisposition more than to really attract her attention, but the other replied with a warm smile in return, and that gesture looked great to him. She was a beautiful young woman and had a traditional dress on, made up of a vest worn over a whitish blouse and a black skirt that appeared full, lying close to the body. Who knew what kind of job she had within the company or what her real occupation was, but Bořivoj was curious about her. He promised himself that he would ask around about her, for sure, as it would be great to get to know her better, as soon as possible…

Tomorrow was going to be the day he would start his new life in that circus as a skilled juggler. He was eager to show-off his ability to all of his new colleagues, of course. After all, wasn't that why he had been hired by his new chief today?

"I've always gotten great results with all the youngsters I have trained…!" Rehor had exclaimed. Tall, well-muscled and with an imposing figure, the blond man wore his usual black outfit made up of a dark gray shirt with full sleeves under a sort of wide, heavy jacket that set off his pale features and his light beard. "I have never failed to achieve the goal I have in mind for those people I train. I'll get out of you whatever is your true potential. None of the students I have taught ever missed the opportunity to become good acrobats, but it cost them a lot of practice and bloody effort in order to get there. You'll be no different, you'll hate me in time, for certain, but you'll also learn that you need lots of exercise and hard training, be sure about it!"

Young Hubert, who was only seven, listened attentively to Rehor's speech in silence. The tall Serbian of sixty years was reputed to be very severe and extremely demanding. Many of the people he had trained also said that he was evil, because he wasn't used to giving any compliments to his students, nor did he ever forgive their mistakes or wrong movements over the course of his difficult training. A few young trainees even said that he was a sort of *sorcerer*, but such gossip was hard to believe—even though, at times, you could really think he was a strange individual when you stared directly into his deep, wild eyes.

Before stepping onto the stage as artists, all the young recruits and the new members of the circus had to go through a period of training that varied in length according to their discipline and level of experience. It had always been that way.

Rehor always told his trainees that everyone contributed their special skills to ensure acrobats from backgrounds such as acrobatic gymnastics and circus arts made a successful transition to the stage, so that everyone could reach their full potential. Depending on your previous experience and the act for which you were selected, training could last from a few days to several months. At times it would even take years and, no matter how famous or capable you became, you also needed to keep your body in great shape and exercise on a daily basis, of course, in order to be at your best for the next shows. The main training program focused on different areas and the young ones had to completely master each part of it before they could join a real show in front of the paying customers. Acrobatics required that you made sure each act was technically perfect and thoroughly spectacular in the end, if you wanted to keep your job and please the trainer and, after all, the viewers.

In particular, "acrobatics" covered: floor tumbling, acro-balance (including hand to hand balance), banquine, trampette and springboard work, and so on. Forward roll, backward roll, handstand, handspring, flyspring and round off were all examples of the moves you had to be able to perform well, from the first day you were admitted by the Serbian trainer—and things became harder and harder, day by day, certainly.

As in most places like his circus at that time, acrobatic programs required children start as young as seven years old, as was true in Hubert's case. The young aspiring artist, blue-eyed and slender, had a well-proportioned body and an attractive face encircled by a head of fair hair, but he hadn't gotten his growth spurt yet. He would eventually get taller, he knew, but his interest in getting to the top and being famous was larger than his patience, actually, or so many of the other students said. He was there thanks to his elderly uncle who was a poor circus caretaker and the only living relative he still had around. That man didn't spend too much time with him, but it was thanks to his money that Hubert had eaten daily since he was a small child, and he didn't want to disappoint his uncle in any way, nor cause him to worry because of his problems.

The style the boy wanted to specialize in was properly called *acro dance*, which combined classical dance technique with precision acrobatic elements. It was defined by its athletic character and its use of acrobatics in a dance context. Actually, in a way this was in contrast to traditional acrobatic and artistic gymnastics, and it was known by various other names including *gymnastic dance*, though it was most commonly referred to simply as *acro* by all the dance professionals. Dancers had to be trained in both dance and acrobatic skills and they had to be in excellent physical condition as well, because it was a physically demanding activity.

Acro also combined the skill of deftness with the beautiful

moves of a dancer. In history, acrobatic acts and individual dance had already been performed in vaudeville for several years prior to 1860 in the eastern countries of Europe. This was long before it emerged in the United States and Canada, and it was definitely not until the early 1900s (that is, much later than the time of Hubert) that it became very popular worldwide to perform such a peculiar style. As a matter of fact, no individual performer could be cited as its originator, strange to say but true.

Acrobatic training taught flexibility, balance, strength, muscle control, and above all, discipline and concentration. There were many kinds of physical programs that could help youngsters in learning the acrobatic and performance skills needed to become circus acrobats. These included gymnastics, dance and many other activities. Gaining experience was also necessary to help performers in working with multiple partners or developing more useful skills. The high degree of discipline and concentration required was top grade and not everyone proved capable of getting there in the end. Great tumbling skills could be an added virtue for any dancer and, with quality instruction, anyone would gain more flexibility and upper body strength, giving him or her a substantial advantage in such a demanding activity.

Even though vaudeville acrobatic performances were often little more than acrobatics set to music, Acro had always been a real dance since the first time it appeared. Using its acrobatic movements —within a dance context—the young one wished to create a new special style of his own, a sort of sequence of movements that could define him and become recognizable as uniquely his. In it, you were allowed to add elements from several contemporary music fields, even though all the trainees that were accepted within the circus over the course of this period were mainly the more traditional ones. So you had to prove to be incredibly good if you wanted Rehor to allow you to make your dance an expression of your personality. There were no rules limiting the movements you might perform, the length of your dance, or the type of music you preferred to use, if you were famous, undoubtedly capable and the customers showed that they loved your style, certainly. But there was a long road to go ahead of Hubert before he could get what he really and deeply wished.

♣♣♣

Prague was the historical capital of Bohemia proper, situated in the north-west of the country on the Vltava River. The name of the town was derived from an old Czech word, *praga*, which meant 'ford', referring to the city's origin at a point along the ancient waterway. Actually, the location of their circus was just not far from the river bank itself.

The Revolution of the new steam-powered industries had a strong effect in Prague, the same that had occurred within the British Empire and in France. Many modern factories took advantage of the coal mines and ironworks of the nearby region. Also, the main suburbs had soon reached a population exceeding a hundred thousand because of the new activities, and that meant people with a job and some money to spend, and all of that was very good for the circus income, of course. This meant that shows in such entertainment venues were allowed to get more and more customers every single time they happened, with an undoubtedly growing appreciation over the course of the week-ends throughout the whole area.

Beyond that, the Czechs were also going through the Czech National Revival movement: political and cultural changes demanded greater autonomy and many things were going to be deeply modified in a matter of a few years, even though the revolutions that had shocked all of Europe around 1848 had been fiercely suppressed in town and in the surroundings. The situation had started to improve only after 1867, when the Emperor established the Austro-Hungarian Monarchy of the Austrian Empire and Kingdom of Hungary. After a massive flood had caused extreme damage to the suburbs, finally in 1891 things were being restored with difficulty and everyday life seemed to have taken the right path, at least for the moment. It was a time full of promises and great things ahead for everyone, or so most of the population thought.

Thanks to its wondrous palaces and several ancient sites, like Saint Nicholas Church and Písek Gate along with the main sights of old Wenceslas Square or the Powder Tower, the town itself had become one of the world's most popular destinations for the richest tourists and the most famous authors, artists, and poets. Their circus was not one of the most important attractions in the surroundings in comparison to such beautiful ruins from a great past, but it was certainly something worth seeing. This was thanks, of course, to the many efforts and the undoubted skills of the capable workers that put their colorful show on stage every single night.

As Bořivoj was going to train early in the morning the next day, heading for an open area close to the river, he happened to see that young woman again. She sat at a table in a meadow and had a beautifully-embroidered costume on, something that was no longer commonly worn and that she probably was accustomed to wearing when she did her job each day. This costume seemed to be something connected to the activity of a sort of medium for the paying customers or something like that, as far as he had heard. Because so many areas of the Czech country had their own traditional costumes, as far as the juggler could recognize, that was a Blata traditional dress —common in the past in the region between České Budějovice, Jindřichův Hradec and Vodňany. It was very lavishly decorated by using white and red beads and sequins that were typical of those places. There was also a large headband functioning as a peculiar head covering, a wide collar, or '*výkladek*', around the neck above an embroidered shirtfront, and two wondrous chestnut mid-calf boots just below the knee. *She is very beautiful...* the man considered. *Here she is again. It must be destiny...*

As Bořivoj chose a spot and positioned his ordinary equipment on the ground, he removed his wide shirt and began some speedy exercises in order to prepare for the training. Juggling was, in a way, the throwing and catching of objects, where there were more objects than there were hands (or sometimes other parts of the body) doing the throwing and catching. Clearly, three balls thrown and caught between two hands was a very simple thing to him, but it was enough to start from, of course, before trying something more complicated over the course of the next hours. There were three easy sequences in juggling with many variations, some exceedingly complex that were based on these principles.

At first the *shower* came, which was a series of movements where objects juggled followed a circular pattern with one hand doing higher throws and the other passing or doing low ones to the first hand. Then, there was another where many objects juggled followed a figure of eight pattern with each hand throwing the object to the same height when the previous throw had reached its peak.

Afterwards, it was the turn of the so-called *fountain* where each hand threw and caught objects and didn't transfer to the opposite hand. Of course, other more elaborate sequences and tricks were put to use when a juggler was already experienced, exactly as Bořivoj was. One of those was the *robot*, which gave the impression that the balls thrown were connected to each other or to the juggler's body and it had become very popular especially over the course of the last years. Many new steam-powered inventions had brought innovations in every field of everyday life and had made most of the people well acquainted with what the metallic automata were. Many thought the powerful airships in the sky of many countries were the most visible example of the modern period the whole world was going through, but there was much more than that. Besides, by adding elementary skills to any juggling pattern the effect the circus artist got in the end could be greatly increased in complexity, and the young man loved to try some more difficult patterns that were variations of the common movements all jugglers had to conform to as ordinary principles.

Little by little, exercise after exercise, Bořivoj had started increasing his heart rate and respiration that morning. Juggling proved to be just perfect to develop good hand-eye coordination, perception, visual reaction time and neuromuscular balance. While the almost continuous rising and falling of the objects became seemingly unending, the attention of the juggler was incredibly expanded as he focused on the pattern and nothing else around mattered in the end.

While he kept doing his movements, a thought crossed his mind, in a way: everyone usually wanted to become stronger, faster, and more powerful, that was a common wish of the people, but what good were all these qualities if you lacked the coordination to use them? Circus performers who didn't spend any time working to improve these attributes or that didn't take a moment to review their weekly training plan weren't allowed to get any further, it was certain. This was just what Bořivoj didn't want to happen to him…

As the juggler kept training, he noticed that the young woman in the traditional dress sitting nearby was staring at his movements with an interested look on her pale face. In truth, he had tried to impress her by using his noteworthy ability, that was clear, but the man didn't think that he could really attract her attention so quickly.

As the other smiled at him during a pause, he took advantage of the opportunity and put his objects aside in order to go to her and introduce himself. That was going to be the time he would finally know her name, after all.

At first, Bořivoj was a bit ashamed to approach the woman so directly and start talking to her, but he had always been lucky in love, at least so far. Actually, the young juggler had a pleasing face, but he didn't consider himself to be really handsome—well, at least *not too handsome*, after all. He had been involved in a few love affairs previously, of course, but nothing really serious. As a matter of fact, living the life of a traveling circus performer or a juggler always on the move wouldn't help anyone to in creating a stable family life, that was for sure. In a way, the man hadn't even tried it in reality, as his career and the need to gain more and more money by continuously changing jobs had always been more important than anything else until today.

"Hi, there!" he exclaimed, addressing the young woman. "I'm Bořivoj. I was hired just yesterday by the owner of this circus."

The other seemed to weigh him for a brief minute, and then said, "I'm Silvie. Welcome to our home."

"What kind of act do you perform at the circus?" the young juggler asked..

"I work as a medium," was her plain reply.

"Do you mean the kind that stages a sort of otherworldly séance and makes the customers think they can talk to the souls of the deceased?" Bořivoj inquired after her activity.

"Actually, I'm a real medium…" the other stated, but her face appeared strangely a bit vexed. She seemed to take her job very seriously, at least according to her demeanor.

At that point the man looked surprised but thought better than to immediately clarify that perhaps he had misunderstood her. He didn't want to upset her nor did he want to seem like an individual who had no religious beliefs. Other than that, he was trying to win her over and not to appear as an offensive newcomer. It was clear that she really believed in what she did, so why should he doubt her words, after all? "Sorry, I was ill mannered… The fact is that I have never met anyone like you." Bořivoj soon specified the significance of his phrase. "I mean, I've never seen a real medium before, but I've heard about such things. You can overhear a lot while living in a small built-up area like the place where I am from."

Silvie stared at him and a tiny smile seemed to show off on her delicate mouth, as if she was having fun because of his embarrassed look. "Where were you born?"

"In Litomyšl, it's just a small town in…"

"In the region of East Bohemia. Yes, I know it, as my father was also born there."

"Oh, well, I would never have thought that someone else might have heard about my small hometown. And where is your father now? Is he working for the circus, too?"

"He died five years ago," she replied in a low tone.

"Oh, I'm very sorry. Have you ever visited my town?"

"Only twice, and I was very young then, but I liked it, certainly. I still have some clear recollections of its imposing Renaissance castle and the lovely houses."

"And, those are great sights, for sure! May I ask you a question?"

"Why not?" the woman said.

"Do you ever talk to your father now that he is in the afterlife? I mean, by means of your medium powers?"

There was a prolonged silence, and the man considered that he had said something inappropriate again. Perhaps he should have thought about it more before saying it, but he began stuttering in a strange way and his behavior looked very funny to her in the end. "At times I do talk to him," Silvie finally revealed. "But I never imagined someone might ask me such a question so soon after meeting me."

"Sorry if I was coarse… Maybe I am just a stupid. Sorry again!" a worried Bořivoj said.

"Don't mind. You were sincere, at least. How old are you?"

"I'm thirty-five. I just joined your circus yesterday, but I hope I'll get on well here. I've worked for some other entertainment parks before, but this place seems to be very large and influential, you know."

"Did you frequently change jobs in the past?"

"Not that frequently. Actually I think my previous experiences led me here for a purpose, and from this moment on my real career will start, as I really like this circus. It's possible that I could settle here once and for all, for the present time and the foreseeable future, you know."

The young woman smiled at him and relaxed her expression. Probably his last answer had attracted her interest in some way. From that moment on, things were easier and their talking became more and more pleasing, sure thing. She told him a few things about her family, even though all of its members were already gone by now, and Bořivoj took the opportunity to let her know more and more about him in return. They had lunch together, along with a few young members of the circus company that were training at the same site. Silvie introduced them to the juggler and made him feel better. It was a great, pleasing time and in the end the man thought that something very good could come from all that. Maybe he was going to have another love affair, who knows, as Silvie was really an interesting woman and he liked her very much. And it was only his second day working at this circus!

Bořivoj didn't know if it had been that first long morning of training, the late evening he had spent with that woman along the river, again, the same day, or if he just had caught cold, but he felt weak later on and so he understood he might have taken a flu in the end. So, the young man was forced to go to the show and do his job even though he was not in a good shape. Nonetheless, things went along in a great way and the many viewers were pleased with his excellent juggling. The same thing happened the following night, though with much more difficulty to the juggler, but the third day his health deeply worsened to the point he had to stay in the house and he, regretfully, completely lost the next circus show.. His boss wasn't happy about that, and Bořivoj was also very embarrassed and didn't know what to say. But there was nothing he could do about that, anyway.

It was that night that everything started, unexpectedly—while he was laying on his bed and all of his body was aching because of the flu he had caught. *When you just told yourself that a good night of rest would help you to recover quicker and completely...*

Hubert had kept training hard for eight months, and he had

to admit he had greatly improved his skills in all the fields of acrobatics, even though he wasn't completely satisfied yet—and nor was his exigent Serbian trainer pleased either.

The boy still remembered very well the day he had received a custom-made costume thanks to his uncle, of course. Even though, as things went on, he had never had too many opportunities to enjoy it or be happy about all that.

In reality, most of the long training was very exacting and Rehor turned out to be an unpleasant individual as he beat the students, and the young boy especially, in a very harsh way. He did it at times just to make him follow his orders exactly and accomplish all the difficult movements and the steps he asked for every single time.

There were days when Rehor didn't show any respect towards the youngsters like him—*especially to him*—as he had once dared to reply to the trainer in a way that the one hadn't liked, nor was able to ever forget.

"You'll eat only after you have shown me you have learned how to properly jump and dance!" the Serbian had cried out that time and nobody among the students tried to oppose him.

But Hubert had said that he and his young colleagues needed to eat if they wanted to grow up, be in good shape and become more experienced and skillful. "We must eat lunch and dinner, trainer! We need to be strong to improve ourselves and try harder." That's what he told the man that day, but the Serbian hadn't allowed the boy to say it ever again. Nor had his teacher taken his age as an excuse to prevent himself from beating Hubert's body hard on the face and the back, for a few long, painful minutes.

That was something that all the students thought or had on their mind, but no one was ready to claim his rights nor to openly move against the terrible trainer. All of them knew better: that they could go back to living the poor life of orphans and be sent back to the streets. That was where many of them had been found and collected as very young children before being brought to the circus in order to discover if they had some useful skills to let them make a living. Most of them, apart from the few who were sons and daughters of artists already living and working within the circus, had been starving for a long time before they were offered this great opportunity, so they didn't want to be abandoned again—and one day or two without eating was much better than a whole week of hunger, certainly. A beating was an acceptable tribulation in comparison with other worse things that might occur to them all if they weren't silent or talented enough.

From that moment on the Serbian had started looking at Hubert with hatred, and the boy thought he had been put in a bad light, with no hope to change it all in the end, unfortunately. He was sure about it the evening before what would have had to be his first real show on the stage, with real paying viewers inside a sold-out crowd inside the Big Top. The young boy had been training hard, doing his best, in order to make the exigent man appreciate his improvements and forgive the things he had said. He could already taste how it would be in front of the crowd, but the decision the Serbian made and then told him was really very disappointing and cruel, after all.

"You're out!" the trainer cried out. "You are not at the right level to perform publicly tonight, I'm sorry."

"But, trainer! You're wrong! I feel ready today…" Hubert dared to exclaim, but he immediately closed his mouth and restrained himself.

"What?" Rehor looked at him with two evil eyes that didn't expect a reply. "It will happen exactly as I said. And now go away, don't bother me anymore! We'll see your new moves next time, maybe…"

Those hard words had remained engraved in Hubert's mind as if they were a physical wound made by a sword, piercing the skin, reaching inside of your body, causing great damage… and all the sneers he could notice on the faces of the other youngsters who were allowed to perform instead of him, especially Dobromil and Radek who were even younger, made the boy understand that they were making a fool of him. They were going to be in the show while he was out, as a matter of fact, with no chance to change things!

He didn't know if it was the same day that he started thinking of that terrible act for the first time, but certainly such a decision made him become angrier and even more worried about his career and his future. Some time afterwards it would become clear what such words would really have caused, and eventually he would see the sad outcome that was put into motion—undoubtedly with some very bad, regretful consequences..

That strange fact occurred the night the young juggler was forced to stay in his lodgings at 9:00 pm, because of the bad cold he had taken, being incapable of going onto the stage. Bořivoj thought that it was really very bad luck as he had just joined the show only three days before, and to miss such an opportunity or let his colleagues down was not what he wanted or supposed that could happen any time, but that was the way things had gone. So the young juggler had stayed lying in the small single bed, very thoughtful and with his head aching and it was exactly at that moment that he saw *it* for the first time.

Just as the band of musicians outside began playing and their music spread around—*the unexpected thing began*, all at once. And it kept going on for a while, as long as the music was heard nearby.

At first it appeared to be *a shadow*, a dark shadow against the dim wall on the opposite side of the room, then he noticed that it looked more like a short figure resembling a man, or a small boy (*but it could be even a dwarf, how could he be really sure?*) and it started moving backwards and forwards, very slowly, being illuminated by the small oil lamp positioned next to his bed.

"What the hell?" the young man asked himself as that shadow kept moving along the wall, seemingly engrossed in a strange stroll. Bořivoj thought he was having a sort of dream, at first, but then he noticed that the strange figure was walking in time to the music played by the musicians outside, as incredible as it seemed… It was a dance! Beyond that, the gestures and the steps of the strange presence actually conformed with the sounds that came from the open window, just next to the shed where he was staying at present.

All that looked like a strange, unexpected shadow play, that ancient form of entertainment which was very popular in various countries and had also spread to Europe in the mid-18th century. Shadow play used a figure or some shadow held between a source of light and a translucent screen to create the impression of moving humans and other three-dimensional objects. Usually various effects could be achieved by the capable hands of the artists moving both the figures and the light source. A skillful artist was able to make those appear to walk, dance, fight, nod and laugh, too.

The shadow he was seeing presently was executing some well-balanced movements, as if it wanted to clearly emphasize body lines and picturesque extension. It was a clear display of strength and flexibility, with an extensive use of conditioning and stretching over the course of the show. The figure seemed to be very capable of blending dance movement and tumbling—it went back and forth, up and down, right and left. That was a really spectacular and startling performance; it was a demonstration involving great agility and complexity, apparently without physical limitations which could hinder its actions. But *what kind of trick was that?* How was that fictitious shadow able to move that way? Maybe some circus worker was playing a bad trick on him. It was also possible that somebody was taking him for a ride. But was that really probable, anyway? There was nobody else inside the shed now—the young juggler was sure of it.

Then at a certain moment, Bořivoj didn't know why, he thought that such a ghastly show was bound to be more than a common shadow play, *as it just seemed that something otherworldly had been brought back to life!* All that black shape, the obscure features he could perceive on it and the overall feeling he sensed, was that this was something much darker than the darkest night, more desperate and lasting than the saddest impression or the strongest tingling he had ever had. This was not a form of entertainment: he really was watching *a thing connected to the afterlife*, a sort of incredible, sullen presence, and all that sent a strange sensation back down his already tired and feverish body. Now, he was completely terrorized.

"Oh my!" he cried out in a hoarse voice, because of his weakened condition and the illness he had, and then repeated it again. But the shadow didn't seem to be worried by his anxious tone, nor did it stop his dance performance. It kept going on and on for a few minutes, as long as the musical instruments livened up the night and spread their tunes around.

It required all of his strength for Bořivoj to stand up and move as quickly as possible away from his bed. In doing so, he made the oil lamp hit the floor and so it was destroyed, but luckily no serious flames spread across the room. Then he headed for the door

REACH FOR THE SKY
CATCH ME IF YOU CA
MAY I HAVE
this...
FALL

and went outside, still barely dressed and partly nude. *What was going on inside that shed?* What could he do now, he asked himself without a reply, of course… And most of all, *who was going to believe him?* Or who could help him get rid of such an incredible thing once and for all?

Since that original painful rejection, many others had followed and Hubert had been unwillingly forced to swallow a lot of bitter pills because he was never allowed to get to the stage during a real show, while his young colleagues jeered at him. But might they really be reputed colleagues of his, as the boy never performed publicly even though he always did his best in order to please the requests of the trainer? He supposed not, actually…

One morning, the man in the kitchen called the students who were training in acrobatics at half past five to eat a sumptuous breakfast—just before starting the usual first exercises. The meal was composed of a tough steak, muddy coffee and stale bread. For another time, Hubert wasn't allowed to eat—these were the orders of the Serbian. Actually, this way he would be better able to comprehend the lesson, according to what the exigent trainer thought, but the boy thought the only consequence was that he was going to be very hungry all day long. He believed that the only thing waiting for him was hunger, along with the many exercises to do, and his rest would be even worse than the evening before. Much worse and much more demanding, certainly…

The young aspiring *acro dancer* applied himself in spite of everything, but notwithstanding his results nothing he did seemed to be enough to make Rehor change his mind. The reality became clear before the poor student's eyes the day he completed what he thought was his best training morning ever. The Serbian took him aside and started speaking to him. "I'm not satisfied with your exercises, again," he stated. "I see that you're doing all you can, but it is not what viewers will like nor does it appear to be on the same level of your fellow students. Take Dobromil and Radek for example: they're younger than you but both of them are really better, and the paying customers appreciate their spectacular performance during the shows."

At that point, Hubert was very dejected and felt that something was simmering under the surface of his skin. The boy felt himself growing weak in the knees, as he believed he could never pull off better exercises than the ones he had already done! He wished that he could say that he was disappointing only in the trainer's mind, that it was the Serbian who was wrong, certainly. He wished he could also express his resentment in clearer words: the young dancer was sure that Rehor deeply disliked him, and that he didn't want him to ever be on the stage and only wished him bad luck. And this was all because of his rebellion on that one day, because he had dared to hinder his cruel orders! And that had come after many slaps, punts and blows he had received from that man over the course of those hard, terrible weeks, along with the deprivation and degradation he had suffered every single time the trainer believed that he was slacking off or didn't put forth his best effort for the day. The young artist was sure he was good enough to perform, as a matter of fact, and some of the youngsters who trained with him at times told him so! But there was no way to change all that, no means to finally start the career he had been wholeheartedly dreaming of for so long.

Probably, it was exactly one of those dark evenings of deep despondency when he stayed alone in a corner of the circus area, still licking the wounds of the last beating of the previous day, that he devised what had already started being on his mind… and so things completely deteriorated in the end.

It had been a stormy night and a heavy downpour had hit the countryside surrounding the town, so the show had stopped early the previous day. The morning after, the circus workers found his dead body at the border of the area where the trash bins were kept, to the left of the circus tent. It was easy to figure out what had happened. Many said that the young boy had simply jumped off a tall lamppost he had previously climbed, or that he had simply overestimated his capabilities and had fallen down inadvertently while training in a dangerous place. Others thought that he wasn't very good at climbing and that may have been why he hadn't completed his training. Perhaps he had never been allowed to perform on stage for good reason given his limited skills, as that unlucky accident clearly showed… but his desperate uncle didn't believe all the gossip. Whatever the truth, he was hurriedly buried and soon forgotten by all the other members of the circus, along with those artists who had finally missed their opportunity to become famous or had left the entertainment field in order to look for some other better jobs in town, or even elsewhere.

But his death was followed shortly after by another find, something that had a serious impact on all the rest of the circus activities, and that made many other performers within the entertainment park remember those events for a while, after all, because poor Hubert had not passed alone...

There was a lot of skill displayed by the performers at Viewegh Circus before Bořivoj's turn under the big top that night, so he was a bit worried, but he did very well in the end. As he completed his juggling show and exited the stage in order to reach the tent which served as dressing rooms for the company, he went outside and got just past the temporary quarters for the horses. He wasn't looking too attentively at the many vendors' stands in the area nor was he listening to the voices around.

The apprehension he had had for his oncoming performance a few moments before was still tormenting him, and there was also something else... The juggler knew it wasn't just nervousness that really upset him, but it was the reflection that he had to go back to in that shed. Thinking about sleeping there late at night greatly troubled his thoughts. Certainly, the moving shadow he had seen previously was still deeply engraved on his mind as a ghastly presence he couldn't explain.

Actually Bořivoj had discovered that, after that first fearful night, the presence had never appeared again while he was in the bed, but he was sure that he had clearly seen it that day, and it hadn't been due to his cold or for the terrible flu he had gotten at that time! All the other nights he had been forced to sleep there nothing else had happened, though he couldn't figure out why. Then a thought came to his mind and the young man remembered that all the following nights he had gone back to the shed very late, after the end of the last circus show: when it was that late no musicians were playing next to the house, as at that hour all the entertainers had already completed their duty or were closing down in order to have some rest before the next working day.

So, maybe he had seen that figure only by chance, as he had been forced to stay in that shed because of his illness and his overall weakness. It might also be that *such a ghastly thing only happened early at night*, for some unknown reason, *and at a time when he was commonly performing on the stage*—even though there was no easy explanation for such an occurrence.

Then, the young man stumbled into Silvie, and she appeared like a ray of sunlight after a storm, taking him away from the many worries that he had on his mind at present. Their love affair was going on very well, and he was pleased to have found such a wondrous and kind woman in that place.

"Well met, very good juggler!" the young woman greeted him, as he came nearer.

"Glad to see you!" the young man replied, trying to smile, but he frowned in the end.

"What's up?" she said, noticing his strange look.

"Well, it's nothing, only that something worries me…"

"Something worries a tall, strong man like you?" the other exclaimed, complimenting him with her surprise. Then she added, "Shall I use my otherworldly power as a medium to solve your troubles and help you? Shall I do it now, before I do the same show tonight on stage for paying customers in the Big Top? I'm certain tonight's séance is going to be a fantastic display of my ability to contact and deliver messages from ancient seers and relatives long gone…" Her words didn't get the result she was waiting for, that was a deep laugh from him, so she appeared a bit thoughtful in the end. "Maybe there's really something that worries you, and I'm very curious about it…just tell me—what's the matter?"

Bořivoj stayed in silence for a while, staring at her with a perplexed look on his face, then he dared to ask her: "Would you like to help me to find out the truth about a strange presence?"

"A presence? Oh, well, it seems like the perfect job for me… tell me everything!" The woman had tried to get him excited about his tale, but the tone used by the man, along with the almost imploring look still on his face, didn't promise anything good.

As the juggler completed his account, Silvie's eyes showed

some interest, along with a sort of apprehension.

"So, will you help me?"

"Will it make you sleep peacefully at night, in the end?" the other smiled at him.

"Please…" he insisted in a low voice.

"Well then, why not? I've never heard of such a thing happening within the circus, but I haven't lived here all of my life, anyway. I'll do what I can, be sure."

So it was that later same night, after the conclusion of the overall show, the two met just outside the shed that functioned as a house for the young juggler. Then, they went inside in order to stage the restricted séance she had proposed to him. The two were already tired, but Silvie had told him that the attempt to find out the truth was worth half an hour of sleep, after all.

They sat at a small table in the darkened room, the only one inside the shed, and the woman positioned a few specialized tools for conducting such activities. She had with her a board (known as a talking board, according to what she told him) that was just a flat tablet, made of wood, that had on it pictures, numbers and words. The board was accompanied by a planchette which had the form of a pointer in glass.

"Won't it be dangerous?" he asked her before they started, being a bit scared after all.

"I haven't ever been harmed yet…" she replied in a calm tone.

"Another thing… there was music playing outside when I saw the unusual shadow that night. Do you think that could be important? Obviously there are no musicians playing music now…"

"It could be important, but this will not stop my research, be sure…" She calmed him down immediately after.

As Silvie ordered him to do, the man placed two fingers on the planchette which was in the middle of the board. Then the woman said something in a strange language the juggler didn't understand, a language he had never heard before. She focused on the board and attempted to communicate for the first time. The medium seemed to be fully conscious and awake while doing so.

After some moments, a dark shadow appeared against the dim wall on the opposite side of the room, just as it had happened that fearful night. For sure it had to be the one of a short man, or a small boy and it started walking backwards and forwards.

Silvie was watching it for the first time, and took the opportunity to attentively examine it. The shadow kept moving along the wall, and seemed to be involved in such strange walking. "Who are you and why are you here?" the medium dared to ask the figure. Her voice was deep and still calm, but a sort of trembling in her words could be noticed, so much so that the juggler was actually almost unable to recognize it as her own, and all that seemed to be very strange to the young man.

"I was Hubert, an acro dancer," the shadow revealed.

"How old are you and when did you die, my dear?" the woman continued.

"Seven years old; I entered the afterlife many years ago," the presence said.

"Tell us your story, my dear. What happened to you? Why did you die so young?"

"I wished to become an acro dancer. I really liked it. I trained hard, but unfortunately…" A few words were spoken from the dark figure with some difficulty.

"What really happened to you? Why are you still here, after your passing?" the young woman insisted in the same calm tone.

"I'm here because of my actions; I did a thing that I should not have done. One day I killed myself, and…" Then a sort of wind started blowing into the shed, and an oppressive sensation reached the two who were seated there for the séance. "I'm not allowed to say anything more. I can't do it because…"

"What's happening?" the man asked Silvie, becoming afraid. But the medium didn't reply, as she wasn't certain about what was really going on at present.

As the presence of the boy stopped speaking suddenly, he was soon overshadowed by another voice that came along with a bulky, tall figure, an unexpected one.

"Who are you? Reveal yourself before us," Silvie ordered the newcomer immediately, but her mind wasn't as resolved or as stable as she wanted to outwardly. That new appearance represented something unusual, an unwanted change that worried her a great deal.

"I'm Rehor," the new voice burst out. "And Hubert was just a young student of mine!"

After being bewildered at first, the woman looked at the juggler next to her, then asked the new presence a question. "So you were his trainer…but why are you here now? We have not called for you; I didn't invoke your soul…"

"Whenever you call for one of my dead students you also call for me…"

"How is that possible?" She appeared to be very surprised.

"Because of my sorcery, clearly…" the other stated in a hard voice.

"Your sorcery?" the young woman exclaimed. Then she said to herself 'Oh my…!', as she was beginning to see that things might turn out for the worst…

"Yes, I was also a practitioner of sorcery, and I mean dark sorcery, certainly."

"So, why are you here, then?" Silvie repeated, as she wanted to know something more about all that as quickly as possible, before it was too late, or before the situation could become too dangerous to them all.

"Because I have power over my students even after their passing…"

"What are you saying?" she said. "What kind of power? What's the bad blood between you and that dead boy, Hubert? Why don't you leave him alone? He's just an unlucky soul of a young boy…"

"Because before very stupidly dying, he killed me, too! Hubert poisoned me by deceiving me!"

There was a very deep silence in the darkened room, and no one dared to add anything or to reply. Then Silvie forced herself to continue and asked the Serbian trainer's soul. "If this is true, what do you want from him? Are you asking for vengeance against him? What happened to the youngster? Did the police take the responsible person into custody before he died?"

"Oh, no! He killed himself as he was unable to live with the guilt of the crime he had done. He was a foolish boy, a weak one, I always thought so, and he proved I was right! But he didn't know that he was already mine, *body and soul*, as he couldn't get rid of me because of my sorcerer's tattoo on his body…"

"A tattoo on him?" the woman asked of the presence.

"Exactly!" the other stated. "And now his soul is forced to follow my orders even in the afterlife and to dance according to my will, thanks to my power, now and forever!"

At that point Bořivoj cried out. "What are you saying?"

"Release him, now… please!" Silvie cried out. "What you are doing is unfair and very evil…"

"Absolutely not—his soul is mine now as was his life when he was alive, thanks to my tattoo being on his skin, even after his passing. It's my power that allows me to do so. This was a practice I always used on all of my students. Beyond that, the anger between Hubert and me is not your business, anyway…"

"Do as I ask you…" Silvie repeated her request again, her mind focusing on the present situation as her energies tried to force the presence to follow her orders now.

"Never!" the other replied in a harsh tone. "And you are not going to order me to do anything from now on…"

With that said, a strange convulsion seemed to immediately seize the body of the young woman, and Bořivoj became very worried, as she looked incapable of stopping his power. He also noticed a strange luminous tattoo appearing on her neck…

"Stop it! *Damned man…*" the juggler cried out, approaching Silvie because all that was very terrifying and he feared for his beloved life.

"Don't move, dear," the medium said. "His sorcery is too strong; you could be seriously harmed, seriously, and I simply… I can't…" Teardrops were streaking down her cheeks and a sort of trembling had gotten hold of her body. Her face was pale now and it seemed obvious that she was going to faint soon.

The man tried to touch her, to help poor Silvie in some way, but he was thrown back against the wall as he put his right hand on her shoulders and he cried out in pain. A deep wound appeared on his skin and also in his mind, or so it seemed to Bořivoj it had occurred, anyway.

When the juggler came back to his right mind, and he felt strong enough to stand up again, he rose to his feet and hurried to reach Silvie, who was down on the floor. Great was his sorrow when the man discovered that she was already dead and cold. Incredibly cold! How was it possible? What had happened? Bořivoj was simply unable to resign himself to the terrible fact of the medium becoming the soul of a dead woman. He couldn't ever accept such a loss, and one that had been caused by his request, as he himself had asked Silvie to help him to discover the truth about that dancing shadow.

That evil shade! It was him! *Damn' him, damn' him...* the desperate juggler repeated to himself for many long minutes.

A long laugh was heard in the dimness of the room of the wooden shed as the man was crying for the death of his woman, and madness seemed to seize his lost and regretful mind in the end.

After that event, no one dared to enter the shed again, and Bořivoj stayed in another wagon where he tried to sleep and rest throughout many terrible days, but with no good result. The young man was very sad, incredibly dejected, as he wished he would never have asked her to perform that séance that sad day. He was certain that it was due only to his request that his love was now dead. *If only he had kept to himself the thing he had seen in the shed, if only he had not had her involved in it all!* But now it was too late.

One day, the young juggler was received in the office of the proprietor of Viewegh Circus, a man named Jakub of about sixty with receding hair, who looked to be a bit stout. He asked him about what had really happened in the shed and his impressions about it all. As he started telling him the truth, the other looked pensive and stopped him.

"And what is the name you heard?" the circus proprietor asked him all at once.

"It was something like Hubert," the young man replied with a sorrowful look on his face.

At that point, the proprietor stopped filling out the papers he had on the desk and raised his eyes in order to look directly at Bořivoj. "I know that name"

"What?" the juggler exclaimed.

"It happened many years ago. I was only twenty at that time and my father was the previous proprietor of the circus. But it is a sad story..."

"Can you tell me something about it, please?"

"He was a very young aspiring *acro dancer*, if I remember it correctly, and he stayed in that old shed at that time. His uncle had built it. He probably had some respectable skills, but he ended up killing his own trainer finally, a Serbian who had a bad reputation because he was very demanding towards his students. Anyway, that man used to get some good results with his young acrobats, even though only by means of some terrible ways and a difficult training that often included beating the boys and girls and forcing them not to eat if they failed a test or if their movements and dances didn't please him. He also claimed to be a sorcerer."

"It's exactly what that evil presence told Silvie! He's the one who killed her!" the young man cried out as he heard all that.

The other remained in a deep silence for a while.

"Why is that shed still in the circus? Why didn't you destroy it long ago?"

"Well, at first it was my father who let that old uncle of the dead boy bring it along during the stops the circus had on its way across the country. That man thought that it was the only thing he had left of his nephew, and after that old employee died some years ago, the shed just always remained our property," Jakub explained.

"And what do you plan to do with it now, after everything that has happened? The evil being living in that place killed Silvie! Why don't you do something about that?"

The other raised his black eyes and spoke in a soft tone. "We'll see. Some steps should probably be taken to destroy it. As for me, I have already ordered that the shed has to be closed, and no one is to enter it anymore."

"This will not bring Silvie back to us, unfortunately…" the young juggler added. "… But at least no one else will stumble into that terrible creature again."

"Exactly. Whatever it is…" the proprietor nodded. "I always told Silvie not to make use of her powers after working hours, but she wouldn't listen to me. I've always been afraid that some accident could occur some day. Actually, Silvie was very gifted, but she tended to overuse her special skills at times."

"Actually, it was me that asked her to help me to find out the truth about that shadow I had seen in there."

"Don't condemn yourself. You didn't know what was going to occur that night."

"That still doesn't make me feel better," Bořivoj burst out. Then he stood up and left the office before starting to cry again, as he didn't want the proprietor to see him that way.

Then, one night, just a few days later, when his many worries and tears of the day finally left his mind and he fell asleep, the young juggler happened to see a known face, *or was it just a dream of his?* It was the face of Silvie, as he knew her well: such a pleasing smile and wavy hair seemed to invite him to follow, to come along with her. Two pale hands reached for him and touched his fingers, then reached his wrists and started pulling him to her body.

So, Bořivoj finally stood up and moved towards her, as his feet proceeded along in the dimness of the night while he went to the opening of the wagon, stepped down to the ground and kept following her. *Or was it all a dream,* again? He wasn't sure, but what did it matter anyway? He was allowed to see Silvie again, and he was so happy for that moment…

The juggler found himself before the front door of the barred shed, the same bad place where Silvie had died that night. At that point, he seemed to wake up, but his tiredness was too deep, his senses being still asleep, so he tried to move backwards, but he found he couldn't escape. At the same time, the presence of Silvie waved his direction and incited him to come on, to stop his doubts once and for all. So, the young man removed all the worries from his mind and forced his body to go on, and he finally got to the door, removed the wooden planks that kept it closed and then opened it before entering inside.

The darkness filled everything in there, but he was sure he could still see the presence of Silvie anyway. The woman touched his hands, then he felt a sort of warmth, but it wasn't something coming from a human body certainly. It was something else, a sensation that he couldn't comprehend completely. Then the front door suddenly closed behind them, and an old oil lamp was lit. Much to his surprise, the juggler noticed that it was the same lamp he had used in the shed before—but it was impossible, as he had knocked it off the table and it had been destroyed. *How was it really possible?*

And then he heard that harsh voice, the same damn tone he

had already learned to hate: *the Serbian trainer*, that unholy individual! "You've come, finally. Now you're mine,body and soul, the same as your dead woman…"

It was at that point that the stand of musicians began tuning their instruments outside. A luminous tattoo began appearing on his left hand and the juggler was able to see his shadow reflected on the wall, along with the one of the presence of Silvie. *What the hell…?*

"Come into my collection of souls, forever!" the presence ordered. And so the musicians started playing their music, the same they used to when there was a circus show on stage during the week.

On command, the shadow of the young man began dancing, along with those of the dead woman and a shorter figure nearby, the long gone acrobat named Hubert. And the music played on unceasingly for a very long time…

— FIN —

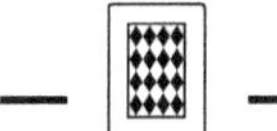

It takes a moment for you to realize that it is silent in the tent, that the music was only in your mind, and you see the juggling balls sit still in the host's hands as the next mirror chimes its demolition. Xe places them with the growing collage of bric-a-brac, and looking at the arrangement, you try to reach back in time, to remember with clarity the series of images and events signified by each object… but already each narrative has the quavering quality of a dream or a trip, a faded photograph in your memory compared to the sensory feast each tale presents in the moment.

The cat hops once again up onto the table, crossing to you, and you reach out, rubbing against the mottled skin, surprised at how soft it is. Your host smiles again, this one even softer than before. "Didi likes you," xe says. "Granted, he likes most people, but still."

The hat is flipped off of xer head, and this time it sits on the table before xem as they reach down inside of it with both hands. When they emerge, they are grasping a tarnished silver crown, rimmed with what might be real rubies and might only be costume glass. "Our next tale is a game of thrones, of ascension and of actualization," xe says, the gemstones catching the flames much the same way as the juggling balls. "A tale of taming the teeming masses, of being tamed in turn… a tale of abandoning the familiar to become…"

VII. The Queen

performed by Diane Arrelle

Melinda licked the cotton candy crystals from her fingertips and wished she were enjoying herself. The sky was ominous, the midway overcrowded with people, and the pain in her stomach was growing worse by the minute.

Why'd she come here anyway? she wondered, and fingered the car keys in her pocket. She dreaded the circus and everything it represented, and yet when she found the free ticket in her mailbox, she knew she had to come. After years of avoiding the big top, she found herself here.

She studied the giant, full-colored posters lining the corridor created by tents and the little trailers selling food. Faded, painted acrobats swung from trapezes, leotard clad-men carrying long, balancing poles were frozen for all time gingerly stepping their way across the high wire, young women in sequins held hoops for performing dogs who were probably long dead. Every poster was a cliché, and yet—and yet, something eerie and not quite human surrounded those images.

Melinda quickly averted her gaze and stood in the middle of the midway, staring at the ground, trying to decide whether to go home or stay and try to discover why she needed to be here. That was when she felt the first raindrops like a gentle tap on her shoulder. She spun around and realized no one had touched her just as the sky opened up and the rain fell all around her in skin-soaking sheets. A flash of lightning lit up the area, then plunged it into a dull, dark premature nightfall. Without thought, she rushed into the striped tent to her immediate right. She dashed through the flap and almost ran into a woman with caked make-up and large rings on every finger.

"It's you!" she said. The woman's heavily-lined face registered instant recognition. "At long last, it's you!"

Taking an awkward step back, Melinda shuddered. The old carnival teller was smiling through ruby red lips and pointing at her. Her cry of *"It's you!"* echoed in her head as she backed out of the tent and stood in the rain for a full minute before realizing that she was soaked.

Melinda began to shiver even though the late afternoon was warm. Teeth chattering, she looked around, but couldn't get her bearings. Striped tents were everywhere and she entered one at random, making sure it wasn't the one she had just fled.

The flap swished closed behind her and her eyes slowly adjusted to the dark, musky interior. She could see racks of costumes: spangled leotards, silly clown suits, short red jackets and a long ringmasters coat. Melinda relaxed and grabbed a deep rich purple velvet jacket, a jacket that fit so perfectly it seemed to mold itself to her and exude warmth. In a few minutes she stopped shivering and in a few more, the dark and the new-found warmth lulled her to sleep.

It was a deep sleep, filled with images of circus life: animals, clowns, fortune tellers, clowns, trapeze artists, clowns, elephants, clowns and faceless people who wanted her and frightened her, yet were not ominous. She awoke, feeling uneasy and confused. She tried to think, but couldn't get all the visions out of her head. Why'd she come to the circus anyway?

Oh yes, she remembered—to prove to herself that there was nothing to fear. She'd never been to a circus, hated playing big top with the other kids as they hung upside down on swing sets. She'd always been afraid of the big top, ever since she was a child, moving from foster home to foster home.

She felt the heavy weight of disappointment. She hadn't defeated or even confronted her demons. She left the dark protection of the costume tent and decided to sneak away before anyone discovered her. Everything was so quiet, no noise filtered in from outside, no laughter, no midway barkers calling to the crowd, no ringmaster's demands to look left or right or center ring, no calliope of tinny music. Just silence, silence as thick and impenetrable as the darkness enveloping her.

The midway was closed, the rides still, the animals asleep. It felt as if she were the only living soul at the circus. She looked over the midway, the food concessions were closed up tight and the games of chance silent. She saw a slit of light coming from the tent she had run into the first time, the fortune teller's tent. Why had that card reader acted like she knew her?

Gathering up all her courage and ignoring the weakness in her knees, Melinda went over, lifted the flap and walked inside.

The teller was seated at the table with two cups of tea and cookies. "Come and sit, dear. I'm sorry I frightened you earlier. It was just the shock of seeing you again. We'd almost given up hope, even though the cards foretold you'd come back."

Melinda took the chair. The tea looked inviting and she was hungry. "You know me?"

The teller laughed, "Yes, of course, dear. Do you know you?"

Melinda shook her head. "No," she whispered. "No, I don't really know me at all. I don't have a past."

"Yes, dear, you do. How much do you remember?"

"Living in foster homes, but not knowing anything more about me than my first name."

"Well, Melinda," the teller said in a soft, kind voice. "Here: take my hand."

Fearfully grasping the ring-covered, red-nailed hand that looked like a vicious talon but felt like soft velvet, Melinda was suddenly engulfed in images. Memories. This was her home. She tried to remember why she'd run away, but all she could recall was the clowns chasing her, clowns hunting for her, all these years, hunting for her... Wanting her.

She let go and gasped. "I remember! I ran away. Ran from all of you! Oh, the clowns, the clowns. I've got to get out of here!"

The reader reached for her hand. "No, don't try to leave. You're home now."

Melinda jumped up and ran out. She saw them then, the clowns, lurking, hiding in the shadows. She had to get away. She ran,

no one followed, but she could sense them all around her. So many clowns—why would such a small circus have so many, many clowns? She ran down the midway, blind to everything. Searching for a way out, she felt them closing in, drawing their circle tighter.

A doorway! Without thought, she ducked inside to find herself surrounded by herself. She reached out and touched glass. The house of mirrors! She ran, blindly bumping into the walls, confusing herself, losing herself. She was everywhere, reflecting back at herself, hundreds of Melindas.

She sank to the floor and wept. *What did all this mean?*

She heard them, saw them wandering the maze in search of the real her. There were hundreds, no, thousands of clowns, surrounding her as they reflected endlessly in their quest.

"If I just stay still, maybe they'll never find me," she whispered.

"Ah, Melinda, they will find you. They have to, they need you to come home." Melinda looked up and saw the fortune teller standing before her. The older woman smiled and held out her hand. "Come, it's time to come home and take your rightful place."

Tears streaming down her cheeks, Melinda took the old hand and suddenly another memory flooded in. "Mother? Mother!"

The reader smiled, and her once ominous face was suddenly warm and caring. "Oh, Melinda."

"Oh, Mother… Momma, I ran away… I was scared… terrified. I didn't want the responsibility. I was… I was just a dumb little kid. Then I forgot… I think I wanted to forget."

"I know, Melinda, it is hard to accept who we are, who we sometimes must be. A hard road for a sensitive child. My poor baby. All those years, I've missed you."

"Me too, Momma, I got lost and didn't know how to get home." Melinda smiled and hugged her mother. The last puzzle pieces fell into place. She was a part of the circus world, an important part that was never known by the mundane world outside.

She looked down and with a shaking hand, lifted a bright red nose from the floor at her feet, pulling it over her small one. A perfect fit.

She was Queen of the Clowns, and clowns the world over would soon hear of her return, and all would once again be right, All clowns worldwide would finally be united once again. That was what had frightened her as a child, made her run away: Too much responsibility for a child who hadn't even understood the word responsibility.

That's right, you are our Queen!" the clowns all shouted in a roar as they filed out into the night. "Long live the Queen!"

Melinda crossed the midway and they bowed. She came to a huge golden tent and entered. The clowns followed her, then the rest of the circus family entered as well. She walked to the end, to the throne, her throne. She took the gold crown covered in garish, brightly-colored glass jewels from the velvet seat and placed it on her head.

Smiling at her cheering subjects, Melinda sat, picked up her scepter and squeezed the bright orange rubber bulb at one end. As the horn blared out *ARRUUGAH,* she laughed, knowing she was finally home where she belonged.

— FIN —

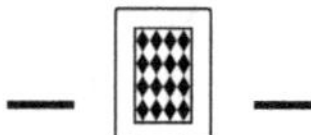

The weight of the crown presses down on your skull, and you raise your hands, touching the metal in surprise that isn't really surprise, running your fingers over the gems whose authenticity you still can't determine as the seventh mirror falls to pieces. The host smiles at you across the table as you lift the corona from your brow, xer nails slipping down the notches of the sphinx's spine. "Some truths are terrible… but some terrors are sweeter than the fear. Sometimes, the even the infernal lessons bring something other than strife."

You gently toss the crown across the table, landing at an angle against the chunk of meteorite. Another cannon burst of thunder roars, this one louder than all the others, and the electric lights on the sign above explode in a fountain of sparks, leaving the room lit only by the standing candles. Didi growls in displeasure at the noise, hissing at the sky, and your host's grin returns, pearly whites glistening in the flames. Xer hat remains in place again this time as xe flicks xer wrists, each hand producing a prop from within xer sleeve: one hand a masquerade mask, ribbons dangling, and the other a dagger, shining and sharp. "On one hand, a prison of one's one making…." xe says. "On the other, a prison snapping shut around you… Together, this next pair of tales forms a deadly…"

VIII. A Double Act

performed by Corrie Haldane

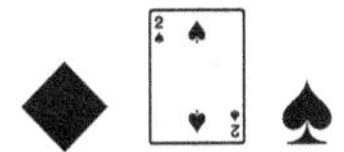

Freaks

When I reach the front of the grub line, Cook points at me with his wooden spoon. "You the new man?"

What has he heard about me? What does he know? I study my worn, dust-caked shoes rather than meet his eyes. "Yessir. Laborer."

He tilts my chin up with a greasy finger and studies me. I grit my teeth and let him, hoping he didn't visit the post office in the last town, where I signed on with this outfit. Hoping he didn't see a certain *"wanted"* poster by the door.

After a moment, Cook nods and ladles stew into my bowl. "You're gonna fit right in," he says.

I turn and scan the cookhouse for somewhere to sit, not sure whether to feel relieved or offended at Cook's declaration. Maybe he recognized me, maybe he didn't, but either way, every freak in the goddamn show is in here. I'm supposed to fit in with *this* crowd?

I squeeze between two of the strangest folks I've ever seen. On my right is some sort of animal man, completely covered with thick, black hair. Even his face is hidden behind a coat of coarse fur, though the pale blue eyes peering out at me aren't animal-like at all. He grunts in my direction but doesn't bother with me otherwise.

The man on my left is an astonishing height. I'm usually the tallest in any crowd, yet this man would have to slouch in order to rest his chin atop my head.

Boss had told me to eat quick, that I'd best not be late if I hoped to keep my job. He needn't have worried; I shovel the food in so fast, I barely taste it. Working and traveling with the circus is one thing; it puts money in my pocket and miles between me and my past. Eating with the freaks is something else altogether. I don't belong here. I am not one of them.

I drop my empty bowl into the washtub with a clatter and hurry past Cook. He's seasoning the Fat Lady's grub with spice from a small, ornamental box.

The Fat Lady licks her lips, chin slick with drool.

I shudder, and walk faster.

My traveling companions are strange, but as the days pass, I grow used to their oddities. The Siamese twins. The Four-legged Woman. The Bearded Lady. All of them.

They're the ones that bring in the money. Boss fawns over 'em and Cook does, too.

Me and the rest of the crew eat well enough, but Cook seasons the freaks' suppers extra special. He never brings out that pretty little box with the stained-glass lid when he's filling my plate. As I spoon up bland, over-cooked potato, I daydream about what that spice might taste like.

We all eat together in the cookhouse, but I mostly keep to myself. The other workers don't trust me yet, and the freaks don't mingle with the muscle.

Supper is mostly a cheerful affair, everyone stuffing their faces, laughing and talking. But one night, one of the roustabouts pins down Isaac the Human Skeleton while Cook force-feeds him. "You know you want it, Isaac," Cook croons as he shovels in another heaping spoonful.

In the days that follow, Isaac wolfs down plate after plate of Cook's carefully prepared meals, tears streaming down his face. But no matter how much he eats, he just gets skinnier and skinnier.

One night, I line up for grub behind Jack the Gentle Giant, one of my dining companions back on my first day. I tilt my head, look up at him. "If I didn't know better, I'd swear you've grown since I got here."

Jack laughs. I laugh. Cook laughs, too. He's still laughing when he slips the pretty little box from his pocket, and he winks at me as he sprinkles a pinch of seasoning over my meal.

For the first time since I joined up, I feel like I belong. I wink back.

Annie, a voluptuous young woman with a luxurious beard, beckons me over and I sit down beside her on the long wooden bench. As I dig into the grub, she squeezes my thigh and smiles up at me. Supper tastes especially good that night. So does every meal thereafter.

Cook makes sure of it.

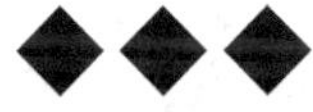

Although Cook has taken a shine to me, Boss still pushes me hard. Everything hurts, but my right shoulder throbs ferociously, and I reach across to massage the aching joint. The skin, stretched taut over muscle and bone, is hot to the touch.

Teardown, set up. Over and over, town after town. The demands upon my body are constant and I fall into my bunk each night with relief.

In time, the freaks come to accept me, as I've come to accept them. They laugh with me over meals in the cookhouse. They invite me to sit by their fire in the evenings. And Annie the Bearded Lady shares my bunk at night.

"You belong to the circus," Cook says one night as he hands me my plate. "Always."

NOT
LIKE TH
NOT LI
NOT LIK
OF SWORDS

I grin at him, thank him for the grub, and find a seat at my regular table. *You're gonna fit right in,* he'd told me back when I first signed on. I hadn't believed it then, but it had turned out to be the truth.

Zip the Pinhead sits down beside me, crazy eyes rolling in opposite directions. He gestures at my plate. "You shouldn't eat that."

I ignore him, relishing the taste of Cook's special seasoning, marveling at how it seems to change flavors with every bite: sometimes sweet, other times savory, but always delicious. I mop my plate clean with a hunk of bread.

"Big man gets bigger. Hairy lady gets hairier. Zip gets zippier." He points to his tiny head, laughing and crying at the same time. "What happens to *you?*"

I rub my shoulder as I glance around the cookhouse. Ten minutes ago, I saw a room full of friends, folks I'd come to know and like. But as Zip stumbles away, I shake my head and look again. These aren't regular folks, and I don't want to belong with them. They're a bunch of wild-eyed freaks stuffing their faces. The food turns to sawdust in my mouth.

What happens to me?

I don't mean to find out.

That night, when Annie comes to me, I send her away. And when the circus finally sleeps, I make my escape.

A shadow among shadows, I dart between the tents and wagons. When I reach the edge of camp, I wait for a cloud to drift across the moon. Then I run.

Dawn breaks as I reach the woods. I push on, rubbing my aching shoulder as I stumble over tree roots and rocks.

The birds are noisy, and then they are not. *Is someone following me?*

I head deeper into the brush. My shirt snags on a branch and rips. I pull it off, throw it away, and keep going.

As the sun climbs across the sky, I slow, finally stopping to catch my breath beside a small pool. All is silent. I am alone.

Free.

I take a deep, shuddery breath and bend over the water for a drink. Before I can dip my hand into the pool, I catch sight of my reflection and freeze. An enormous growth protrudes from my right shoulder.

I hesitantly reach up to touch it, leaning forward for a better look.

The surface of the pool is calm. My reflection is clear. The painful mass on my shoulder swells, pulsates.

And then, it opens its eyes.

Cook's voice echoes in my head: *You belong to the circus. Always. You're gonna fit right in.*

When I scream, the sound is doubled as a second voice joins mine in hellish harmony.

Iron & Ink

The fat man, pockets heavy with my gold, unlatches the padlock on the circus wagon's door. He ducks inside and beckons me to follow.

"You ain't *never* seen the likes of this." His boast is barely more than a whisper so as to avoid waking the ringmaster, who sleeps in the next wagon over.

He lights a lantern and our shadows dance along the wall. I incline my head towards the tattered sheet that blocks off one end of the caravan. "Is she… behind there?"

He nods, pulls the curtain aside, and holds the lantern high. "Feast your eyes, sir!"

A woman lies naked upon a wooden platform, blinking against the sudden light. Her skin is elaborately tattooed with flowers, vines, and runes. Her wrists and ankles are bound with iron cuffs. Her golden wings are spread out beneath her, pinned to the wood with delicate iron nails.

Iron. I can feel its hateful bite, even from across the room.

The man grins. "Told ya, didn't I?"

A single tear traces a salty track down my cheek. "Yes," I say, sliding my silver blade between his ribs. "You did."

The fat man collapses at my feet. I snatch the key ring from his spasming fingers. The iron burns, even through my calfskin gloves.

I unlock the manacles and tug the nails free. She sits, curling her wings round herself, concealing the ink upon her flesh. The same designs decorate my own body. The needle's burn binds us, always.

"Husband," she sighs. "I knew you'd come."

She tugs the curtain free, wraps herself in it, then plucks the bloody knife from my fingers. "I hope you saved the Ringmaster for me."

— FIN —

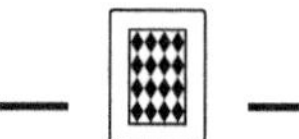

The tip of the knife pierces the nose of the mask, and then the fabric flutters to the table as the eighth set of shards falls to the floor. Immediately Didi pounces on his new domino-print toy, getting tangled up in the frilly ribbon as his claws extend. You hear your host laugh for the first time, and as you hear the sound, you find yourself wondering for the what xer story is—and then you blush, as the question feels indecent, like undressing xem in a perverse mental exercise.

As if to punctuate the point, the blade lands tooth down in the table's surface, sticking up like Excalibur in its hunk of rock. "For this next story, I'd like to try something different," xe says, and then xe beckons to you with a spindly finger, biding you come to xer side of the table for the first time. "Kneel," xe says, and you have an uncomfortable feeling of being hunted, as if Didi is not the only cat in the room and one is much bigger than the other. Xe reaches again under the table, and produces a palette of paints and a brush. "Try not to wiggle too much," xe instructs, and begins to apply paint to the brush and then to the tip of your nose. "This next tale is one of trial and tribulation, of the truth willing to out itself, of walls closing in as we partake in…"

IX. Clowning Around Big Top Where Wishes & Nightmares Come True

performed by Alicia Hilton

The clown at the ticket booth was crying green tears and smelled like formaldehyde, but Joseph bought two Fun Plus Passes for *Clowning Around Big Top*. It was Emily's eighth birthday, the first birthday they'd spent together without her mother, and he wanted the day to be perfect.

"Thanks, Daddy," Emily said.

He leaned down and kissed her cheek, then grasped her hand.

His daughter's flesh felt as cold as ice, and her fingers trembled like a frightened bird about to fly away, but her smile was radiant.

One of Emily's canines was chipped. Joseph made a mental note to call the dentist and see whether it should be filed or capped.

As they walked through the tunnel that led to the circus tent, Joseph smelled manure, cotton candy, hotdogs, and something musty.

There was no ticket attendant at the end of the tunnel, but joyous roars and bright lights greeted them. The bleachers were packed with spectators.

Splat. Gelatinous goo dropped on the ground near Joseph's left shoe.

He looked up and saw bats swooping around the ceiling, flitting around lanterns like giant black moths.

Joseph glanced at their tickets—F17 and F19. Their seats were on the left, six rows from the railing. "Do you need to go potty before we sit down?"

Emily shook her head. She turned towards the central arena.

Four clowns who wore skeleton costumes were harnessing two donkeys to wooden chariots. Each clown had whips and cudgels strapped to their belts.

At first, Joseph thought the donkeys were real since the masks were so realistic, but he noticed that the animals wore human shoes instead of having hooves. Joseph said, "Do you think they're going to race like gladiators?"

"Can I ride in a cart?" Emily asked.

"It's not a pony ride. They're people in costumes." He chuckled.

She squeezed his hand tighter until her little nails bit into his skin.

Joseph's flesh stung, but instead of chastising his daughter for cutting him, he felt a surge of excitement. He enjoyed experiencing pain almost as much as inflicting wounds.

Emily fidgeted. "Where's Mommy? I want to go home."

"Mommy's gone on a trip. Don't whine, Princess."

One of the donkeys brayed and kicked sawdust in a clown's face, then lifted its tail and farted, making a sound like a trumpet.

The tallest clown turned towards the spectators. "Shall we punish the beast?"

A woman with a flowered hat yelled, "Flog him."

A teenage boy in the front row raised his fist. "Bite. Don't let 'em hit you!"

The naughty donkey brayed, but didn't attack the clowns.

The tall clown uncoiled his whip. *Crack.* Leather lashed the donkey's hindquarters, cleaving a scarlet stripe in the fur.

The man in the donkey costume screamed, "Stop. Mercy!"

The clown gave him another lash.

A tear rolled down Emily's cheek. She asked, "Why did he hurt him? The donkey was just being silly." She let go of Joseph's hand and wiped her face.

NO
EXIT
FACE
YOUR
FEAR

Joseph ruffled her hair.

She flinched when he touched the bald spot on top of her head where curly tresses had been yanked out.

Joseph didn't apologize. The child needed to toughen up. He said, "Silliness can be dangerous. The clowns are teaching the donkeys to behave."

Emily looked down at her feet.

"Hungry? I'm working up an appetite," Joseph said.

She sniffed. "My tummy hurts."

"Ice cream would make you feel better. I'll bet they've got strawberry."

She raised her chin. "I'm not hungry. Can I get my face painted?"

"Princess, they don't do face painting at the circus."

She pointed towards a sign that said *Restrooms*. "Over there, Daddy. A clown has lots of pretty colors. She'll paint my face."

Joseph saw people queued up for the toilets, but no booths or shops.

Emily said, "*Please.*" She grabbed his hand and tugged it. Her skin was warm, so hot that he almost jerked away.

"Okay, Princess. We'll make a pit stop if there's no face painting."

They'd walked about thirty feet when a man strolling in the other direction jabbed his elbow into Joseph's ribs. "Watch where you're going," Joseph said.

The man turned around, and Joseph got a better look at his face.

A long diagonal scar bisected his ugly mug, leaving a deep notch in his nose. The left eye was so bloodshot, the sclera looked more crimson than white.

Joseph rarely apologized for anything, but tightness in his belly prompted him to say, "Sorry, my mistake."

Emily said, "Daddy, hurry. I'm next!" She pointed in the direction of the bathrooms, but the queue of people had vanished. Instead of the *Restrooms* sign, there was a pink neon light that said *Face Painting*, hanging above a door.

Joseph blinked. When he opened his eyes, the neon sign was still there, but the color had changed to yellow, Emily's favorite color. "How did you know it was here?" he asked.

"The bats told me." Emily smiled, flashing her chipped canine. Giggling, his daughter ran towards the sign. Her legs were much shorter than his, but she sprinted like she was turbo charged. Emily got to the door and grasped the knob.

"Wait for me," he shouted, but his daughter ignored his plea.

By the time he'd run to the door, Emily had vanished.

The hallway was darker than the tunnel they'd walked through to enter the Big Top, a hell of a lot darker, and it was filthy. The concrete floor was cracked, the walls were stained, covered with spatter marks, and Joseph couldn't see a damn thing ten feet in front of him. He smelled something musky, like a wet dog.

"Emily," he called. "Emily, answer me!" Of course, the little fool didn't respond. She was turning into a headstrong bitch, like her mother.

He pulled his smartphone out of his pocket so he could turn on the light, but the battery was dead.

As the hallway got even darker, he shuffled forward, pausing periodically to shout for his daughter. Soon, claustrophobia set in, and it got hard to breathe. He bumped into a wall and swore. Holding his hands out, he felt around himself and breathed a sigh of relief when he realized that the hallway had curved to the right. As he made his way around the bend, the hallway brightened. He saw two figures ahead of him.

A woman wearing a frizzy red wig and white face paint was sitting on one side of a table. Another woman, a brunette with long hair, was sitting in the chair opposite the clown.

"Hello," Joseph said. "I'm looking for my daughter. She's eight."

The brunette turned around.

When Joseph saw her face, he gasped. "Emily?"

She had his daughter's green eyes, and a mole on her left cheek, just like Emily, but she wasn't a little girl. She looked like she was twenty-one. *Impossible!*

The woman who looked like Emily said, "We were waiting for you, Daddy."

Joseph's eyes watered. "Princess?"

Emily said, "I'm not a princess, I'm a lion."

The clown dipped a paintbrush in yellow paint, leaned towards Emily, and stroked the brush across her cheek.

Miraculously, fur and whiskers appeared.

Joseph leaned against the wall, fighting a sudden wave of dizziness.

As the clown painted more of his daughter's face, her visage transformed, becoming feline. Even her eyes changed, the irises transforming to amber.

"Purrrfect!" the clown declared.

"This can't be happening. I—I'm dreaming," Joseph stammered.

The lion said, "I'm hungry, Daddy. Pay the clown."

Joseph's hands shook when he pulled out his wallet. "How much do I owe you?"

"Your money's no good here. Truth or dare?" the clown said.

Joseph laughed, but it was a brittle sound that bordered on hysteria. "What're you going to ask me to do? Walk a tightrope?"

Emily growled, a rumble so loud, the floor shook. Her mouth opened wider as she roared again, baring her canines—fangs at least four inches long.

Joseph's bowels gurgled. He clenched his groin but couldn't stop urine from dribbling down his leg. He hadn't pissed himself since he was in second grade.

When Emily's horrid roar finally stopped reverberating, the clown said, "Your daughter wants you to tell the truth. Why did you kill her and your wife?"

Joseph wanted to deny the accusation, but his lips and tongue moved as if someone else controlled his body. "Money," he said.

Emily extended her paws and attacked. Claws raked across Joseph's throat, turning his scream into a gurgle.

The last sound that Joseph heard was the clown's laughter.

— **FIN** —

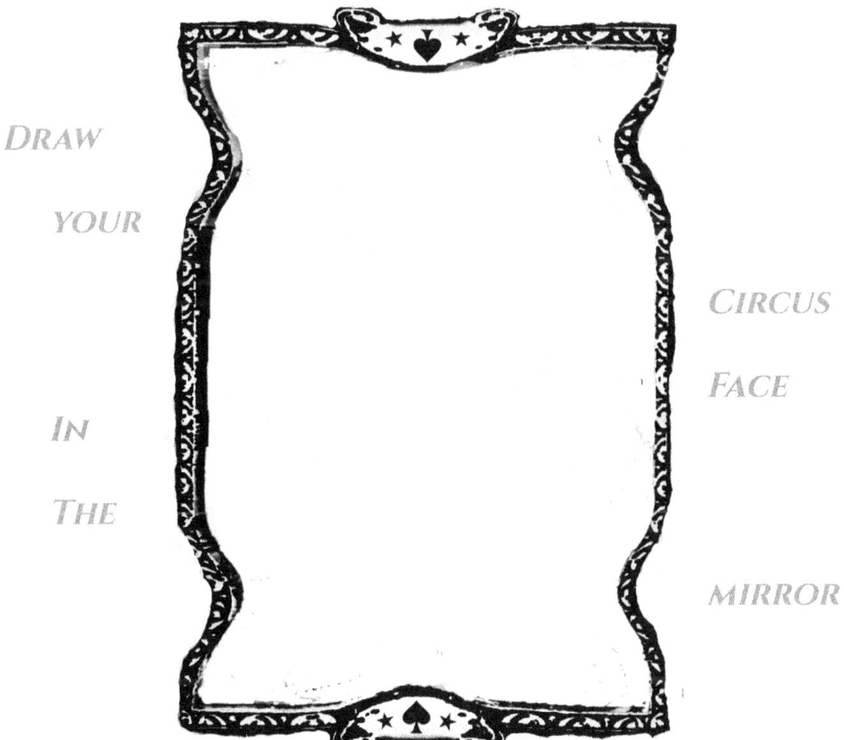

The story ends and the sinister laughter fades, leaving only the tittering of your host; it's a wonderful lilting, teasing sound, and you look up to see xem smiling down at you. "There," xe says, dotting you one final time on the nose with xer brush before producing a hand mirror as another of its larger brethren bites the dust. You take in your painted visage, carefully considering the geography of the face under the makeup:

You smile back at xem, feeling at home here with this strange storyteller, feeling like you're looking under your skin rather than at makeup covering it. In a moment of boldness, you kiss xer knuckles in thanks, leaving the slightest streak of paint against their knuckles. For the first time, it occurs to you how odd it is that in a festival as crowded as this, that no one else has wandered into the tent this whole time.

"Halfway through your trial," xe says, pulling you to your feet and leading you back to your side of the table, standing behind you, a hand on your on shoulder. "Half the locks picked." Xer breath tickles your ear, and you suddenly remember your glass of lemonade on the table, the acidic saccharin nearly the same taste as xer whisper. "No prop to prompt this next tale," xe says, placing a palm on the small of your back, the other hand gliding against your wrist and raising it into the air. "Follow my movements. Sense the next story in your lungs, in your ligaments, in your limbs. Close your eyes. Don't see this one. Feel it. Breathe it in. Breathe it out. Stretch. Feel yourself let go, bending, becoming more…"

X. FLEXIBLE

performed by Corinne Pollard

"Have you worked at a circus before?"

The manager threw the question over his shoulder as we entered the tent. Wide-eyed from the tall ceiling of red and white stripes, it caught me unawares and I shook my head, knowing my interview was hanging on by a thread. Sure enough, the manager frowned, but his stride did not falter.

We proceeded to the ring, where he pointed out the seating structure, the amount of sand covering the stage and other details he needed athletic men for. I nodded at every pause, but my mind wandered. I darted glances everywhere, eager to spot any anomalies, proof that I was not insane. Once I passed the interview, the hunt could begin.

"... questions?"

"Yeah." I bent closer to his tobacco-scented jacket. "I've heard men have been disappearing without a trace."

"No, no, the men have been coming down with the flu. You've nothing to worry about. Now, do you want the job or not?"

I accepted without delay, eager to begin my undercover operation.

Back at the hotel, I double-checked my equipment until confident that each machine was functioning well. As I put away the thermal camera, my phone buzzed.

"When are you giving up this ghost-hunting malarkey?" My wife's annoyance burned my ear. "Come home, Reggie. You've missed too many birthdays on this."

"I know and I'm sorry, but this is it. I can feel it. Too much unexplained weirdness is going on."

My wife snorted. "When are you going to grow up? Ghosts aren't real!"

I sooth-talked her, murmuring the usual that it would be my last operation if I couldn't find anything, but her fiery temper refused to be blown out even after I had wished the children goodnight. I promised to transfer funds to replace the broken stove before she hung up with a grunt. She's never understood why it's important to me. I need confirmation of an existing afterlife alongside ours. The objects that moved without me touching them and the flickering lights I experienced growing up needed justification. My skittish mind needed the answers as much as I sought to breathe.

My phone buzzed again. Sweet Elsie. An angel. Her golden curls always smelled of strawberries, strong enough for my tongue to taste it. She giggled, as I whispered how much I missed her and the things we would do in bed once I was back.

The next day, I armed myself with the EMF gauge. Its aerial poked out from my pocket, silent, as I fulfilled each task the boss assigned me. The device was quiet all morning, but on my break, I struck gold. A loud humming erupted, and I dragged the noisy device out into the open. No one else was around, as I scanned the staff room, but the hum then died.

I retraced my steps, confirming that the signal seemed stronger, emanating from a corridor. I followed the sound-waves as butterflies fluttered inside my belly.

A closed flap in the canvas pulled my gaze, and I leapt inside. Each canvas wall was coated red, a bloody chamber. Lockers and benches chopped the musty space in half. It appeared undisturbed, but the EMF gauge screeched.

A sudden drop in temperature stuttered my lungs.

"What are you doing here? This is the ladies' changing room!"

She was gorgeous, with a river of black hair tied in a high ponytail and generous curves enhanced by her skin tight leotard. It

wasn't good enough.

represented her Asian heritage, with a golden dragon coiling around her crimson torso. For a second, the dragon's scales looked like they shimmered while slithering.

She noticed me staring, and with a smile, she raised her arms, stretching them. In a blink of an eye, she bent her waist unnaturally backwards and flipped her head. There were no cracking sounds from her bones as if her limbs were made of elastic.

She righted herself and winked. "Like what you see?"

The EMF gauge slipped out of my fingers from my amazement. I stammered an apology and picked up my now silent device. It didn't seem to be broken, but the sudden silence was louder than its previous screeches. Something was amiss.

"I'm performing later and was practicing a new contortion requested by the manager. He is very demanding." She crossed her arms, almost pouting.

Once again, her body sucked in my attention. I spied her curves, delectable hills against the spandex. My hands flexed as my mouth watered.

I coughed. "You're good. I like what I see."

A flash of anticipation flickered across her face. She was interested. "You like, huh?"

I nodded, stepping closer into her personal space.

"Do you want to bend with me?" Her sultry words tasted spicy. An addictive drug. It rushed to my head. I reached out to grip her shoulders while nodding.

Intense pain struck me, and I collapsed onto the carpet with a cry. Glancing at the cause, I almost vomited at the sight of my arm contorted into a fleshy spiral. Bones had popped, skin had ripped, and blood dripped.

"Bend with me." She giggled, and my arm tightened as it twisted. I screamed for it to stop, and miraculously, it listened. "*Aww,* I thought you liked flexibility."

My other arm bent backwards, hard enough to snap the bone in two. I yelled for help as my stomach roiled. Vomit spewed out of my mouth and soaked down my t-shirt.

The contortionist leaned over me, tutting, as her dragon glared, fangs bared. "If you don't like being flexible, then why have an affair?"

"I'm sorry!" I wept, but a glint sparked in her eyes.

"Why do men do this to us? We're women, not objects to mess around with." Her petite face darkened as she spat. "And yet when we find out they're married, they make us stay, because they love us and not their wife. They lie and lie. We just accept it, because we love them."

My leg folded in the wrong direction. It tore apart at the knee, shredding skin, arteries, and ligaments. Blood sprayed like a fountain and then pooled underneath me. I wanted to black out, but fear and adrenaline that flooded my remaining veins kept me alert.

Without using my butchered arms, I tried to crawl flat on my stomach towards the exit. My weak squirms led me nowhere. I changed tactics again, pleading for the contortionist to release me from this agony, but her mind was elsewhere.

Her dark eyes were fixated, lowered to peer at her chest, and before my eyes, slices ruptured, staining the leotard a more sinister shade of red. The wounds spread, an assault beyond my comprehension that churned my stomach.

She glanced at me and smiled with crimson splattered teeth. "He said he loved me and he lied."

My eyes widened as I felt an invisible force gripping my neck, and for a brief second, I wished I'd taken my wife's advice. My neck twisted with a thundering snap.

— FIN —

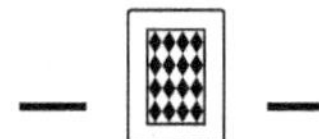

You exhale in a long, gentle breath, feeling the stretch in your extremities, feeling centered and grounded. By the time the tenth mirror does its familiar trick, you find that you are scarcely even startled anymore by the sudden sound, which has become as familiar as the sounds produced by your own body. You are slow to open your eyes, and when you do so find that you are on the floor, once again looking up at your host, gathering your limbs back around you. You do not know how you twisted in your reverie, only that your arms and legs and spinal column now feel loose and free and relaxed.

As you get to your feet and take your place back on the stool, xe crosses back over to the other side of the table, this time producing from xer hat a closed wooden box. The crank on the side is wound, and xe sets it on the table as it pops open, revealing a tiny, rotating big top accompanied by a tinny reproduction of calliope music, the tinkling tune mingling with the continued drumming of the rain above. You take in the little striped tent in its tiny world, turning a pirouette on its spindle, and xe places xer palms against the table on either side of the box. "Miniscule worlds that are bigger on the inside, turned inside out and let loose to run amuck in the big, grown-up universe," xe intones. "For our next story, we bend and we stoop, making ourselves small enough to step into a child's brand new..."

XI. Circus Tent

performed by Kerry E.B. Black

Brad and Lynn set up the miniature circus tent in the center of the living room. A blue flag topped the red and yellow striped canvas cylinder. Scallops and dags dripped cheerfully, adding to the festive feel.

Adam clapped his chubby hands as he jumped and laughed. "I wuv it, Momma! Fank you, Daddy!"

Proud parents grabbed hands in silent congratulations, pleased by their three-year-old's enthusiasm.

Adam climbed through the door flap, blue to distinguish it from the rest of the tent, and vanished from sight.

His parents knelt at the entrance.

The interior was large enough for Adam to stand. If he reached up, he could not touch the spire. Light filtered through the material cast zebra-like stripes of gold and gray. He took his crustless peanut butter and marshmallow whip sandwich inside, chatting with imagined companions.

Brad sniffed. "I swear I smell roasted peanuts."

His wife pointed out the sandwich, raising an eyebrow. As she walked to the kitchen to tidy up the lunch dishes, he patted her rump. She giggled.

Brad caught a whiff of fresh-spun cotton candy.

"Yippee!" Adam's voice accompanied a thudding sound inside. "I wuv horsies."

Brad tuned the television to local news, ignoring his son's boisterous exclamations. He crinkled his nose. An herbal scent, almost like the alfalfa hay Brad used to feed livestock when he was a teen, drifted through. His wife must have lit a candle. Strange scent, though.

A phrase uttered by his son registered on his distracted parental consciousness. "Uh oh, she's naked. I can't look."

The boy backed out of the tent, eyes covered with sticky hands, his tongue sticking out in a *yuck*.

Brad pressed the remote's off button. "Son, what're you doing?"

"I don't want to see the naked lady, Daddy. I'm going to the baffroom." The boy rushed down the hall. Under his arms was tucked a small stuffed clown doll Brad didn't recognize.

Naked lady?

Adam certainly had an active imagination. Still, Brad bent and pushed aside the blue door flap to look inside the tent.

On the canvas floor rested the plastic superhero plate, topped by the mostly-eaten sandwich and corn chip crumbs. Brad collected the lunch left-overs and straightened, feeling the gentle caress of the canvas against his cheek as he stood. A whiff of jasmine and sandalwood made him think of belly dancers. He closed his eyes, picturing a bonfire around which swayed tanned hips barely clothed in silks and tinkling bells.

"Daddy, you're in my way."

Brad snapped out of his reverie, stepping aside to allow his son to enter.

"Did you light a fire, darling?" his wife inquired, taking the plate and kissing his flushed cheek.

"No, I thought you did."

She looked over her shoulder, head cocked to one side, but said nothing.

"I want an elephant ride!" Adam shouted.

Brad shook his head and sank into a comfortable position on his brown leather recliner and turned the news on again. Soon, he

SERPENS
CAPUT
SERPENS
CAUDA
AQUILA
EQUULEUS
DELPHINUS
M13
HERCULES
CORONA BOREALIS
LYRA
CYGNUS
M27
M13
Cap
Algol
LYNX
PERSEUS
ARDALIS
TRIANGULUM
Double Cluster
URSA MAJOR
LEO MINOR
M33
M81
CASSIOPEIA
M31
URSA MINOR
ANDROMEDA

dozed and dreamed of feather and sequence-clad beauties whipping lions until they obeyed each command. He awoke, aroused.

His wife's legs stuck out of the tent's entrance. She sang a silly song with their son inside.

With a lecherous smile, Brad ran his foot up the fleshy protruding curves of her calves and thighs, wiggling his toes at the base of her pink shorts.

"Ahem, I'll be right back, Adam." Her face appeared between the tent flaps. "May I help you?"

Smile crooked across his face, he leered, wagging his finger to entice her to follow.

She sighed, disappeared once more to kiss his son loudly ("Ah, *Mom*!"), then emerged to grab her husband's hand. He guided her to their bedroom and lavished kisses on her eager mouth and delicate neck. She gasped and responded, met the kiss with passion until they collapsed, spent and tangled in sheets no longer neatly arranged upon their queen-sized bed.

She deposited little kisses like pops on her husband's cheeks and forehead while he admired the pert bosom jiggling beneath her freshly-donned, white cotton t-shirt.

"Lynn, we haven't taken Adam to a circus. How do you suppose he knows so much about them?"

She stopped, eyes narrowed. "I don't know. What do you mean?"

"Well, he was talking about tigers and trained puppies and tightrope walkers. How does he even know the word trapeze?"

She laughed, shaking her head. "Adam is such a clever child." However, her brow was knitted.

Adam's shrill voice interrupted the short silence that followed. "Momma? Daddy? Watch what I can do!"

Brad wondered how long Adam had stood in the bedroom doorway, but more startling were the three kitchen knives in his hands.

"I can juggle. The cwown told me I can."

Lynn reacted first, her voice quivering with concern. Her hands shook as she reached toward him. "Honey, you know you're not allowed to touch knives."

"I know, but watch. I am a circus p-former!"

The child threw the utensils into the air.

Lynn screamed.

Brad froze in horror.

Garnet splattered the white sheets and tan carpet as the child attempted to catch the blades.

— FIN —

The music box grinds to a halt in time with the breaking of the next mirror, the shards tumbling like the juggled knives that had occupied your mind's eye a moment before. The miniature tent has stopped its spin, and xer fingers snap the lid shut. "More hard lessons," xe says, moving the box to the pile of spent items. "More's the pity."

You remember a childhood injury—cutting your hand trying to open a Christmas present with scissors, or maybe trying to climb something you shouldn't have and slicing your palm to shit. Your body remembers, twitches in empathy, even if your brain can't recall the exact wound. The innocence of childhood and the vulnerability, the smallness that comes of being and the ease of breaking.

For the first time, you realize that somehow, it seems that the tent has become smaller as the mirrors have broken, as if the canvas around you has constricted like a boa. Surely, you reason, it's just a trick of the darkness, an optical illusion caused by the electric lights above going kaput.

One, two, three rings xe plucks from the hat with xer nimble fingers, landing them in front of you with a repeated flick of the wrist. Xe holds the hat in the air, not smiling now, looking gravely serious. "Again we travel into the realm of image, of experience, of dynamic flow, logic be damned..." One of the rings soars through the air, missing the hat by almost a foot. You flinch, shake it off, and ready the next ring. "Swing once, swing twice, swing three times, a series of dazzling acts that make up a stunning..."

XII. Triple Threat

performed by Trevor Wright

Of Beast & Blood

The ring feels too small tonight,
the lion's eyes locked on yours,
glowing with something
you've tried to ignore.
You raise the whip,
but your hand trembles,
and deep down,
you know
this was always coming.

The lion paces,
its body tense,
muscles rippling beneath golden fur.
It was once tame,
obedient.
You made sure of that.
You beat it down,
broke its spirit,
forced it to bow beneath the

crack of your whip. But

nothing stays broken forever.

The crowd cheers,
but the sound fades,
drowned out by the low growl
that rumbles deep in the beast's throat.
Its eyes burn,
not with fear,
but with rage.
You taught it that.

You step forward,
cracking the whip,
but the sound is hollow,
a useless snap in the still air.
The lion's lips curl back,
revealing sharp teeth,
teeth you once trusted
to stay hidden.

You made it this way.
You starved it,
pushed it,
drove it mad with hunger and pain,
and now,
the hunger turns on you.

The whip falls from your hand,
useless,
as the beast lunges.
Its claws dig deep into the dirt,
its eyes burning with fury,
with the fire you stoked.
You try to run,
but you can't.
You can only watch as the beast closes in,
its jaws snapping,
its breath hot against your skin.

You taught it to hate.
You made it savage.
And now,
it's taking back what you tried to steal
its freedom,
its power,
its soul.
The lion roars,
and the sound shakes the ground beneath your feet, the air
thick with the smell of blood.
Your blood.
You created this monster,
and now,
it's the last thing you'll ever see.
The crowd gasps,
but it's too late.
The beast you tried to tame,
the hunger you created,
has finally devoured you.
And the cage you thought would hold it
was always your own.

SHATTERED SELF

At dusk, the fun house hums,
lights flickering against the cold glass.
I step inside, surrounded by
twisted reflections, faces
pulled wide,
bodies stretched and warped,
distorted but harmless, at first.

The deeper I go, the air thickens.
Laughter echoes,
faint and distant,
a mocking sound that bounces from

mirror to mirror. My reflection
turns before I do,
its grin sharp, eyes unblinking.

I freeze,
its gaze pinned to my chest,
fingers pressed to glass that chills my bones.
I back away, but it lingers,
moving when I don't,
a shadow detached from its source.

The lights flicker,
and suddenly there are many of me,
each one wearing the same twisted smile,
each one watching, waiting.

I run, but I am everywhere—
reflections split, refract,
filling the space with versions of myself
I've never seen before.

The mirrors close in,
surrounding me like hungry mouths,
the glass no longer cold,
but breathing,
and I am no longer the one outside looking in.

THE LAST TOSS

The barker pulls me aside,
away from the noise
and crowds,
his voice low, smooth.
"How about something
a bit more… special?"
His eyes gleam in the fading light,
and for a moment,

DREAM

I hesitate.

"Three tries," he says,
"three rings,
that's all you'll need."
His smile widens,
promising,
enticing.
"One perfect throw,
and the prize of a lifetime
is yours."

I glance at the booth,
hidden in shadow,
away from the bright lights.
The game is simple,
a ring toss like any other—
except for the promise
of something grand.
It sits in the center,
a thing of beauty,
radiant under the carnival glow.

"Your wildest dreams," he whispers,
"within reach, if you're willing to play."

I take the first ring,
its weight heavier
than expected,
but the rules seem clear,
the goal
within reach.
I throw—
the ring spins through the air,
glinting under the twilight.

It misses.
But the barker's grin

never fades.
"Two more," he murmurs,
"you're so close."
I can feel it—
the lure of the prize,
its shine pulling at me,
the promise of dreams made real.

Another toss,
the ring just shy
of the mark.
But I'm in too deep now.
The prize seems closer,
more vivid,
its glow pulsing
like a heartbeat.

"Last chance,"
his voice smooth,
encouraging.
"One more try."
I throw again,
and this time
it lands.

The barker claps slowly,
his smile widening
as he steps closer.
"You've done it," he says,
"take what's yours."

I reach for the prize,
its surface cold,
but I barely notice.
All I see
is the life it promises,
the future I've longed for.

But as I pull it from the shelf,
something shifts.
The prize feels different,
heavier,
colder.
The shimmer fades,
and beneath the surface,
darkness stirs.

The barker's voice tightens
around me
like a noose.
"Did you think it would be so easy?"
His eyes glint,
sharp as glass,
and I realize too late—
the game
was never about winning.

The prize, once radiant,
now writhes
in my hands,
alive with something ancient,
something hungry.

I try to let go,
but it clings to me,
its promises unraveling
into curses.
The life I dreamed of twists into shadows,
and the barker fades
into the dark,
leaving me
with the weight
of what I've won.

— FIN —

The second ring lands amongst the rest of the memorabilia, looking around the handle of the knife still stuck in the tabletop, but you watch the third glide through the air, finding its mark as the sound of breaking glass cries out for the twelfth time. It disappears back into the shadows from whence it came and the hat rolls down xer arm before being flipped back on top of xer head. "Bravo, brava, bravissimo!" xe exclaims, deadly countenance breaking back into a riotous smile. You breathe a sigh of relief, and then laugh at yourself a bit—for a moment you had almost believed the game had mortal stakes, was more than a silly contest.

"Twelve tales, twelve times we've danced so far," xe says, and xe again reaches beneath the table, this time withdrawing what looks to be the coffin of an infant. The door opens, revealing a porcelain doll inside, her pale cheeks and glass eyes making her seem not just inanimate, but indeed like something no longer alive. The doll's ballroom dress is musty with cobwebs, and there are spiders caught in her fountain of black ringlets. "Another story, then—the thirteenth stroke of the clock. An account of impersonation and retaliation, the thrilling tale of…"

XIII. The Living Corpse

performed by Kevin Hopson

"**H**ow do you do it?" Sebastian asked.

Georgia sat inside her stagecoach, meeting Sebastian's gaze. "Do what?"

Sebastian eased into the leather-padded bench seat across from her. "Die and then return to the world of the living."

A chuckle escaped Georgia's lips. "I don't really die. I simply slow my heartbeat and breathing to the point where I appear to be dead."

"But everyone believes it."

"That's the point," Georgia said.

"I suppose."

"If you must know, it took years of practice to master."

Sebastian's brow furrowed. "So, you're implying that someone such as myself could do it?"

Georgia shrugged. "Perhaps, but it's possible that not everyone possesses the ability. Much like your gift. You can bend your body in unfathomable ways, and I'm certain I can't do the same."

"But my gift is purely physical. Not to say that yours isn't, but there must be a mental skill to it as well."

"Of course. As I said, it took me years to perfect."

Sebastian nodded, inspecting the stagecoach with a keen eye. "This is a very nice stagecoach. Much better than mine. How do you afford it?"

BREATH
IT IN
BREAT
IT OU

Georgia debated whether to answer. "I have a side business," she finally said.

Sebastian raised an eyebrow. "What type of business?"

"Impersonating the dead."

"I'm afraid you've lost me."

"Have you ever wanted to disappear and start a new life elsewhere?" Georgia asked.

"The thought has crossed my mind."

"Well, I help people do just that. For example, wives who want to escape their abusive husbands. Or gamblers so far in debt that they can't possibly pay up. These people are desperate. Desperate enough to fake their own death. But it's only convincing if there's a body, which is where I come in."

"How so?"

"It's carefully planned out," Georgia replied. "The proper people are paid off, and I disguise myself as the deceased when the time comes."

"Men included?"

Georgia nodded. "Makeup and props do wonders. I can even alter my height and build by wearing certain apparel."

Sebastian's mouth hung agape. "Have you ever been buried alive?"

"Only once. Thankfully the pastor dug me out shortly after. It was Johnny Moore's funeral."

"My cousin?"

Georgia's eyes bulged. She hadn't meant to let the name slip. "He'd run up quite the gambling debt. But if it's any consolation, he's in California starting a new life."

"Well," Sebastian said, taking a breath. "I suppose I can take some comfort in that." He hesitated. "Are there any others I should know about?"

"I'm usually sworn to silence, but I do feel a little guilty for keeping Johnny's secret from you."

Georgia leaned forward, and Sebastian did the same.

"Do you remember Governor Poole?" she whispered.

"He's alive?"

"No. He actually died, but not until after faking his death. He planned to run off with another woman but his wife found out and killed him for real."

— FIN —

This time, when the haze fades, you're sure of it—somehow, someway, in the midst of your reveries, the tent has shrunk. The thirteenth mirror falls to pieces, only five left standing like the points of a pentagram with you and your host at the center. The coffin door shuts, once again sealing the little doll inside, and together they join their ilk, the spreading collection of items by now taking up a fair chunk of the surface area. Seeing the miscellany, you frown for just a moment—how long have you been sitting here, playing mind games with this stranger? The hallucinatory nature of the experience has left you unmoored from any sense of passing time, and though part of you feels that you have eaten enough, that you should go discover what else the festival has to offer that it is time to cut this short, you find yourself rooted.

Only a handful of stories left. So what if you miss out on the rest of the event? Isn't that the nature of this sort of thing, to make your own fun? And besides, what are you—chicken? You were given a challenge, told the stipulation if you wish to leave. In for a penny, in for a pound.

Again both hands reach down into the hat, and when they emerge this time they are grasping a ceramic dragon, coiled and painted with watercolors and craning its neck at a leering angle. As one of xer hands dips back into the hat you notice an opening at the base of the statuette, and indeed, xer fingers reappear with a cone of incense between them. Placing it inside the dragon, xe looks towards you. "Mind lending us a light?" xe asks, pointing to your stool. Looking beneath it you find a box of strike anywhere matches that you had not noticed before, and with a handful of failed tries you watch as the head flares to life, moving it to the figure's base. "The burning desire to touch, to be touched, without the fear of immolation," xe says, smoke beginning to curl out from the wyrm's head, the smell of hot cinnamon and clove drifting into the air. "A story of isolation and of unmasking, a tale as crackling hot as..."

XIV. Dragonsbreath

performed by Warren Benedetto

The woman's head lurched forward as her SUV slowed to a jarring stop, its bumper only inches from the police car parked sideways across her lane. Half a dozen emergency vehicles crowded the street ahead of her. There were police cars. Fire trucks. An ambulance.

She watched with mounting horror as a pair of paramedics lifted a gurney out of the ambulance and began wheeling it up the driveway of a nearby house.

Her house.

"Oh my God," she breathed. "Lila!"

The woman threw her car door open and leaped from the driver's seat, ignoring the urgent chime warning her that the engine was still running. Darting across the road, she pushed her way through a crowd of onlookers and ducked under a strip of yellow police tape.

"Ma'am!" The police officer manning the perimeter of the scene reached for her. "You can't—"

"That's my house!" she yelled as she twisted away from his grip.

The place looked like it had been hit by a missile. A large portion of the front wall had caved out onto the lawn, spilling charred beams and scorched pink insulation from the collapsing attic like innards erupting through an exit wound.

The woman sprinted to the front porch and vaulted up the steps two at a time. Shards of broken glass crunched under her feet as she rushed into the house.

A thin veil of smoke hung in the air. In front of the couch, a man in a black windbreaker squatted next to a sheet-draped form. The back of his jacket was emblazoned with large white block letters: CORONER. The woman's stomach dropped.

"Lila! Oh, no, no, no..." She rushed over to the body, fell to her knees, and reached for the sheet.

The coroner's hand shot out and grabbed her wrist. "Don't."

"She's my daughter!" The woman wrenched her wrist from the man's grasp then yanked the sheet back. What she saw punched the air out of her lungs. She recoiled in horror. Her hands flew to her face, fingers trembling. A tortured wail rose in her throat.

It was her daughter, her angel, her Lila. Her precious, beautiful, perfect baby girl.

Dead.

The lower half of the teen's face was destroyed. Most of the skin had been burnt away, revealing scorched muscle and bone underneath. The burns extended down into the darkness of her mouth then emerged through a smoking cavity in the middle of her chest. Her ribs were splayed outward as if something had exploded them from the inside. Smoke drifted lazily upward from the hole where her heart used to be.

The woman felt numb, senseless, confused. The sounds in the room began to fade, becoming muffled and far away. Her vision grew soft around the edges. Through the fog, she was dimly aware of the coroner drawing the sheet back over her daughter's ruined face.

"Sorry," the woman said vaguely.

A hand rested on her shoulder, steadying her. A man's voice spoke. "Ma'am? Are you the mother?"

She nodded, never taking her eyes off her daughter's lifeless body.

"Do you recognize this?"

The hand held a large plastic evidence bag in front of her face. Inside was a black fabric mask. It resembled a ski mask made from a thick fireproof material with ovals of dark tempered glass protecting each eye.

The woman's heart kicked in her chest. She *had* seen the mask before, on a boy at her daughter's school. As far as she knew, Lila had never spoken to the kid. He was an outcast, always wearing that creepy mask wherever he went. The woman assumed he had been disfigured somehow, but she didn't know for sure. She had never seen his face. But she knew his name.

The woman's lips moved in an inaudible whisper. The officer holding the evidence bag leaned in closer.

"What was that?" He looked at the coroner. "What'd she say?"

The coroner shrugged.

"Ash," the woman said again, louder this time. "His name is Ash."

Ashton Gale had been sweeping for what felt like hours. The bleachers were an endless sea of stale popcorn, broken peanut shells, and crumpled churro wrappers. A tacky mixture of spilled soda and dissolved cotton candy seemed to coat every surface.

The job wasn't what he had in mind when he signed up. He imagined he'd be out on the midway, manning one of the game booths. Or spinning cotton candy. Or collecting tickets on the Ferris wheel. Instead, he was basically a janitor.

It was working out okay, though. The job paid less than minimum wage, but his employers paid in cash, let him eat for free, and gave him a tiny run-down trailer in which to live. That was more than enough for him. All he cared about was that he had escaped his shit-heel town sight unseen, and that he wasn't out on the street begging for change. Or in jail. The rest was gravy.

As Ash swept, a pair of crumpled beer cans flew through the air and clattered onto the bleachers in front of him.

"Incoming!" a voice shouted from above.

Peals of raucous laughter echoed down from a trio of rowdy carnival barkers hanging out at the top of the bleachers, a foam cooler full of cheap beers between them. They were shit-faced as usual, fresh off another night of convincing stupid people to play rigged games for worthless prizes.

"Hey, Lecter!" a barker named Higgins slurred. "Trash those for me, will ya?"

Ash picked up the crushed cans, dropped them into his trash basket, then continued sweeping. A few seconds later, another crumpled beer can whizzed through the air. It collided painfully with the side of Ash's head, dinging his ear through his mask.

"Duck!" Higgins yelled after the fact.

Ash threw down the handle of his broom in frustration. "Dude! What the hell?" He pressed his hand against his ear to dull the pain. "What's your problem?"

"What's my problem?" Higgins stood up, swaying on his feet a little. "What's *my* problem?" He began lumbering down the bleachers toward Ash, his heavy footfalls booming on the wide aluminum steps. "What's *your* problem?"

"Some asshole won't let me do my job. *That's* my problem."

He tried to swallow down the intense heat rising from his chest into his throat. He had dealt with guys like Higgins before. It never ended well. He couldn't let himself get too heated, or he would end up in more trouble than he was already in. He had to calm down. Cool off. Relax.

He took a deep breath then bent down and picked up his broom. When he straightened up, he found himself nearly face-to-face with Higgins. The barker lunged at Ash, grabbing at his mask. "Take that thing off."

Ash batted Higgins' arm to the side. "Get away." Another flare of searing heat swirled in his chest. He strained to choke it down.

"Little freak. What're you hiding under there? Huh?" He reached for Ash's mask again.

Ash dodged backward out of Higgins' grasp. He wielded his broom defensively, holding it crosswise in front of his chest. "Don't do this."

As Higgins readied himself to lunge at Ash again, a hand seized his shoulder and yanked him backward.

"Higgins!" a female voice shouted. "Back off!"

Higgins spun around. Behind him was a diminutive girl of about eighteen. She was wearing an oversized gray hoodie with the Fairway Amusements logo emblazoned across the front. Her emerald-green eyes sparkled under the string lights hung overhead.

"Leave the kid alone, you old drunk," the girl said with a smirk. She tossed Higgins a fresh can of beer. Higgins caught the beer against his chest. "One for the road."

Higgins shot a glare at Ash then looked back at the girl. "He a friend of yours?"

"He is now."

Higgins grunted. "All right." He cracked the beer open and took a sip. "We cool?" he asked Ash.

"Yeah." Ash lowered his broom back to the ground. "We're cool."

Higgins' buddies stomped down the bleachers from where they had been watching the drama unfold. One of them patted Higgins' shoulder. "C'mon, mate. Chow time."

Higgins nodded. He drained his beer, wiped his bottom lip with his sleeve, then crumpled the can and tossed it at Ash's feet. "Missed one."

Ash looked down at the can. His chest burned like molten lava. He swallowed hard. He couldn't wait to kill the guy.

Without another word, Higgins followed his friends through the exit.

"Sorry about that," the girl said to Ash once Higgins was gone.

Ash picked up Higgins's can and dropped it into the trash bin. "You didn't have to do that. I could have handled him myself."

"Meh. He's not worth it." She looked Ash up and down. "You're new, huh?" She extended her hand. "I'm Esmé."

Ash wiped his palm on his pants then shook her hand. "Ash."

"Ash. Nice." She nodded approvingly. "When did you join?"

"About a week ago. You?"

"Oh!" Esmé laughed. "I'm a Fairway original."

Ash tilted his head, confused. "What's that?"

"Carnival kid, born and raised." She indicated the Fairway Amusements logo on the front of her hoodie. "Home sweet home."

"Wow, so you were born here?"

"Not *here* here—my parents were down in Florida for the off-season—but, yeah."

"That's crazy. I didn't even know 'carnival kid' was a thing."

"Well, now you do."

"Yep. Now I do." An awkward silence fell between them. Ash began sweeping again, his eyes on the floor. He could feel the heat of Esmé's gaze as he pushed the broom in her direction. "Excuse me."

"Oh, sorry." She stepped up onto the bleacher bench, placing her hand on Ash's shoulder for balance. Her touch sent an electric jolt racing along his skin. He looked up at her. She had fair skin with a light spray of freckles across her nose. Her eyes were ringed with heavy black eyeliner. A pair of candy-apple red braids poked out from under her hood.

Esmé smiled down at Ash. From the way her eyes were darting around his face, he could tell what she was thinking. He had seen the look before.

"What do you want to know?" Ash said.

Esmé quickly averted her gaze. "I'm so sorry. I didn't mean to stare."

"No, it's okay. I'm used to it. Go ahead. Ask."

Esmé hesitated, then spoke. "What happened?"

"Nothing. I have a condition."

"Do... do you ever take it off?"

"It's best if I don't."

Esmé nodded. She looked at the mask again then plucked a stray piece of string from the side of it. "Well, I like it. You're like a cross between Deadpool and Darth Vader. It's badass."

Ash was speechless. Nobody had ever complimented him on the mask before. Some people stared. Some laughed. Some tried to ignore it. But badass? That was a first.

"Hell," Esmé continued. "I'd wear one if I could. It'd be like my secret identity."

"Nah, you definitely shouldn't."

"No? Why not?" She cocked an eyebrow.

"Because..." He paused. He wanted to compliment her, to tell her she was too pretty to cover her face, but he knew that, no matter how he said it, it would come out completely desperate and weird. "You'd be really hot," he said instead.

"Wow, thanks." Esmé laughed. "I'm flattered."

"Inside the mask, I mean."

"Ah. Right."

"Anyway." Ash lifted his broom, desperate to extricate himself from the awkward mess he had created. "I better get back to work."

"Oh, yeah, sure. Don't let me stop you." Esmé walked along the bleacher bench like it was a balance beam then jumped down onto the stairs. "See you around?"

Ash smiled under his mask.

"Definitely."

"Hey, Vic!" Esmé bounded up to the antique carousel and leaned on the battered metal fence that surrounded the empty attraction. "Can you run it for us one time before you go?"

The elderly man in the faded Fairway Amusements polo smiled, his weathered face crinkling around the eyes. "All right, Spark. But no music, okay? It's past quiet hours."

Esmé clapped her hands and squealed gleefully. "Thank you!" She tugged on Ash's sleeve. "Come on, hop on."

Ash followed Esmé through the gate and onto the carousel. "Did he just call you Spark?"

Esmé rolled her eyes. "Yeah. That's his pet name for me, since I was a kid."

"Why?"

"Because I light up his life. Duh."

Ash snorted out a laugh. Esmé moved along the rows of wooden horses until she found the one she was looking for: a black steed with a fiery red mane. "Ah, there she is. My spirit animal." She dug her toe into one of the metal stirrups attached to the horse's side then swung her leg up and over the saddle. "Giddy up."

Ash grabbed the tarnished brass pole that speared the horse next to Esmé's. The metal was cool and slick with condensation. He pulled himself onto the horse and settled into the saddle. "Spark should be your superhero name."

"Ugh, no way. Sounds more like a Care Bear or something." Esmé changed her voice to a peppy, enthusiastic squeal. "C'mon, kids! Let's all use our imaginations!" Ash laughed. Esmé switched back to her normal voice. "Nah, screw that. If I'm gonna be in a comic book, I'm gonna be a supervillain like Selene."

"Selene?"

"From *Dark X-Men*?" she asked. Ash shook his head. "The Black Queen of the Hellfire Club? She's like Jean Grey, but in bondage gear."

"Badass."

"Exactly." She leaned off her horse to look at Vic. "All right, Vic! Start her up!"

Vic punched the button to start the ride. The carousel lurched then began to pick up speed. Without the calliope music blaring, the ride was a cacophony of turning gears and hissing pistons playing over the low rumble of the engine that powered the ride.

Ash raised his voice above the racket. "So, you know everyone around here, huh?"

"Pretty much, yeah. I mean, sometimes new people come and go, but most have been around forever. Vic's been with us for like fifty years. Right, Vic?" she yelled as the carousel swung past the old man. He raised his head and waved. She laughed. "He has no idea what I just said."

"Is there anyone else our age? Other carnival kids?" Ash asked.

"Not anymore."

"They left?"

"You could say that. There was a fire. In the Haunted Castle."

"Oh, shit. I'm sorry."

"Yeah, it was a bad time."

Ash thought for a moment. The incident sounded familiar, like something he had seen on the news as a kid. He could picture the flames raging from the windows of the faux-stone turrets of the castle and the face of the giant fiberglass demon over the front entrance melting in the heat.

"Where did that happen?" he asked.

"Greensville."

"Yes! Right. I thought so. I grew up right by there. I vaguely remember hearing about it when I was little. My mom would never let me go to the carnival anymore after that."

"And yet here you are."

"Yeah. Ironic, I guess."

Esmé lapsed into silence. Ash stole a glance at her. Her hoodie had fallen backward onto her shoulders, revealing her vivid red braids. The loose baby curls around the edge of her hairline danced in the breeze. The golden glow of the carousel lights made her face seem luminescent, as if she was lit from within. Ash felt a familiar pull in his chest.

God, she's beautiful.

Every night for the last three weeks, Esmé had shown up outside the big top toward the end of his shift. At first, their conversations were awkward. Ash wasn't sure why she was hanging around or what she wanted from him. But after a few days, the awkwardness began to dissipate. They started to talk more freely, to laugh more easily.

Esmé was hilarious: irreverent, clever, and brash. She was also brilliant. She had been homeschooled—more like self-educated—so she seemed to know everything about everything. She was like a walking Wikipedia. Plus, she had read every comic book he had read—and more. She knew every hero, every villain, every origin story. Ash never got tired of talking to her. He was spellbound.

"Why *are* you here?" Esmé asked.

The question caught Ash off guard. He blinked, coming back to the present. "Hmm? Here? You asked me—"

"No, I mean with Fairway. Why did you join?"

"I needed a job."

"Yeah, but... the carnival? Why not, like, Starbucks or something?"

"I don't know. It's hard to explain. I needed to get away."

"From what?"

Ash didn't answer. He hadn't talked with anyone about the incident. The memory was still too fresh. Too painful. He wanted to block it out, to forget all about it. If he didn't, he was afraid he'd lose his mind.

What happened to Lila was... God, it was awful. And it was all his fault. He had been weak. He let his guard down even though he knew how risky it was and what the consequences might be. He just wanted so badly to believe that it would be okay, that he could be normal.

But he was wrong. And Lila had paid the price.

"Forget it," Esmé said, noticing Ash's hesitation. "You don't have to say."

The churning of the carousel's machinery began to wind down. The attraction started to slow. Vic waved his hand as the carousel rounded the curve where he stood. "All right, kiddos! Time's up."

"One second!" Esmé chirped. She swung her leg over her horse's saddle and climbed off. "Come on," she said, beckoning for Ash to follow her. "Real quick. I want to show you something."

Esmé walked along the inside edge of the carousel, in the opposite direction of its rotation. Ash slid off his horse and followed.

The center of the carousel was stationary, like a wide octagonal pillar around which the platform turned. Each of the pillar's panels was painted with an intricate old-fashioned carnival scene, with roaring elephants, mustachioed strongmen, and balloon-wielding clowns. Above each painting was a large mirror that reflected the carousel's glimmering lights. It made the ride seem infinitely bigger than it was.

As the carousel slowed to a stop, Esmé jumped down into the space between the platform and the center pillar. She stepped up to the painting of the elephants and slipped her hand into the narrow gap between the panels. There was a solid click of a latch opening. The elephant panel swung inward. It was a hidden door.

Esmé stepped through. "Watch your head." Ash ducked his head under the low-hanging door frame as he entered. Esmé closed the door behind them.

Once inside, Ash stood up straight. "Whoa," he said, his voice full of wonder.

The inside of the pillar was hollow, forming a small hidden room in the center of the carousel. Most of the space was taken up by the ride's motor and gearbox along with a sound system with several large speakers. Most interesting to Ash, however, were the mirrors: he could see straight through them, to the carousel horses on the other side. They weren't mirrors after all; at least, not from the inside.

Ash turned around slowly, looking out through the one-way mirrors in all directions. As he came full circle, he found himself almost face-to-face with Esmé. "Sorry," he mumbled. He tried to take a step back, but his heel knocked into the speaker box directly behind him. There was nowhere for him to go.

"It's okay. I don't bite."

Ash pretended not to hear her loaded comment. "I had no idea this place was here."

"Yeah, most people don't." Esmé leaned back on the speaker box behind her. "I used to sneak in here every night when I was younger. I'd sit for hours and just watch the world spinning around me." She gazed out through the mirror beside her. The carousel lights glinting through the tinted glass flickered across her face like firelight. "There were so many kids out there, laughing, having fun, having friends." She looked back at Ash. "I just wanted to be one of them, you know? Doing dumb shit. Living in a house, going to school, hanging out with other kids my age." She looked out through the mirror again. Her eyes had a glassy, faraway look. "I used to try to make friends with them, but..." She trailed off.

Esmé stood and stepped closer to Ash. She was nearly toe-to-toe with him in the tiny space, so close that he could feel the heat radiating off her skin. She didn't say anything.

Ash laughed nervously. "What?"

"Hug?" She extended her arms to her sides.

"Oh. Sure." Ash awkwardly wrapped his arms around Esmé. She hugged him back. He could smell the warm vanilla scent of her shampoo through his mask. Her face felt warm against his chest.

After a few seconds, Esmé loosened her embrace. She kept her hands around his waist and looked up at him, her eyes sparkling. "Nobody can see us in here, you know."

Ash felt his pulse begin to accelerate. The hidden room suddenly felt impossibly small, claustrophobic, as if a sudden fire had sucked all the oxygen out of the place. Heat waves distorted the air, threatening to suffocate him.

"Yeah. We should go. Vic's probably wondering where we went." He fumbled for the doorknob.

"Right," Esmé said, disappointed. She dropped her hands from his waist. The heat began to dissipate. As Ash unlatched the door, Esmé stuck her foot out and blocked it from opening. She put her hand on his arm. "You know you can trust me, right?"

"Yeah, sure. I know."

"Whatever your condition is, I don't care. You don't have to hide from me."

"I'm not hiding from you," Ash insisted. He opened the door. "I'm protecting you."

He ducked out, hoisted himself up onto the carousel platform, then began weaving his way between the rows of wooden horses. Esmé called after him.

"Protecting me? From what?"

But Ash was already gone.

Ash walked quickly across the carnival grounds. He made his way along an orange plastic storm fence then turned left into the dark alley between two 18-wheelers. The fastest way back to his trailer was to cut through the parking area where the carnival's vehicles were staged: a maze of flatbeds, box trucks, and recreational vehicles of every shape and size.

As he navigated the maze, he heard loud voices and raucous laughter. He recognized the sound. It was Higgins and his crew of sycophants, the same guys who had harassed him the night he first met Esmé.

"Hey, Lecter!" Higgins bellowed when he spotted Ash. "C'mere for a second."

Higgins and his friends were sitting on the edge of a flatbed, passing a bottle of whiskey back and forth between them. A kerosene camping lantern cast a dull white glow in the dusty air. Ash had learned the names of the other two barkers since their last encounter. There was Orsi, a short, fat Italian with thinning hair slicked back across his sunburned scalp and Freed, an ex-con with ice-blue eyes and a tattoo of a flaming skull on his neck.

Ash quickened his pace. Higgins swiped the whiskey bottle from Orsi then jumped down from the flatbed. His boots kicked up puffs of dust as he landed in front of Ash.

"I was wondering when I was going to see you again," Higgins said. "Come and have a drink with us." He took a swig from the whiskey bottle then held it out to Ash. "Consider it a peace offering."

"Thanks," Ash mumbled. "But I'm good."

Behind Ash, Orsi and Freed jumped down to the ground.

"It isn't polite to turn down a drink from a friend." Higgins took an unsteady step closer to Ash. His speech was slurred. "We're still friends, right?"

"Sure." Ash looked over his shoulder. Orsi and Freed were close behind him. With the long flatbed trucks to his left and his right, Ash had no place to run. He was trapped. "I'm just not up for it right now. Long night."

Higgins nodded understandingly. "Girl trouble?" He held up a finger to Orsi and Freed. "Give us a minute." Then he slung his arm around Ash's shoulder and started walking with him. "Talk to me," he said, his voice lowered. "What's the problem? She's not putting out?"

"It's not like that," Ash said through gritted teeth. He twisted out from under Higgins's grip. Higgins let him go. "Man," Ash said, shaking his head in disbelief. "You are such a piece of shit."

He tried to walk past Higgins. Higgins shot his arm out across Ash's chest then pushed him backward. "Hang on. That's no way to talk to a friend."

"Then I guess we're not friends anymore."

"No? That's too bad." Higgins shot a look over Ash's shoulder. Orsi and Freed lunged at Ash from behind. Each of them grabbed one of his arms. Ash struggled to pull away, but they were too strong. They twisted his arms painfully behind his back.

Higgins stepped up to Ash then threw a punch directly into Ash's stomach. Ash doubled over, gasping for air. Orsi and Freed pulled him upright. His head hung down as he tried to catch his breath.

"That's for your smart mouth, *friend*," Higgins said. "Now..." He reached up, grabbed the top of Ash's mask, and pulled. The mask

stretched then slipped off. Higgins tossed it aside. "Let's see what we've got here."

Ash's chin sagged down to his chest. His dark brown hair hung down over his face. "Give it back," he whispered weakly.

Higgins grabbed a fistful of Ash's hair and pulled his head up so he could see the teen's face. His disappointment was palpable. Ash was a normal-looking kid—good-looking, even. There was no disfigurement. No scarring. Nothing worth covering up at all.

"Well, shit," Higgins complained. "Look at Johnny Depp here. Why're you hiding that pretty face, boy?"

"I have a condition." Ash's lips curled back from his teeth in an angry sneer. His voice sounded deeper, more guttural, as if his throat was full of hot coals.

Higgins didn't seem to notice the difference. "If you say so." He motioned to his friends. "Let him go."

Orsi and Freed released Ash's arms. Ash pulled away, rotated his sore shoulders, then walked over to where Higgins had dropped his mask. As he bent down to pick it up, Higgins planted his foot on Ash's backside and pushed, sending him stumbling forward.

Ash fell to his hands and knees. A bright flash of flame ignited underneath him with a *whoosh*, like lighter fluid being splashed on a grill. The flames lit up the night with a blinding white flare of light.

Higgins jumped backward. "Whoa! What the hell?"

"I tried to warn you," Ash said as he climbed to his feet. He raised his head to look at Higgins. His irises were glowing like cinders in a campfire.

Before Higgins could react, a bluish-yellow jet of flame erupted from Ash's mouth and engulfed Higgins in a torrent of liquid fire. Higgins's clothes and hair were vaporized almost instantly. Higgins opened his mouth to scream. Instead of air, he drew in a lungful of superheated gas, incinerating the delicate tissues in his mouth and gullet. His lungs seized, trapping the searing heat inside his chest. Oily black smoke poured from his throat. No sound escaped his lips.

Like a flood of napalm from a flamethrower, the blaze gushing from Ash's mouth consumed Higgins completely. His body became a twisted black silhouette, a ghoul writhing grotesquely in a white-hot pillar of fire. His flesh began to bubble and melt, stretching and blackening over his bones like burnt taffy. Steam hissed from his eyeballs as they ruptured in the heat then sunk back into his skull. The acrid stench of burnt skin poisoned the air.

Orsi and Freed stood paralyzed, watching Higgins' immolation in numb horror. Higgins stumbled blindly toward them, his expression frozen in a rictus of agony. Just as he reached them, his lifeless body crumpled into a smoldering heap at their feet.

Ash snapped his mouth shut, cutting off the jet of flames. He glared at the two terrified men, his eyes pulsing with an ember-orange glow.

A flood of urine spread across Orsi's pants. "P-Please. D-don't."

Ash pulled the mask over his head. The heat waves dissipated.

"You tell anyone, and I'll find you. Understand?" Orsi and Freed both nodded. "Then go," Ash said.

The two men ran, disappearing into the shadows between the 18-wheelers.

Once they were gone, Ash slumped against the flatbed then sat on the ground and drew his knees to his chest. His head hung heavy on his neck. He felt weak, drained, as if every ounce of energy had been spilled from his body.

A crunch of dry grass made him look up. His stomach twisted into a knot.

Esmé was standing over him.

"Hey," she said quietly.

"Hey." Ash's voice felt thick and raw in his throat. "You saw." He could tell from her face that she had.

"Yeah. You okay?"

"No." He struggled to his feet and dusted off his jeans. "I better go."

"Where?"

Ash looked down the row of trucks at the empty carnival grounds. Lights from a distant highway traced a line across the darkened rural landscape. "I don't know."

"Then stay."

"I can't. Someone'll find him."

"So what? Let them." Esmé bent down and picked up Higgins' whiskey bottle. She began pouring the caramel-colored liquid onto his smoking corpse.

"What are you doing?"

"Such a terrible accident." Esmé sighed with mock remorse. She emptied the bottle onto the ground next to Higgins then dropped it on the dirt by his hand. "He really should've been more careful."

Ash watched as Esmé grabbed the camping lantern that was still glowing on the flatbed truck nearby. She tossed the lantern underhand, landing it next to Higgins's body. Its glass shattered. Fresh flames whooshed up as the glowing wick ignited the spilled alcohol. The fire sped along the ground then up and over the corpse.

"You don't understand. It's only a matter of time before someone else gets hurt. Before *you* get hurt."

"You won't hurt me."

"Not on purpose, no. But that's the problem. I can't help it. The only thing keeping you safe right now is this stupid mask. If I take it off..." He backed away from her. "I'm sorry."

He started walking in the direction of the highway in the distance. He would hitch a ride. Find a new job. Start over someplace else—alone. Again.

Esmé spoke from behind him. "I know what happened, Ash. To your friend."

Ash froze in his tracks. He turned around. "How?"

"The police. A few days after you joined. They were looking for you."

"What did you tell them?"

"Nothing. But they... they had pictures."

Ash closed his eyes, suddenly overwhelmed with a flood of images from that night. Lila, on the couch, removing his mask. Leaning in, eyes closed, lips parted. The soft brush of her mouth against his. The beating of his heart. The burning in his chest. Then, the flames. Raging past his lips, down her throat, through her ribs, an explosion of liquid fire tearing her open from the inside. Her body tumbling off the couch, sprawling on the floor, eyes wide, face ruined. Dead.

"I wasn't sure if you were who I thought you were," Esmé continued. "But I knew I had to find out."

"She was my friend." Ash exhaled a shuddering breath. He felt nauseous. "She wanted me to feel normal, just for a second. And it killed her. *I* killed her."

"But you're *not* normal. You're special. You have a gift. A beautiful, wonderful gift."

"Yeah. Great gift. Thanks, Dad." His voice dripped with sarcasm.

"You just need to learn to control it. If you can harness it, use it to your advantage... you'll be unstoppable. *We'll* be unstoppable."

"Don't you think I've tried?" The desperation in Ash's voice was plain. "You think I want to wear this thing for the rest of my life?" He tugged at his mask. "It's the only way."

Esmé reached into her back pocket and pulled out a colorful slip of paper, about half the size of a postcard. "Stay. Just one more night."

"Why? What's the point?"

"Trust me." She handed the paper to Ash. "There's something you should see."

The midway was awash in light and sound. Squeals of glee accompanied the rumble of the rollercoaster as it roared around a bend and into a towering loop. The music from the carousel blared over loudspeakers, while barkers implored passersby to test their luck at games of skill and chance. The tantalizing aroma of hot kettle corn and fresh roasted peanuts wafted through the air.

Ash weaved his way through the chaos, past the Mirror Maze and the Giant Slide, to the sideshow tent behind the big top. He looked down at the slip of paper Esmé had handed him the night before.

It was a ticket.

The Amazing Esmeralda, it read. *Death-Defying Feats of Wonder.* *8:00 PM.*

Ash hadn't realized Esmé was a performer. He had just assumed she was with the carnival because her parents were there. She never said otherwise, and he never thought to ask.

Ash passed the ticket to the girl at the gate then entered the sideshow tent. There were no bleachers inside, just folding chairs set up on a carpet of bright green Astroturf. The front of the tent housed a small black stage between stacks of loudspeakers. At the back of the stage was a large banner featuring the same *Amazing Esmeralda* logo as on the ticket.

Ash dropped into his seat. The lights dimmed. The crowd grew silent. Dramatic music began to thrum through the loudspeakers followed by the booming voice of an announcer.

"And now! Ladies and gentlemen! Prepare yourselves for the most death-defying feats of wonder your eyes have ever seen! I give you Fairway Amusements' brightest new act! The hottest talent under the sun! Behold! The Amazing! Esmeralda!"

A massive gush of flame erupted out of the darkness, directly at the audience. The crowd screamed with surprise and delight. The flames quickly dissipated, replaced by a pair of whirling, spinning wheels of fire that rotated around each other like the rings of orbiting planets. Sparks ricocheted off the stage. The rings changed size, each alternately growing and shrinking and growing again. The crowd *ooh'd* and *aah'd* with appreciation.

Finally, bright red spotlights faded in from above, illuminating the performer at the center of the stage: Esmé. She froze in a dramatic pose, holding her flaming torches aloft. Her red hair was twisted into a tight bun. Irregular red and black stripes were painted diagonally across her face. Her sleeveless black bodysuit and knee-high boots reminded Ash of something that would be worn by a comic book hero. Or a villain. She looked fearsome. Dangerous. Wild.

"Badass," Ash whispered to himself.

Esmé placed the torches into black metal stands on either side of her then touched the flame of each torch with a fingertip. Fire raced across her upturned palms and along the tops of her bare arms to her shoulders. With her arms held out at her sides, the flames looked like feathers on the wings of a phoenix.

Suddenly, the stands holding the torches seemed to collapse, each tipping inward toward Esmé. The torches hit the stage at her feet, igniting a column of flame that consumed her body, from her feet to her neck. The crowd cried out in surprise. Esmé raised her arms toward the ceiling as if summoning the fire higher. Then she clapped her hands over her head. The flames raced up her body, along her arms, and into her hands, leaving her body undamaged and unharmed.

Esmé held her hands cupped over her head then brought them forward in front of her. A small, bright flame danced in her palms. She blew on the flame, sending a torrent of fire from her lips into the air. Then she inhaled, drawing the fire back into her mouth.

The lights dimmed almost to black. Esmé opened her mouth. A brilliant yellow glow emanated from her throat. The fire appeared to still be burning, deep inside her body. Esmé tipped her head back and spat a bloom of fire into the air. The flames formed the shape of a dragon in the air over her head. The beast flapped its blazing wings, flew out over the heads of the audience, then disintegrated into a shower of sparks.

The crowd leaped to their feet, giving Esmé a standing ovation. As Ash stood and clapped, Esmé's words from the night before came flooding back to him.

"You just need to learn to control it," he heard her say. "If you can harness it, use it to your advantage... you'll be unstoppable. *We'll* be unstoppable."

We'll be unstoppable, Ash thought again.

We.

"Why didn't you tell me?" Ash asked.

He and Esmé walked through the shadows between the 18-wheelers, passing the circle of burnt grass where Higgins's body had been recovered earlier that morning. Remnants of yellow police tape trailed along the ground and flapped in the breeze. The police hadn't asked too many questions. It was just a freak accident as far as they were concerned. An open-and-shut case.

"How's that conversation supposed to go, exactly?" Esmé said, arching an eyebrow.

"But you knew about me. You must have."

"I thought maybe I did, yeah. But I couldn't be sure. Lucky for me, Higgins outed you before I had to figure out how to bring it up."

"How did you know, though? Because of the mask?"

Esmé stopped and looked up at Ash. "You don't remember me, do you?"

"From where?"

"The carousel. You were eight, maybe nine years old. I saw you riding alone. I asked if I could ride with you."

A blurry image flickered at the edge of Ash's consciousness, just out of reach. He remembered... something. But he wasn't sure exactly what.

Esmé continued. "I snuck you on all the rides. The Ferris wheel. The Tilt-A-Whirl." She paused. "The Haunted Castle."

Ash's eyes widened under his mask. He remembered. "That was you," he whispered. Esmé nodded. "Those kids. They were so mean to you. I... I got so angry."

"We both did."

The heavy veil Ash had cast over the memory began to lift. That night was the first time he had become aware of his powers. The first time he had lost control. The first time someone had gotten hurt. The first time someone died.

Somehow, he had escaped from the inferno unharmed. His mother found him wandering through the stampeding crowd, his face smeared with soot. She asked if he was okay. He said he wasn't feeling well. His chest hurt. His throat burned.

His mother's face had gone bone white. She warned him never to tell anyone what happened. Then she hustled him past the arriving fire engines and out to the car, never to return.

A few days later, she gave him the mask for the first time. It was the same kind his father had worn before he died. "You'll need to wear this from now on," she had said.

"For how long?"

She didn't have an answer.

Ash walked with Esmé in silence, too overwhelmed with the force of the memory to speak for a bit. They arrived at Esmé's trailer. As Esmé fished for her keys in her backpack, Ash stared at his reflection in the darkened window. His mask stared back at him.

Esmé found her keys and unlocked her trailer door. She turned back to Ash. "Now what?" she asked quietly.

Ash looked at his reflection again. He reached up and slipped the mask off his head, then leaned forward, took Esmé's face in his hands, and kissed her softly on the lips. Waves of heat distortion rippled around them.

After a few seconds, Ash pulled away. He opened his eyes. Esmé smiled at him then tilted her head back and exhaled a column of fire into the air. The flames morphed into a giant dragon several times larger than the one from her show. The creature hovered overhead for a moment then flapped its wings and soared away into the starless night sky.

"You've gotta teach me how to do that," Ash said as he watched the dragon disappear into the distance.

"Tomorrow."

She kissed him again, then took him by the hand and led him into her trailer. As Ash passed through the door, he let the mask slip from his fingers and onto the ground outside.

— FIN —

Another shuddering crash of thunder shakes the tent, calling you out of your haze of dreamy warmth and mingling with the by now almost comforting sound of breaking glass. Only four left, you at the intersection of the crossroad, the embrace of the canvas around you growing tighter. Didi hops up in front of you yet again, seeking attention, and you watch the last wisps of smoke spiral out of the ceramic dragon's snout as the incense cone peters out. The host pushes the statue aside, meeting your gaze.

"It can be a gamble," xe says. "Trusting yourself, especially when you've seen what you're capable of." You can still feel the heat, even now, and you watch the candles flicker in the remaining mirrors, considering the fragility of fire and its ravenous and immediate potential to become so much more than its size. You imagine the candelabras tipping, falling against the walls of the tent, the flame spreading up the walls, consuming and cavorting…

The image of destruction is counteracted by xer fingers repeating their well-rehearsed dip into the hat of wonders. Hanging from their hooked index is a chain of red plastic monkeys rising up, up, up, the kind that one expects to find in a barrel. "Animal or beast, man or monster…" xe say, and the linked arms keep coming and coming until xer hand is as high as it can reach, the linked primates dangling like an unwound entrail. "A lineage of service, a reversal of roles, a festival of fools and a festival of flesh, the story of a world weathering the grisly consequences of…"

XV. THE TAKEOVER

performed by Glen Held

Zom Kong was the ridiculous, but pretty accurate, name they gave the fifty-foot-tall dead ape. There were shrieks and gasps from the audience as the thing strained against its bonds, but all the creature accomplished, all it *could* accomplish, was to move a few yards in either direction. When the crowd realized they were safe, sighs of relief and scattered laughter filled the half empty tent.

I stood in my usual position on the far side of the tent, the shadows obscuring me as I watched the show. Suddenly, the zombie ape quit straining, its milky gaze going across the big tent until it alighted on me. I threw my hands up to my mouth, realizing I'd unconsciously been whistling. It was an old-time tune, "Beautiful Dreamer", that my mom had sung to me, and the creature usually responded to it in a positive way.

But my actions were too late; Colonel Carter was already headed my way, and he was not happy. Dressed in an all-white Wild West outfit and drawing up to his full height of six foot seven, Colonel Carter towered over my five foot nothing. I wasn't intimidated. Compared to what I'd gone through in my life, stuff like this was inconsequential.

"How many times do I have to tell you not to whistle that infernal song?"

"Sorry, Colonel," I said quickly. "I didn't even know I was doing it."

He opened his mouth to say something, then thought better of it and looked at Zom Kong. Luckily for me, the creature had gone back to trying to pull free. The Colonel grunted and turned back my way. "Give me today's attendance."

"It's a little over four hundred," I told my boss, and he raised a shaggy white eyebrow. The Colonel was not an "approximate" type of person. "Four hundred seventeen paid admissions, two hundred twenty of which were children. A hundred and twenty had the five dollar off coupon. There were also a hundred and fifty separate admissions to the Burning Pit, to see where zombies were disposed of."

I saw him doing the mental calculations. "Decent," he declared. It was decent, although two years ago, right before I was hired, the Colonel would have ripped out his long, flowing white hair to see this amount of people in his thousand seat tent. But back then the Zombie Circus had five times the number of dead and they were a lot more mobile.

"Candy, food, and games of chance sales are doing what you'd expect from this size crowd." I gave him the figures. There was something else I had to talk with him about, but the time wasn't right for that. I went on with my report. "Zom Kong and Boris merchandise are selling at a twenty percent pre-show clip. I project intermission sales of thirty-two percent and exit of another thirty with the digital picture option."

The Colonel looked down at me. "What about the merchandise for the zombies who aren't with the show anymore? Your so-called 'dearly departed' dolls," he said, and my mouth went dry. "Well?"

"They're not selling," I admitted. "But I have an advertising campaign set to…"

"Set to lose me more money!" His demeanor grew worse by the second. This was not going to be one of his good days. "You know, if not for me, you'd still be in that freak show over in Coney. You remember what that was like? You remember the kind of life you led there?"

I lowered my gaze. "It was humiliating."

Before getting this job, my resemblance to a cave man with long, muscular arms, a broad chest, short legs, a sloping forehead and entirely too much hair on my body had only allowed me to get sideshow work as a missing link or, rarely, a strong man. Unfortunately, my sloping forehead contained lots of smarts, and I had been born way more ambitious than my station in life allowed me to hope for.

Things changed when Colonel Carter bought my contract and promised me I might one day take over if I worked hard. And work hard I did, doing everything he demanded and much, much more. My taking over was a promise I would hold him to.

"You'd better step it up or you'll be back in Coney in a New York minute!" he continued, but I could see his anger winding down. The Colonel was nowhere near as cruel as he'd been when I first got here. Those physical and verbal beatings had been bad, especially when he used the "equalizer". That was a telescoping rod he carried and used to dish out punishment. I shuddered just thinking about it. "Understand?"

"I understand," I quickly answered, not wanting to meet the equalizer again.

The Colonel snorted, giving me a look of contempt that I'd seen too many times before. "If not for your father, I would never... Damn!" He fell silent, shaking his head and mumbling curses.

"My father?" I asked, heart pounding. My father had supposedly taken one look at me and left, never to be seen again. Mom tried to raise me but died when I was a child. With no other family, I was sent to an orphanage, my looks keeping me from being adopted. "You knew my father? How did you know him?"

Colonel Carter looked at me for a minute, then sighed as if he had made a decision he wished he didn't have to. "Your dad was a good man, worked for me until Z-Day when he became infected. That's it."

My jaw dropped. I had hoped to one day find my father, but if he'd been infected, it was best he was dead. Ironic that the plague which had given me the opportunity to take over, had taken my dad from me. But how did he work for the Colonel?

And why hadn't I been told this before?

"How did you know my father?" I begged the Colonel. "Tell me about him, please!"

Colonel Carter's eyes narrowed. "I don't have time for nonsense like this!" Whatever good will he had was gone. "He did his job competently and didn't disappoint. Because of him I hired you and because of him I think you can take over. That's it."

That took me away from wondering about my father. That was my past; this was my future. "When will that be?"

"When will that be?" the Colonel mimicked me, then grew angry. "It'll be when I say it'll be. Now what else have you got to report? You're wasting my time!"

His imitating me brought back memories of my time in the orphanage. All I wanted to do was hurt him like his remark hurt me. I had a way to do it also.

"I've got something else to tell you," I blurted out. "It's bad, really bad."

His bushy white eyebrows went up and he gasped. "It's not about Boris, is it?" he asked. I knew why his mind immediately went there. Our remaining giant human zombie had recently become stiffer and more listless than usual.

"No," I said. "He's failing, but it's nothing we didn't expect. By adding more brains to his diet, we should be able to fend off his being permanently dead for months."

The Colonel let out a sigh. "You know, I was acquainted with Boris when he was alive." This was a story I'd heard before, but when the Colonel got on a nostalgic roll, it was best not to interrupt. "Boris was a big guy in life too, although obviously nowhere near the twenty feet the Z plague brought him up to. When he got infected on Z-Day and entered the delirious stage, he infected and killed three of my men before another restrained him."

A thought entered my mind. "Was one of those dead men my father?" I looked to where the giant Boris, clad in only a dark colored loin cloth, stood in a thirty-foot high cage.

"No, Boris didn't kill your father," the Colonel said and dismissed talking about that anymore with a wave of his hand. "So what's this bad news you want to tell me?"

"It's Zom Kong," I said. "The latest lab report says his DNA is breaking apart."

The Colonel blanched and looked over at the fifty-foot-tall ape. The creature, hair mottled, skin covered with scabs, was quietly staring straight ahead. Although the beast had once been an object of terror, since the eradication of the Z plague and destruction of most zombies, the crowds now loved it... from a distance, of course.

"How much time does Kong have?" Colonel Carter's eyes teared up slightly.

"About a week, then we'll have to take him to the Burning Pit for disposal."

The Colonel staggered and would have fallen if I hadn't reached forward and grabbed him. Other workers started to come over to help, but he feebly motioned them away.

"Get me to my office, boy." His voice was weak, and his body trembled. "Hurry."

Quickly, I brought the Colonel to his garishly painted trailer/office/living quarters. As everybody was tending to the show, we encountered no one along the way. The Colonel and I staggered up the steps then inside. I'd never been there before, and was surprised to see it was very plain. There was a bedroom, bathroom, and office area with a few pictures on the wall. He motioned for me to bring him to the office area where he lurched over to his desk and collapsed in his chair.

"Take it out," he said, pointing to the top drawer. I did. Inside was a cigar shaped silver tube. Something rattled inside and I opened it to find a dozen dully glowing, green pills.

The Colonel yanked the tube from my grasp, then greedily swallowed as many of the things as he could get down. The rest fell to the floor, hissing away in a puff of smoke.

"Damn!" the Colonel, back to normal, cursed. He stared at the fading green fumes, sighed, then took out his phone and called a number. Whoever was on the other side answered immediately, reciting a substantial number. "Done. Just get those pills here as soon as possible. What? I don't know. How about Excel? Good." Then he hung up.

"What just happened? Are you all right?" I asked. He ignored the questions and motioned me to sit.

"Before the Zombie Circus, before Z-Day, I was a big game hunter. On one African trip, I found a female gorilla caught in a poacher's trap. Her baby was crying nearby." He pointed to a photo on the wall of himself in hunting gear, then one of him with a baby gorilla. I had heard the story before, in one form or another, but never seen these pictures. "I released her and had her wounds tended to, but she didn't survive. Her baby took to hanging around our camp and I brought him back to the states as a pet."

One of the photos caught my attention. "That picture there," I interrupted, indicating a grainy shot of him and a group of natives. "Those men tower over you and you're six and a half feet tall. Did you find a race of giants?"

The Colonel, as was his custom, didn't answer any question he didn't want to. "When the infected Boris attacked, I would have been his victim if the then grown ape hadn't leaped forward and saved me. It was bitten in the process. Since it saved my life, I didn't want to kill it," he stated. While I thought there probably was some loyalty involved, I had no doubt the real reason was because the Colonel hoped to make money off it. "As the infection continued, the ape began to grow, getting so big that no cage could hold it! I staked the poor creature here, in the middle of nowhere, and put a tarp over it.

"When the plague ended and there were no new zombies, I came up with the idea for the zombie circus. It took a while to convert the tarp to a tent, and I had to pay off local officials to get it done, but get it done I did! I had Zom Kong and Boris and was able to get my hands on another half dozen, those who you named the 'dearly departed.'"

"My marketing strategy should have worked," I said, but he wasn't really listening.

"At the start, the zombies were hardly the docile creatures they are now and so I built safeguards into the arena; safeguards that nobody but myself knew about. Suffice it to say that even if one of the zombies were to escape their bonds, they wouldn't get far. I'm proud to say though that I never had to use any of them," he said, and that was the first time I had heard of any *safeguards*. "The Burning Pit also insures that the government lets me continue here without too much interference. You should see some of the things they send here to get rid of, but that's another story.

"Our first couple of years were great, but ever since my dead lost most of their mobility and a bunch have truly died, well, business isn't what it used to be. When *you* take over though, things are going to be different."

My heart started pounding at the news. "When will that be?"

"Soon," he said with a wink. "Very, very soon"

But it really wasn't soon at all, or at least not soon enough.

The Colonel uncharacteristically wasn't at breakfast the next morning. I went to his trailer looking for him, but he didn't answer my knock. I knocked again and this time he did answer, screaming to be left alone or everyone would be deeply sorry. Okay. As he had said I would take over, I told everyone the Colonel had said I should run things while he was laid up. That's why I was the one called when a hard-looking man arrived demanding to see the Colonel.

"I've got a delivery I can only give to Carter," he said, giving me a disgusted look. "Take me to him now."

I shook my head, not about to be intimidated by him. "Colonel Carter isn't available. Give it to me and I'll get it to him."

The man scoffed. "Look, I know I'm a day early, but that's not happening, shorty," he said. "I'll wait, unless you know his password."

Password? How would I... then I remembered the strange ending to the Colonel's earlier phone conversation.

"Excel," I said.

The man held my gaze for a second, then shrugged and tossed me an oblong shaped box. Without another word, he turned and left. The smart thing would have been to give it to the colonel right away. Instead, I opened the box to find another cigar shaped tube with green pills in it. These glowed much brighter than the others. As the colonel didn't want visitors, I put the package in my pocket and went off to run the circus. I'd give it to the colonel next time I saw him.

While I went about the daily circus routines, I got the idea of asking the old-timers about my dad. Before I did, I realized that I couldn't. I didn't know my father's name, my mother had not spoken much about him, or even what he looked like. This was just another disappointment in a lifetime full of them.

I watched the show that night from the Colonel's position. The crowd was less than the day before and Zom Kong's health had deteriorated to the point where the thing could barely move at all. I

felt sorry for the creature, especially the sad stare it gave me when I unconsciously whistled that song. I felt bad for me too. What kind of circus was I going to take over if the star attraction was gone?

That night, at midnight when I returned to my cabin after the show was put to bed, I found a note on my pillow. *Main tent in one hour. It's time for your takeover,* it read, and was signed "*Carter*".

I spent the next hour joyfully pacing in my room. My lifetime of pain and suffering was about to turn around!

At the appointed time, I made my way to the tent. It was a moonless night and would have been pitch dark if not for the perpetual flames from the Burning Pit. Inside the tent was black, except for a small, solitary light that barely illuminated the place.

"Colonel?" Nobody answered. The light was coming from a small lantern on the ground, near, but not too near, Zom Kong. I walked over to it, the only sounds in the place being my footsteps and the creaking that Boris and the giant dead ape made. I entered the light. "Colonel?"

Although the Colonel's voice was a whisper, it somehow filled the tent, coming from all around. "It's time," he said.

"Where are you?" I asked, trying not to show how excited his words made me.

"Nearby," he answered, although he kept out of the light.

Now this was getting spooky, and nervousness almost overtook my ambitiousness. "What's going on, Colonel?"

"Before you take over, we have to have a little chat," he said, then paused a moment before continuing. "Remember when I told you that Boris didn't kill your father?"

I shot an angry look up at where the giant stood on the outskirts of the light. "So he did kill my father?"

"No, Boris didn't, but he did infect your dad."

I gasped. "And then my father died from the plague after that?"

"Quiet!" the Colonel roared, and I fell quiet. The only sound now was from Zom Kong and Boris as they moaned and moved away as far as they could from the anger in his voice. "Not everyone died from the Z-plague, but those who did were the lucky ones. Some turned into zombies, some didn't turn but had their minds warped and bodies consumed by pain and agony. A rare few turned into giants like Boris and Zom Kong. Even rarer were those who… well, see for yourself."

There was a movement outside the light and the Colonel stepped into view. "Oh my god," I whispered looking up at the man who was now close to ten feet tall.

"God had nothing to do with this," the Colonel whispered, "although maybe the plague was his wrath on us. We never did figure out where it came from."

I took a step away from him.

"Boris did infect me that day, and I grew a foot taller than my original five foot five. That's why I was shorter in the picture you saw on my wall," he continued. "Luckily, because of something semi-unique in me, I didn't fully turn zombie, but I kept growing, and my mind often gets cluttered. Over time, I found others like me and a cure!"

"The green pills," I whispered.

He nodded. "Yes, they let me lead an almost normal life, but I must keep taking them to keep from turning. I have a shipment coming tomorrow which should reduce the effects of the last day. It comes at a mighty steep price though." He smiled down at me coldly. "But it's one I'll be able to pay, once you take over."

He reached down for me and my resolve broke. I ran, but not more than a few steps before hitting something and crashing to the ground. Dazed, I reached out my hand to discover an almost invisible plastic barrier had risen from the ground. As I stood, I ran my hand along it. The barrier rose as far as I could touch and continued to the side.

"That's the safeguard I was talking about. It completely encloses us and goes up twenty-five feet. Built to withstand zombie attacks, there's no way for someone as puny as you to get out," Colonel Carter said. "Hold still and we'll put an end to all this."

He lunged at me, but I ducked under his grasp. "I don't understand! What are you doing?"

"I'm allowing you to take over," he said, jerking a thumb toward Zom Kong.

"What?" I said, my back against the barrier.

"You really are that stupid. Did you honestly believe that an ape saved me from Boris?"

"Didn't he?" My heart pounded as I again managed to evade his grasp and moved to the other end of our imperceptible cage. Boris edged toward me, and I scampered away from him, realizing he was inside with us. The only thing keeping him away were his chains.

"The ape tried to help, but Boris killed it. Don't you think the authorities would have taken Zom Kong away from me if it were a true ape and the Z-plague was able to cross species?"

I had never thought of that. "Then who saved you?" I asked, hoping to buy some time to think of a way out. "And if Zom Kong's not an ape, what is he?"

"That's an interesting story." He stopped coming after me. "Boris had already infected me when another man raced out and knocked him to the ground. He was bit also, but managed to pull me to safety while others tied the giant down. Now here's the big question: Do you know who that person was?"

I shook my head.

I didn't like the way he was smiling at me. "Here's a hint. If Zom Kong was human, who would it look like?"

I turned to examine Kong. The long arms, the barrel chest, the proportionately small legs… For the first time, it clicked in my head what was going on here. My body grew ice cold, and I sank to my knees.

"You got it!" the Colonel said, clapping. "Zom Kong is your father. The takeover you're going to be doing is *from him*! All I need to do is free Boris and, if genetics hold true, one bite should give me a star attraction for at least another decade. No more half-filled tents; it's prime time for the Colonel once more!"

Colonel Carter reached into his pocket and pulled out a metal baton. I gasped at the sight of the equalizer. Swinging it downward, the thing telescoped into a long rod. Something new was added: at the press of a button on it, there was buzzing, and electricity shot out the front end. Startled, I backed up into one of the invisible walls. I had nowhere to run, but he wasn't coming after me. Instead, he went behind Boris and disconnected his chains from the stake. Then he used the sparking equalizer to prod the giant zombie toward me.

"Bite him, Boris!" the Colonel screeched, then turned to me. "Don't worry; I'll pull Boris off before he kills you. If you're lucky, you won't remember anything about this once you become the new Zom Kong."

Slowly, Boris shambled my way. I moved off the wall, soon finding myself trapped between Boris and Zom Kong, my father, who was still chained to his stake.

"Between a rock and a hard place," the Colonel said with a laugh. "Pick your poison. Either one works for me."

I looked at Zom Kong to see if there was a way around him, but my father was starting to stir and… Wait, maybe there was a way out of this! Trying hard not to let my fear get the best of me, I again began to whistle "Beautiful Dreamer". As I did, Zom Kong turned its decayed stare my way.

"Dad, it's me, your son," I said, a tear running down my face. "You never did anything for me your whole life, but I need your help now. I need you to…"

"No!" Colonel Carter shot a burst of electricity up into the air to get Zom Kong's attention. "I'm the one who helped you! I'm the one who fed and watched over you all these years. If you know what's good for you, you won't listen to him."

The ape just looked at me uncomprehendingly.

"I'm your son," I repeated as Boris finally grabbed me by the arms and raised me toward his awful mouth. Kicking and pulling at his hands didn't work. He was too strong. I felt his hot breath on my neck. "Help me, dad! Help me!"

And Zom Kong did! Its eyes seeming to clear, it leaned forward, breaking its chains and grabbing Boris's head with a mighty hand. My father began to squeeze, and there was a noise like something being pulled out of mud. A moment later, I found myself falling to the floor followed by an ichor-covered, and headless, Boris.

"No!" Colonel Carter screamed and turned the equalizer on my father. Electricity became Zom Kong's dance partner, causing the beast that was my dad to shiver and cook. A foul odor filled the air.

Zom Kong turned my way, its expression sadder than ever. "Son…" he said in a thick voice, then fell to the ground, now truly dead.

"Dad!" I screamed. I had lost the father I had never known.

Colonel Carter spun on me. "I suppose I'll have to do this myself," he hissed and came toward me. I said nothing. Instead, I closed my eyes, trying hard not to pass out, as I felt like I was being ripped to shreds from the inside out. When I opened my eyes, I was no longer looking up at him. We were looking eye to startled eye.

"What's going on?" Colonel Carter asked, stopping two feet in front of me.

There was a throbbing in my neck, and I touched it, my fingers coming back wet with blood. Boris had bitten me! My body creaked as I continued to grow. I was already taller than the colonel… and my mind was beginning to cloud over. He turned to run but I grabbed him by the arm and bit down hard. The Colonel tasted horrible, and I spat him out, then punched him in the mouth, not wanting him to attract any attention by screaming. He went down hard.

With my mind growing less alert by the second, I watched him begin to grow, thick white hair covering his body as he did. Between my new bite and his old infection, without the green pills, the Colonel would…

The green pills! I had brought them with me. Maybe there was a way out of this yet! As fast as my petrifying body could go, I reached into my pocket and managed to pull out the silver tube which now seemed the size of a pen cap. I looked it over, what was this thing? Why did I have it? But that thought soon left my mind to be followed by a new one, an overpowering hunger.

What was there to eat? There was the thing with no head, the dead festering ape, and the foul-tasting white thing. No, none of that. Then something caught my eye, it was the silver object. It was a little thing, but something in my mind told me it would taste good. I shoved the tube into my mouth, my movements becoming stiffer by the second. I bit down hard, and a mist entered my throat, a green cloud forming…

Immediately, my senses returned, and my body stopped growing. My nerves started to tingle as my body prepared to shrink. I wanted to pass out but couldn't. There were still important things to do. While my strength and size remained, I dragged the changed Colonel Carter onto Zom Kong's stake and locked him up. His growth had stopped at fifty feet, white hair now covering his whole body. Although he only vaguely looked like the original Zom Kong, I wasn't worried. Through intimidation, bribery, or pseudo-science, I was sure I could figure out a way to explain the difference.

I was about to bring the remains of my father to the Burning Pit when a moan came from the Colonel, and I returned my attention to him. Even through the tent's darkness, I could see a trace of intelligence remained. Good. "Help... me...," he muttered in a thickening voice.

I shook my head. "You kept my father like this for over a decade. Now it's your turn." He weakly reached for me, but I was beyond his grasp. "Goodbye, Colonel."

"*You* were supposed to...be the one..." He fell silent, his gaze glazing over.

My body shrinking, I left the big tent, barely managing to drag the remains of the original Zom Kong into the Burning Pit. Exhausted, I sat and watched the flames consume the father I never knew; the father who had saved my life.

"Goodbye, dad," I whispered. "Thanks for being there at the end."

Then I closed my eyes, no longer able to fight off sleep. The last thing I saw was the zombie circus stretching out before me. I smiled. Colonel Carter's last unfinished sentence was going to be prophetic.

"You were supposed to be the one to take over," he meant to say.

And, finally, after all this time, that was exactly what I was going to do.

— FIN —

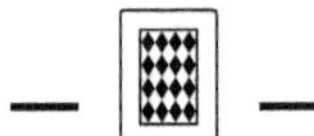

*I*nhuman screeching, the rattling of bars, the trilling screams of the so-called lesser primates seeming to signal the breaking of the next mirror before fading off into the drum of the rain. Only three standing mirrors remain, the table an eye at the center of the triangle. The sawdust around the edge of the circle mingles with the powdered glass, the edges of the tent having grown even closer. The face of your host has taken on an expressionist contrast as the space has gotten more intimate, the candles starkening the shadows as the jungle of toy monkeys joins the other discarded items.

"Our time together nears its end, I'm afraid," the host says, and you try to pin down whether what you feel is dread or relief. Already it feels as if you've spent lifetimes together, this stranger and you, and you suppose, in a way, you have. Xer hand dips into the hat's darkness like a tidepool, and when it emerges, it is holding a spiraling conch. The pearl-peach surface of the shell looks almost lit from within by the candlelight, and again xe circles the table, coming to rest behind you. "Listen," xe says, pressing the shell against your ear. Whispering within, you hear all the sounds of the sea, but beyond the waves and the wind and the gulls you can hear the slightest hint of singing. "Down, down into the depths, kicking up and break the surface only to discover that the world above is as cruel and cold as the one below. Join me as we leap, jump, dive into the sea once more as..."

Carnival Imaginarium Presents:
The Siren from the Deep

performed by Kay Hanifen

Melusine sat below the docks listening to the chatter of humans above her. The past few days had been bustling with excitement as people discussed the traveling carnival coming to the boardwalk. She longed to see it, to learn what a freakshow was and what it meant to be an acrobat. From her vantage point, she had watched them set up the buildings, all painted in exotic colors and depicting bizarre humans and animals. At night, the carnival lit up the boardwalk with bright lights and loud music.

She had taken her usual position observing the people moving in and out along the pier and boardwalk. Though the lights were still sparkling up above, it was getting late, and the crowds were thinning. Overhead, she heard someone with a deep voice speak. "This isn't a place for a lady, Betty, so how about you stay out here while I get Fred and the others?"

"You're too kind, Pierre," she replied in a way that made Melusine suspect she was being sarcastic. It wasn't mean, though, like some of the drunks she'd overheard. Her tone was lighter, more like affectionate teasing.

"Chivalry isn't dead, simply forgotten by most. Enjoy the night and the sea air. This shouldn't take too long."

"Make sure they're all in one piece," she replied. For a minute or two, Melusine watched her standing alone in the moonlight. She was probably the prettiest woman she had ever seen, with raven hair cut to her chin and dressed in a man's coat and trousers and holding a long white stick. A group of drunken men approached.

"Hey pretty lady, how about we show you a good time?" one said.

"I'll pass," she replied. Usually, when harassed on the street, Melusine observed that women either shrank in discomfort or if they were the kind who were paid for a good time, flirted with their body language, but this woman stood tall and confidently as she rejected their advances.

"Come on, don't be like that," another one said, grabbing her arm, "We know you carnies love easy money."

"Let go," the woman snapped, pulling herself free. Boards creaked overhead as she backed down the pier and the men advanced upon her.

"We've got plenty of cash. You can buy yourself a nice fur coat."

"I didn't want to do this," she said, and pulled out a small metal device that glinted in the moonlight and made the men react with fear, "but you leave me no choice."

"You don't have the guts," the first man said.

She aimed down and the men cried out, but it only clicked. "Oh no," she said quietly while the men laughed. Turning heel, she ran until she reached the edge of the pier, the men surrounding her like a pod of dolphins on a hunt. She pressed her back against the guardrail, the terror obvious on her face as she shouted, "Pierre!"

"None of that," a man said and pushed her into the water.

She screamed before falling like a stone. Panicking, she thrashed about, and sinking deeper as her clothes weighed her down. Melusine knew she wasn't supposed to interact with humans, but the woman would most certainly die without her help.

She wrapped an arm around the woman's waist as she went limp and dragged them both to shore. Never having seen a human up close before, she was fascinated. They had similar facial features, but less jagged teeth and softer skin. As Melusine brushed the hair from her face, a hand shot up, grabbing her wrist. The woman's anger, though, was quickly replaced by confusion as she felt Melusine's hand, and then her forearm, gasping as she felt the fin. "You're like us," she whispered in awe.

"Betty," the deep-voiced man from earlier shouted, "Betty, where are you?"

She sat up, coughing some seawater out of her lungs before calling back, "I'm down here. Give me a minute, please."

"We'll be counting down from sixty," another man with a much higher voice said.

Melusine turned to go, but Betty grabbed her hand. "Wait, I want to thank you. What's your name?"

"Melusine," she replied, and the name sounded strange in the human tongue.

"Are you some kind of fish woman, Melusine?"

She nodded.

Betty waited a couple seconds before sighing. "If you nodded, I'm blind. I wouldn't know."

"Sorry. Yes," she replied.

"What are you doing so close to shore?"

"Humans are interesting. I like to watch them."

"Am I the first one you've talked to?"

She nodded again, but remembered and answered, "Yes."

"I owe you, so I want to give you a choice. If you swim away now, I'll never speak of this, and you can spend the rest of your days doing whatever it is you do in the ocean—or, if you think humans are interesting, I'm a part of a traveling carnival. We go across the country seeing all kinds of people. You can join us if you want."

Melusine stared, dumbstruck. She'd always wanted to know more about humanity, and this was her best chance to see all kinds of humans. And it wasn't like she had much left in the ocean. Her pod had left her behind a long time ago when the tear in her back fin made her too slow to keep up with them. "Yes," she replied.

Betty smiled, and it was like staring at the sunrise. "Wonderful! Pierre? Fred? You can come down now."

A tall man with biceps as thick as his head, an incredibly short man, a man with no legs walking on his hands, and a man with rough, scaly skin all approached. The muscular man, presumably

Pierre, ran up to Betty and checked her over. "Are you hurt? What happened?" he asked.

"Went for a dip and met a friend," she replied, gesturing in the direction of Melusine, "Say hello to our new act."

The men gasped. "Is—is that a mermaid?" the short man with the high-pitched voice asked.

"You tell me," Betty replied as she waved a hand in front of her face.

"That's a mermaid alright," said the legless man.

"I'll get Hank," the scaly man said.

"Hank?" asked Melusine.

"The owner of Carnival Imaginarium," Betty explained and then smacked her head, "How rude of me! I forgot to make introductions. Guys, this is Melusine. Melusine, this is Pierre the Goliath—he's our resident strongman—and then there's Fred, but onstage we call him the Lilliputian, and last but not least, Roger Amazing the Half-Man. The guy who just left is Joey, but we call him the Cajun Joe the Alligator Man on account of his skin condition."

"A pleasure to meet you," Pierre said with a bow.

"Always nice to meet another weirdo," said Roger, "We freaks gotta look out for fellow freaks."

Fred grinned. "Don't worry. We don't bite. Well… except for the geek. He bites."

"I'm not used to speaking to humans," she said softly, "but it's nice to meet you. What does it mean to be an act?"

The three men exchanged awkward glances. "Well, it depends," Pierre began, "I'm the strongman, and I show off to crowds. Betty is an expert markswoman—"

"But if you're weird enough, people will pay just to gawk at you," Roger added.

"And you don't mind?" she asked.

Fred shrugged. "I don't exactly love being stared at, and I think my stage name is patronizing, but it makes decent money and it's not like I can get a lot of work as a dwarf. Better than being locked up in an asylum or disappointment room, that's for sure."

Roger nodded in agreement. "Like I said, we look out for each other."

"Carnie life is hard and not for everyone," Betty said, "so if you want to back out, I understand. I'll just act concussed or something when Joey gets back."

She thought of her pod, the way they promised her they'd protect her, but they left her behind when she proved too slow to keep their pace. Of the five humans she met, the cruelties of the sea would have taken all but Pierre and perhaps Joey, but they all seemed dedicated to one another in spite of any weakness. Maybe this could be her new pod. She smiled. "I want to go with you."

Betty grinned. "That's what I like to hear! We'll take good care of you, Mel."

"Jumping Jehoshaphat!" a man, presumably Hank, exclaimed as he ran down the beach, closely followed by Joey. "How on earth did you find a mermaid?"

"Well, she found me," Betty said, and explained the night's adventure.

Hank sat down in the sand, his eyes wide with shock. "Good Lord, Betty, I oughta throw you in the ocean more often."

"Do that and you'll be eating lead for breakfast, lunch, and dinner," she replied and then shivered as the wind picked up.

"Cold?" Melusine asked. She didn't feel the cold, but humans were more delicate that way.

"And she speaks," he said, putting his head in his hands.

"We should get you warmed up," Pierre said, helping Betty to her feet. He turned to Melusine. "Shall I fill a bathtub until we can make a proper tank?"

"Thank you, Pierre," Hank replied, "Use my private quarters, please."

"I'll stay with her," Betty said, "to keep her company tonight." She had a steely expression on her face and her voice carried a note of warning. Hank glared for just a moment before nodding.

Pierre knelt in front of her. "I'll pick you up on the count of three. Ready? One…two…three…" He lifted her as though she were as weightless as the gulls that flew above them. "Let's go."

Luckily, it was the middle of the night, and very few people were out. Those that loitered in the street were so drunk that she suspected that they would assume their procession was a strange dream. When they reached the carnival owner's quarters, Fred drew the bath while Betty went to get changed, and Joey grabbed bedding for her. Without a specific task, Roger headed back to his room. She had never been out of saltwater but realized to her relief that she was comfortable in freshwater. One by one, the rest of the carnies completed their self-assigned tasks and filed out. All but Joey remained, which she was happy about because she hadn't had the chance to properly introduce herself.

"Hello, Joey," she said softly as he set up the bedding for Betty.

The man's skin was scaly and leathery, and occasionally flaked off when he'd scratch at it or brush against something. He jumped when he heard her address him. "Hi, uh…"

"Melusine," she replied with what she hoped was a friendly smile, "it's nice to meet you."

"Nice to meet you too, ma'am," he replied, looking bashfully down at his feet.

Betty returned moments later wearing silk pajamas. "That's the last time I leave my room without extra bullets," she said, letting Joey guide her to the bedding piled on the floor like a bird's nest. "How are you doing, Mel? Hungry?"

She gnawed her lip. It had been a little while since she'd eaten, but she already felt that she'd imposed enough already. "I'm not, thank you."

"Night, Betty, night Melusine," Joey said, shutting the door behind him.

Betty laid back on the bedding. "Thank you again for saving my life."

"Thank you for welcoming me into your carnival," she replied, "You are all so kind."

Betty propped herself up on an elbow. "About that… be careful, okay? You don't know much about the human world, and people who seem nice can be cruel just under the surface."

She furrowed her brows. "But you, Pierre, Fred, Roger, Hank, and Joey are kind."

Betty shook her head. "Be careful of Hank, too. He can be decent, but he only cares about money. Well, money and sex."

"I don't understand."

"A word of advice," Betty replied with a sigh, "the freaks here might look scary, but they're good people making an honest living the best they can. It's the normies you have to watch out for. They shake with one hand and bury a knife in your chest with the other."

"I'll remember that," she said. "If it's so dangerous, why are you here?"

"Because as much as I love Hank, he can get handsy and I don't want you to bite 'em off," she replied, laying back.

Melusine chuckled. "Don't worry. Human doesn't taste very good."

She arched an eyebrow. "You've eaten people?"

"Corpses mostly. Shipwrecks on the open ocean have a lot of casualties." She thought back to the poor souls thrown overboard by the stormy waves above, thrashing and panicking in the water until all the bubbles left and they were still. It wasn't her favorite meal, but it was food, so she ate. She was the only one in her pod who took an interest in humans outside of their status as an occasionally convenient food source. But she was fascinated by their clothes, the little metal crosses around their necks and delicate photographs that she would stare at until the water dissolved the faces staring back at her. After they left her behind, she chose to risk living by a town for two reasons: easy access to food and the ability to watch living humans as they went about their business.

Betty hummed. "Fair enough. But why save me?"

"I thought you would taste bad too."

Betty laughed. "I like you, Mel."

"I like you too," she said, "But you didn't answer my question."

"Why I'm a carnie?" She made an odd sound, her lips flapping as though blowing bubbles. "It's a long story. I wasn't always blind, you know. When Pierre and Papa found me on the streets, I had my eyesight and impressive aim for a little girl. Papa thought I could be the next Annie Oakley. But then the Great Influenza hit. Papa and I got sick. He didn't make it. I did… but it left me blind. As Hank will tell you, blind people are a dime a dozen. People won't pay to see a blind girl, but they'll pay to see one hit a target at thirty paces. We all have to pull our weight around here, so I learned to shoot, and I'm better than most men who can see."

"I could not 'pull my weight' with my pod, so they left me behind," Melusine said softly. She turned awkwardly in the tub so that her tail was right above Betty. "You may feel it if you want. A rival pod slit it, making it impossible for me to keep up with my family."

Betty reached up, and her warm fingers sent shivers down Melusine's spine as the human felt the part of the webbing that had been sliced away. "Does it hurt?" she asked.

"It did, but not anymore. The hurt is now in my heart. I understand why they turned away from me. The sea is cold and harsh, and life is so very precarious. You must do whatever you can to ensure your own survival. I was too weak."

"Bullshit," Betty said, sitting up, "they were your family, and family doesn't turn their back on family. I—I mean, look at us here. We're all weak and deserve to be abandoned, according to your logic. Hell, most of us *were* abandoned, but we're fine. More than fine. Some of us make more money than the people we left will ever see in their lifetime. It's their loss."

She shrank a little under the intensity of Betty's gaze. "We freaks gotta look out for our fellow freaks," she said, repeating Roger's words from earlier that evening.

"Exactly, Mel, and I promise I'm gonna look after you. You won't get left behind again."

"Thank you," she replied, her heart squeezing painfully. She wanted this conversation to be over. Softly, she began to sing an old lullaby in her language. It was a song her pod would sing when welcoming a baby into the family.

"That's beautiful," Betty said sleepily, "You have the prettiest voice I've ever heard."

And you're the prettiest woman I've ever seen, Melusine wanted to say.

The carnies had scrambled to put together a water tank large enough for her to swim inside while still portable. Betty barely left her side in those first few weeks, leaving only to perform and sleep. Once the tank was done, she began her "act," which didn't consist of much. Pierre and Betty would present her and then pull back the curtains, revealing her to a gasping crowd. Then, she would swim around in her tank, eat the fish Betty tossed to her with perfect aim, and play to the crowd. People came from all over to see the "Siren from the Deep," and she took notes, fascinated by the wide variety of humans. Some arrived dressed in clean clothes, others with smudged and dirty faces. There were so many skin tones, eye colors, heights, and weights and she marveled at the astonishing variety of human bodies. And they all reacted differently to her. Children would giggle and tap on the glass while men ogled her bare chest. That made little sense, but she didn't think much of it. Some women would faint while others of all kinds would stare in naked horror and disgust. Those were her least favorite. They made her feel like she was unnatural.

After about a month, while Betty was off performing her own show, Fred, Roger, and Joey entered her tent with a picnic basket. Joey set it up on the platform they used during feeding time. "How're you doing, Mel?" Fred asked, tossing her a tuna sandwich.

"It's very different from the ocean," she replied, "I feel like…"

"A fish outta water?" Roger suggested. The other two carnies groaned.

"Boo," Joey jeered, balling up a napkin and throwing it at him.

"Don't go changing up your act now, Roger," Fred said, his eyes glinting mischievously, "When it comes to comedy, you don't have a leg to stand on." All groaned again, and Melusine splashed him with her tail in protest. He sputtered. "Everyone's a critic."

Hank threw open the curtain followed closely by Betty and Pierre. "Great news, everyone! Guess who got us a private show with Maxwell Haddish."

The guys gasped. "We're gonna meet a millionaire?" Joey asked in quiet awe.

Hank grinned. "Not only that, but we're gonna give him a show, with Mel and Betty as the stars."

"Who is Maxwell Haddish?" she asked, interrupting their excitement.

Betty climbed the stairs, taking her usual seat by the edge of the tank. "A meal ticket. Maybe the last one we'll ever need if we're lucky. He has more money than God, and if we impress him, we'll never have to worry about funds again."

"And Mel, you're our secret weapon," Hank added, "a myth made flesh, a sailor's dream come true, an angel of the deep, a salacious siren, a—"

Pierre cleared his throat. "We will be traveling to his mansion tomorrow. Everyone needs to prepare their best clothes and routines."

As if given an unspoken signal, all filed out to prepare—all but Betty, who removed her shoes and stuck her feet in the water. "What are you thinking?" Melusine asked.

"I dunno," she replied, "I just… I have a feeling. Like how you know when a storm is coming. Not sure how to describe it." Melusine hoisted herself up onto the platform to sit beside her. Betty laid her head on her shoulder and laughed quietly. "It's stupid. This could be our ticket to everything we've always wanted, so why do I feel sick?"

"Sharks are among our most dangerous predators. They're swift, silent, and attack seemingly without warning. Except, if you pay close enough attention to the water around you, you can sense the change in vibration that comes with their movements. Many of us will sense it without knowing what it means until it's too late."

"So, you're saying I should trust my instincts?"

Melusine shrugged. "Instincts are the difference between life and death in the ocean. But not all sharks are looking for a meal. Some need help removing fish hooks or protection from a pod of dolphins. Pay attention to the movements of the water, and if a hungry shark is coming, run."

Betty nodded thoughtfully. "Good point." Picking up her head, she pressed her lips to Melusine's. They tingled from the contact and filled her chest with a fluttery warmth. Betty pulled away and asked, "Was that all right with you?"

"What was that?" Melusine asked, feeling her burning lips.

"A kiss. We do that to show we love someone." Her face turned an interesting shade of pink. "Sorry, I shouldn't have done that. I should go."

Melusine's hand shot out, grabbing Betty's wrist. "Wait. Please."

With a shaking breath, Betty sat back down. "I don't know why I kissed you. I just know that ever since you saved my life, it's like breathing for the first time in a long time. Papa used to say that I'd feel that way about someone someday. He told me it would likely be a man, but unlike most people, he'd love me even if it wasn't. He and Pierre loved each other even though the world says it's unnatural, and I think I might be unnatural like them, and…"

Melusine pressed a kiss to her lips. "We call ourselves freaks, but I don't think you understand what it is to be truly unnatural. If you were born a certain way without any scientific or magical intervention, then you are natural. Fred is naturally a dwarf, Roger is naturally without legs, I am naturally a mermaid, and you naturally love women."

"You feel the same way?" she asked tremulously.

"I believe so. I love the afternoons we spend performing together and the nights where we share meals and talk about our worlds. And the night where we met, I thought you were the prettiest creature on earth."

She giggled. "Then I question your taste in women. But thank you."

Melusine laid back, stretching herself on the platform. "What do we do now?"

"I don't know," Betty replied, "Stay as we are? In all the little mermaid stories I've read, the prince's kiss turns her human, or she doesn't get one and becomes sea foam."

"That's absurd. You're just as likely to become sea foam as I am."

"Both those endings made me sad." Betty laid down beside her. "Most people understand why her becoming a seafoam made me upset. She just wanted a soul and a happy ending. But they don't understand why getting the prince is also sad."

"Why?"

"She gave up everything she'd ever known in the hopes of finding happiness on land, but no one would ever truly understand her. How can they know what it's like to swim through coral reefs and kelp forests like you have, to ride on the backs of whales and sing sailors to their doom? No matter where she goes, land or sea, she's an outsider looking in."

Melusine felt a pang of sympathy and understanding in her own chest. She hadn't fit in with her pod. She was too fascinated by the surface, too slow, the burden on all their shoulders. They all ate first, sang loudest, and brutally beat her down whenever she tried to fight back. Now, even among her unusual friends, she was still an outsider confined to a glorified fish tank to be gawked at by people as proof of the existence of mermaids. "I had not thought of it that way, but you're right. Perhaps her story could only ever end in tragedy." She reached up, brushing a lock of hair from Betty's face. "But for a time, she had love, and perhaps that was worth all the pain."

Her smaller tank had been hoisted on top of a pickup truck and covered with a curtain so no one could stand by the side of the road and gawk, cheating Hank out of his precious money. Betty rode in the back with her, opening the curtain just enough for Melusine to peer out at the rolling hills and fiery autumn leaves. She had told Melusine that Mr. Haddish had made his money off the coal mines that dug deep into the mountainside, bringing industry to the people. His mansion was nestled deep in the woods, far away from town and sat on a cliffside next to a pristine blue lake. It was perhaps the biggest building that Melusine had ever seen and made with intricate carvings along the windows and the tower in front.

An old man stood outside waving a top hat in greeting beside a woman and a bored looking young man as they pulled up front. "Hello there, friends," the old man, presumably Haddish, said.

Hank got out of the car and greeted him like an old friend. "Maxwell! You didn't have to greet us personally."

"I was just too eager to see the specimen. Is she under the curtain?" he asked.

Hank gave a gregarious grin. "Would you like to do the honors?"

"I'd be delighted," he said, hopping up onto the back and pulling it away. Melusine blinked in the sudden light while the old man and his family gasped in delight. "Oh, she's just grotesque." He tapped on the glass, making her wince at the vibrations underwater.

"That's not all," Hank said, "Come on out, Melusine."

She glanced at Betty, whose teeth were gritted, but she gave a short nod and Melusine poked her head above water. Every instinct told her to bite this man's head off, but she had the carnival to think about. They needed the money. "A pleasure to meet you, Mr. Haddish."

He let out a deep, booming laugh. "Well, I'll be damned. She speaks."

Pierre, who had driven separately, hopped lightly out of the trunk, and pulled out a wheelchair. He held out a hand for Betty, but the young man stepped up. "Allow me to escort the lovely lady." He helped her out of the bed of the truck, and she let out an unusually girlish giggle.

"How very chivalrous," she said. Though she was naturally brash and bold, she knew how to play the part of the dainty waif if it suited her needs. Along with her incredible skill, she sold the fantasy of a pretty girl who was helpless when it counted. They all had a role to play in this act.

Pierre set the wheelchair near the end of the car. Melusine wrapped her arms around his neck and allowed herself to be lifted out of the tank and onto the chair. They had discovered that she could spend a couple hours outside of the water before she began to dry out and feel uncomfortable.

"Allow me to give you all a tour," Mr. Haddish said and then to the woman, "Maude, why don't you make sure everything's ready in the dining room."

The woman, who had gone grey at the sight of Melusine, followed by Roger, Fred, and Joey disembarking from their car, simply nodded and went inside.

"She's a touch delicate," Mr. Haddish said to Hank, "Freaks and oddities unnerve her. Don't be too offended if she doesn't take well to your acts."

Melusine hated the hungry way that the millionaire gawked at them, like they were choice morsels to be torn apart and consumed piece by piece. Not once had he addressed any of them but Hank. It was as though they were animals.

"I'm sorry, but there's no way a little lady like you can shoot like Buffalo Bill," the younger man said. He and Betty were just ahead, leading them into the mansion.

just keep swimming just keep swimming just keep

Betty smirked. "I guess you'll have to wait and see."

Melusine gasped when Pierre pushed her inside. The interior was just as intricately decorated as the exterior. The stone floors shone like pearlescent oyster shells and the walls were adorned with silver, gold, and paintings done by an expert hand. Everyone else looked equally awed, with the exception of Betty, who smiled and giggled to maintain the charade, but Melusine could see the way that she tensed when the man put a hand on the small of her back.

"William, why don't you bring Miss Bryant to the kitchen. The ladies can chat while the men talk business," he said.

"Business?" Melusine repeated, "What business?" The rest of the carnies looked just as confused as she was. This was only meant to be a performance, but she had the sick feeling that something else had passed between Hank and Mr. Haddish.

Hank patted the top of her head. "Don't worry about it, Mel. It's just dotting some *i*'s and crossing some *t*'s. You know how it is."

William began maneuvering Betty away, but she stood firm, dropping her flirtatious act like a stone. "I'd like to stay with you, actually. If whatever business you have concerns me or Mel, then I'm gonna be a part of the conversation."

Mr. Haddish sighed. "Fine, if you insist." He muttered something to himself about liberated women. "Allow me to give you the grand tour." He guided them through elaborately decorated rooms, so many that Melusine had no idea what he used them all for. Many were just for sitting and their use depended on the formality of the meeting. The coziest places were for the guests the family was close to while the elaborate and fanciest rooms were for strangers and people they needed to impress. The library was breathtaking, full of books from floor to ceiling, and containing an aquarium built into one of the walls. Fish of all shapes and colors swam around the replica shipwreck, and for the first time, Melusine had an intense feeling of homesickness.

She did not miss the sea or her pod, not really anymore. She had found a new pod and a new frontier to explore, but there were times when she was struck with such a feeling of nostalgia that she could practically hear her sisters' calls. Staring at the tank was one of those times.

"Would you like to go for a little swim?" Mr. Haddish asked, speaking slowly, and enunciating carefully as though she wouldn't understand him.

There it was. That tremor in the water that told her danger was near. Betty seemed to sense it too because she moved closer to her. "Perhaps later," Melusine replied, baring her sharp teeth into something that resembled a smile but carried with it a threat.

Hank quickly defused the tension with a laugh. "Mel doesn't get to spend much time out of the tank. I think she wants to see the rest of your amazing home."

Mr. Haddish lit up. "Right! I haven't shown you my prized collection yet. Right this way."

"You okay?" Roger whispered as they walked through the maze of rooms. Hank and Mr. Haddish were ahead, chatting animatedly and not paying attention to them. Betty was preoccupied by William, who couldn't seem to keep his hands off her, so the rest could whisper among themselves without fear of being noticed.

"I don't like this man," Melusine whispered back.

Pierre leaned down. "Me either. I think Hank's up to something."

"He's always up to something," Fred said. "We're just cash cows to him. He treats us better than most, but I know where we stand."

"What should we do?" Joey asked, anxiously picking at one of his scales.

Melusine took his hand to make him stop before he bled. "We wait, I suppose."

"Ah, here we are," Mr. Haddish exclaimed, opening a large oak door. The room was massive and filled with oddities. The walls were lined with glass jars containing deformed animals and fetuses floating in formaldehyde, a skeleton of a man taller than even Pierre, a photograph of a long-necked monster in a lake and plaster cast of a massive footprint. In the center was a taxidermied two-headed calf, several bizarre statues, guns of all sizes, and various medical instruments. He ushered them inside. "Welcome to my own inventory of oddities. I've always been fascinated by the strange and unusual. You might call me something of a collector, and I am delighted to add you all to my collection."

The clamor of protests was immediate. "What the hell are you talking about?" Roger demanded.

Mr. Haddish looked confused. "Didn't Hank tell you? He's selling the freakshow to me, along with all the acts—well, except for Pierre of course. Unnatural desires like his are not the kind of oddity that fascinates me."

"Bastard!" Pierre shouted, grabbing Hank by the lapels, and slamming him into the wall, "How dare you!"

"Let me explain," Hank began, putting up his hands in a placating gesture.

"Ten seconds…" Pierre growled.

"I wanted out of the game, and when he approached with an offer, I thought it was perfect. We'd all be set for life. I'm looking out for you all! Honest!"

"Yeah, right, selling us to the highest bidder like pure breed dogs is just your way of saying you care," Fred retorted before punching Hank in the crotch.

"Don't worry, you'll be living in the lap of luxury," William said, putting an arm around Betty. She elbowed him in the gut, and he staggered backwards. "Bitch!" he shouted, slapping her across the face. She fell with a surprised cry and all eyes turned to him.

A blinding, white hot rage filled Melusine, and she leapt from her chair, dragging herself as she charged him. She felt a pinching sensation in her neck and pulled out a dart. Eyes swimming, she saw Mr. Haddish holding a small gun.

"Mel!" Betty shouted, pushing herself up and wiping a bit of red from her nose. Melusine turned, and smelling the coppery odor, and seeing the blood, shakily crawled towards her. "Stay awake," Betty said softly as she teared up, "please."

Melusine caressed her cheek, forcing her eyes to focus so she could check for any serious injury. The side of Betty's face was red, but she seemed otherwise okay. Betty got to her feet, pulling her gun. "We're leaving."

"Go ahead, shoot me if you want," Mr. Haddish said, looking pleased with himself.

"You asked for it," she replied, aiming lower and pulling the trigger. There was a loud bang that made Melusine cover her ears, but nothing else. Mr. Haddish didn't cry out or fall over. He hadn't been hit at all. Confused, she emptied the chamber. "Blanks?"

"You didn't think I'd really let you carry a gun around a millionaire, did you?" Hank said, "I replaced your bullets with blanks after yesterday's show."

Pierre's hands moved to Hank's throat, and he squeezed. Hank choked, struggling weakly in his grip. "You didn't think I'd let you take my daughter from me, did you?" he growled.

Another crack like thunder rang out, and the carnies screamed as their strongman fell to the floor with a bullet between his ribs. "Pierre!" Betty shouted, rushing to his side. She felt for the wound, putting pressure on it, and making him cry out. "My beautiful Betty," he choked, gently brushing a lock of hair behind her ear, and leaving a trail of blood on her cheek.

"Pierre, please," she sobbed, "I can't lose you too."

"You won't. I'll just be… watching you alongside… your Papa. I love you." He lifted his head slightly so that he could look at the rest of the people he considered family. At his side, Joey was quietly sobbing while Roger and Fred shook with rage. Pierre's eyes met Melusine's. "Take care… of each other." He coughed up blood. It stained his teeth and dribbled down his chin. And then he was still.

Betty let out a scream that pierced Melusine's heart like a harpoon. She fought against the pull of sleep, dragging herself towards William, who had taken the gun from one of the tables and used it to murder her friend. He aimed it at the sobbing Betty. "Come any closer and I shoot. It would be a waste of a beautiful face, but…"

She snarled and hissed but made no further effort to attack him.

"You…you killed him," Joey whispered, staring in shock at the body. He turned on Hank, punching him in the jaw. "You killed him!" Hank went down and Joey followed, straddling him as he beat him into the ground.

"Guards!" Mr. Haddish shouted, and men with guns rushed into the room. One hit Joey over the head with the butt of a rifle, stunning him enough to drag him away.

Others set upon Fred and Roger, restraining them. They dragged Betty away from Pierre's corpse while three were on

Melusine, who fought ferociously despite the tranquilizer dart. "Betty!" she shouted as they dragged her out the door.

"Melusine!" she shouted back, renewing her struggle against them. The last thing she saw was her friends' tear-stained faces and the cold expressions of Mr. Haddish and William, and then it all went black.

She woke in the library fish tank. For a moment, she was confused and disoriented, thinking she was back in the ocean, but then she remembered what happened. Mr. Haddish sat in a wingback chair sipping tea and reading. With a shriek, she slammed her hand against the glass. That got his attention. He jumped, and then smiled smugly. "Well, hello there, pet. It's good to see you're finally awake. You must be starving." He got to his feet and climbed the adjoining staircase to the top of the tank. The top of the cage was crisscrossed with bars just far enough out of the water for her to poke her head out.

"Where are they?" she demanded, "If you hurt them, I swear, I'll—"

He tsked. "So rude. Your friends are fine, just as I said they would be. I don't mean any of you harm."

"Pierre would disagree."

"Pierre was an unfortunate accident. I'm sorry it had to be that way." He pulled out a salmon steak and dropped it into the water. Melusine stared as it sank while fish swarmed, tearing it apart. Mr. Haddish looked disappointed. "That was a fine fish you let go to waste."

"And he was a good man whose life you wasted like it was worth less than that chunk of meat."

He shrugged and got to his feet. "Fine. Be that way. I'll see if the rest of my new acquisitions are hungry. I'm sure my son is entertaining Miss Betty just fine." Mr. Haddish left her alone, turning out the lights so that she was in complete darkness. With a shriek, she rattled the bars of her cage, channeling all her rage into an attempt to break out. Despite her strength, she could not make them budge, which only enraged her further.

She wasn't sure how long she struggled against them, but eventually, she grew tired. Though Betty thought she had a beautiful voice, she didn't have much talent for the other aspect of her gift. Try as she might, she couldn't lure anyone to her. But she was desperate enough to make the attempt.

She began singing, her voice echoing through the dark library. Her song was in her own tongue, the one she'd stopped speaking when she was abandoned, and sang of her grief and her pain, her desire to be freed and her rage at the injustice of the situation. After hours of her song, the door opened, and Betty of all people stepped in. "Betty?" she called out.

She carried with her a steak knife in one hand and her cane in another. "Melusine?"

"Up here. Follow the sound of my voice."

"It's worked for me so far," she replied with a smirk, feeling around the tank to get to the metal spiral staircase leading upwards.

"How did you get out?" she asked, swimming to the side with the stairs on it so Betty would hear where to go.

"People assume that just because you're blind, you're helpless, but you don't have to see to pick a lock. You just need a hairpin and a whole lot of patience." She slowly began to climb.

"The top is barred. I am not sure how to get out."

"Well, they had to get you in here somehow. Can you see anything that could be like a door?"

She studied the bars above her and noticed a pair of hinges near the staircase. It was a little bulkier a few feet away, probably where the lock was. "Hold out your hand," she said, "and I'll guide it to the lock."

Betty swallowed nervously. Even knowing that she couldn't fall in, the water frightened her. But she held out her hand, allowing her to guide it to the keyhole. Taking a bobby pin, she made quick work of the lock. With a click, it opened, and she was free. Melusine dragged herself out of there and threw her arms around Betty. "I'm so sorry. Pierre was a good man. He didn't deserve that."

"None of us deserve this," she said, her voice choked, "but we should get the others before we figure out what to do next."

Melusine dragged herself down the stairs behind Betty. Though she had powerful upper-arm strength, it was still a hassle moving outside of water. "Do you know where the others are?"

"No clue. But tell me if you spot any guns, knives, or just anything I can throw."

As she passed a desk, Melusine snatched a letter opener. "I think I found something," she said, handing it to the markswoman.

"Beggars can't be choosers," she muttered, testing the balance. "This'll do for now, but keep your eyes peeled." When they reached the door, she stopped short.

"What is it?" she whispered.

Betty clutched the letter opener. "Footsteps coming closer. Four people. And the squeak of wheels?" They held their breath as the four quietly approached. The door handle turned, and Betty took them by surprise, flinging it open. With a cry, she plunged the knife into Hank's arm. He grunted, pushing her away, so she yanked the knife out and raised it to strike again.

"Betty, wait!" Fred shouted. He, Roger, and Joey stood slightly behind him, with Joey pushing the wheelchair.

She froze. "Fred?"

"Yeah, the gang's all here," Roger said.

"Who did I stab?" she asked.

Joey grinned. "Hank."

"Ah, no one important then."

"I'm right here," he grumbled, pressing a hand to the wound.

"I know," she replied flatly.

"You have to believe me," Hank said, "I had no idea he would kill Pierre like that. I'm getting you all out of here."

"Apparently, he has a heart under all that greed," Roger said, "Who knew?"

"Guys, let's finish this conversation on our way back to the carnival," Joey whispered as he stared anxiously down the hall.

Melusine took Betty's hand. "I agree. We should hurry." She got into the chair, and they hurried down the halls as quietly as they could.

"Hold out your hand," Hank said as they walked. Betty did as he asked, and he handed her a gun.

"There better not be any blanks in this one."

"No blanks. I loaded it myself."

"You do see how that wouldn't make me feel better, right?" she retorted as she pulled back the safety, "I'm putting my trust in you for now. But if this is another trick, you'll be my next target practice."

"Understood."

They turned the corner and froze. Mrs. Haddish stood in her pajamas, holding a cup of tea. For a split second, they stared at each other like a rabbit coming face to face with a fox. And then she let out a shriek. Betty fired her gun, shooting her outer thigh. Mrs. Haddish dropped like a stone in a dead faint. They all stared at her for a moment in stunned silence. Betty shrugged. "It's not lethal if she gets medical attention soon, so what are we waiting for? Let's go before they get here."

But it was too late. The security guards were on their way, forcing them to turn away from the front door and try to escape out the back with the gun-toting men close behind. Joey picked up Roger and Fred, putting them in Melusine's lap because otherwise, they wouldn't have kept up. They escaped into the balmy night air. Betty managed to shoot down a few of their pursuers as they ran, holding onto Joey's arm to guide her as they stumbled along the uneven earth.

Security was surrounding them, herding them towards the cliff's edge. Joey stopped short, grabbing Betty so that she didn't go over. She pulled the trigger at the nearest guard, but the cylinder clicked. They were out of bullets and time. But there was still something Melusine could do. Putting all her intent into her voice, she began to sing in her mermaid tongue. She sang her grief for Pierre, her fear for herself and her family, and her anger at the Haddishes. The men began to weep as they felt her pain, collapsing on the ground—but then a crack of thunder rang out.

With a cry, Betty staggered backwards. Before anyone could catch her, she fell into the water far below. William emerged holding a gun, followed by his father. Melusine let out a furious shriek, and they doubled over in agony as it grew higher and higher, their eyes and ears bleeding. Joey grabbed her shoulder, and she stopped. Though the rest of her friends had blood coming from their ears as well, they seemed better off than the millionaire and his son.

With a final glance, she pushed off Roger and Fred, and propelled herself off the cliff. She dove into the water and followed the smell of blood to Betty where she floated near the middle of the lake. Grabbing her by the waist, she dragged her to the surface and then to shore. She wasn't breathing, but her pulse was still there, so Melusine began to push on her chest like she'd seen a lifeguard do to a drowning victim on the beach.

"Betty, my love, please don't leave me," she whispered, blowing air into her lungs and pressing her chest again.

Betty began to cough, retching as she turned onto her side and expelled the water she'd inhaled. Melusine maneuvered her into her lap and applied pressure to the injury. Luckily, it seemed to be only a flesh wound. "This better not become a habit of ours," Betty said with a weak chuckle.

"Stop falling into water and I'll stop needing to rescue you." There were three splashes as bodies fell from above, but no one emerged from the water. Minutes later, Fred, Roger, and Joey ran up. "You guys okay?"

"We'll live. Where are the Haddishes and Hank?" Melusine asked.

Fred grinned. "They won't be bothering us again. Let's just say they went for a swim."

"A pity," Betty said, "and with no mermaid to rescue them."

"Let's get you to a hospital," Joey said, helping her up, but her legs gave out under her when she tried to stand. He glanced between her and Melusine. "I can't carry both of you."

"I'll stay. You can come back for me later." She would be alone again, but that didn't matter if Betty was okay.

"We'll stay with Mel," Roger said, "Go on. We'll be okay." She looked at both men in surprise.

Betty smiled as Joey lifted her up and held out a hand for Melusine. "After all, we take care our own."

Melusine kissed her knuckles. "Freaks look out for fellow freaks."

— FIN —

The musical scales fall away piece by piece, followed by the sounds of the ocean, leaving only the drumroll of the rain and the sound of the standing glass behind you to your left letting go. Your host withdraws the shell, circling back to xer side of the table and depositing it with the rest of its ilk as xe goes. The milieu takes up a large chunk of the table by now, reminding you of the collage melanges presented in the I Spy *picture books you remember reading when you were younger.*

"Sixteen stories. Four sets of four, two sets of eight—however you slice it, your task as spectator is almost at an end." Didi crosses the table to his misstrex, who scratches him behind the ears. "More's the pity." The smile returns, and again you try to tell whether it is mocking or mirthful. "You could stay, you know. Join the show. Surely, there's something you could do here. Pop the popcorn, or sweep the sawdust, or make balloon animals." For a moment you imagine it, indulging the fantasy—flipping your life upside down in an instant, leaving whatever it is that's ailing you here behind, folding yourself up along with the tents and sending yourself down the river to whatever destination awaits down the line...

The brim of xer hat tilts at just such an angle that it resembles the rings of a dark and distant planet, and from those depths emerges a hand puppet, the cruelly twisted face of a Mr. Punch doll. "We've been going in circles for a while," xe says, the bells of the puppet's hat tinkling. "Up, down, round and round and round..." xe says. "The faces change, and the playing field, but the game never does. A reversal of roles, a changing of power. You can dress it up as pretty as you want, try to disguise the shape of the thing with pomp and circumstance, but this penultimate tale reminds us that..."

XVII. You Ain't Fooling Nobody

performed by Jude Deluca

A Week Ago

'Twas the night of the 16th, and all through the dorm room a creature was stirring: more accurately, a creature was *scratching*. He scratched, and scratched, and scratched, but the itch refused to yield.

Peter Dominique threw off the covers with a frustrated groan as he reached toward the lamp on his bedside table. Free from the heavy down blanket, he felt the full force of the radiator. The room was like an oven; he was practically drenched in sweat. He yanked off his soaked shirt to spare himself from drowning. In the glow from the lamp, he saw his roommate's bed was empty. He figured Jake was still out doing God knows what, but could've sworn he heard someone coming in ages ago. Peter chalked it up to being half asleep. *Fucking sleep paralysis…* he thought.

With the darkness of the room abated, Peter saw firsthand the damage he inflicted on himself. Tonight, his eczema was particularly bad. It usually flared up during wintertime, but Peter believed tonight set a record in terms of pain. The heat only made it worse, but with how wonky the pipes could be in the building he didn't dare crack a window. Peter made a motion of rubbing his hands together to alleviate the burning sensation coursing through his digits until they practically felt raw.

As he focused on the watery, blister-like marks on his fingers, desperately popping them like zits to permanently get rid of them, he had to ignore the itchiness of his calves. When at last he felt a momentary relief in his hands, Peter raked his nails up and down the dry skin of his legs.

"Ow!"

Peter brought away his right hand to see red beneath his nails. He had scratched so hard he drew blood, which was nothing compared to the cracked, scabby marks at the base of his fingers having freshly broken open. The sight made him nauseous.

"The hell with this," Peter muttered. Despite how badly he wanted to sleep, he knew he'd be up all night scratching if he didn't apply some lotion. Common sense and experience dictated he should've done so before going to bed, but can you blame a guy for being exhausted? After a long day of classes, exams, and team practice, the sweet siren song of sleep was too alluring. Not to mention, tomorrow was the big day. One of the most important days for Ivy Falls State University.

Peter watched the neon red number on his digital clock blink from 11:59 pm to midnight. It was now December 17th. Saturn Week at Ivy Falls had begun.

Though giddy at what tomorrow would bring and the role he'd play in the festivities, it also made Peter more desperate to get some sleep. There was no way he'd start an ostentatious occasion like Saturn Week with no energy. As he passed by the closet on the way to the bathroom, he thought about what was hidden inside. A great honor had been bestowed on him which he'd carry with pride. He couldn't help but giggle.

It was too bad he didn't hear the matching giggle from inside the closet.

Turning on the overhead light, Peter navigated through Jake's dirty laundry on the tile floor to reach the sink. Opening the cabinet beneath it, Peter removed a large, industrial-size bottle of cocoa butter. Though the budget of a third-year college student was woeful indeed, Peter justified the extravagance on account of his medical condition. For added measure, he wrote it off as a holiday gift to himself.

Popping open the top, Peter generously squirted a heaping dose of lotion into his palms. He vigorously rubbed cocoa butter up and down his arms; he made a motion akin to washing his hands to ensure his poor fingers were coated. With another heavy dose from the bottle, he went about providing relief to his poor legs. The creamy scent alone brought a sense of relief to his mind.

The relief vanished in a microsecond, replaced by screams of agony.

"*AAAAHHH!!! AAAAHHH!!!*" Peter dropped to his knees, but they too felt as though they'd been set on fire. His arms and hands burned, the skin turning an inhuman shade of red. While he screamed, Peter dug his nails deep into his arms. He scratched harder than he had ever scratched before. Blood ran down his fingers, which were starting to blister furiously, and he looked down at his legs, which were similarly red. He wanted to scratch at the marks on his calves, but to focus on them would make the pain intensify in his arms.

Knocking the cocoa butter off the sink, Peter fumbled, trying to turn the water on. He forced his mind to ignore the torture he was experiencing, telling himself water would fix everything.

If only the water would flow.

"What's wrong?! Why isn't anything-aaahhh!!!" Peter tried to understand why the sink wasn't working, why salvation wasn't pouring from the metal fixture no matter how he turned the knobs. That's when he remembered the bath.

Peter threw himself across the bathroom, almost cracking his head on the side of the tub. Sobbing from the pain, Peter crawled into the tub and reached toward the handle. He prayed the water still worked in the shower. Frantically his peeling fingers tried to hold onto the faucet.

His tears of pain became tears of joy as he heard a familiar groan from the pipes. His prayers had been answered.

His prayers were answered by a cruel god, it seemed, as the water pouring forth from the showerhead brought more suffering. He screamed louder as the fire spread to his chest, back, and face. The blisters popped and peeled, the red turning white. He only had enough cognitive thought not hijacked by pain to recognize the familiar scent drenching his body.

Pure chlorine.

As the chemical mixed with his blood, Peter scratched his face. Scratched his eyes. Something ruptured. Blood flowed down his blistered cheeks, the skin coming loose beneath his fingers. He scratched and scratched as his body peeled and peeled, while someone else in the room laughed and laughed.

"That…" Peter choked, having little strength or vision to look at the green-and-silver clad figure standing above him. But he knew that laugh anywhere. "That's not… fun…n…"

"Who cares if *you* think it's funny?"

Tonight—Several Hours Ago

"Ty, c'mon, let's go back to your place and order a pizza or something. Ty!"

Kitrina "Kix" Victoria sighed in frustration as she followed her humiliated boyfriend. She could still hear the echoing laughter coming from L.L. Coffee Bean. The snow had stopped falling, and Ty Cochran's heavy boots crunched the cold white powder beneath them on the ground. The streetlamps glowed, adorned with festive lights of red and green, blue and white, green and silver. Many of them were draped in streamers of green and silver foil or decorated with cutouts of carnival masks hanging from their sconces. Though the lamps brought illumination to the night, they did nothing to brighten Ty's mood.

This is why I hate Saturn Week, Kix thought. *Everyone turns into a five-year-old.*

She easily kept up with Ty thanks to her long legs, the legs of a champion swimmer. "Are you going to spend the whole night sulking?" Kix asked. "You're the one who kept saying Saturn Week's not a big deal."

"When you're not the one everyone's laughing at!" Ty shouted.

"Look at it this way; tonight's the last night," Kix reasoned. *And thank God for that.*

"You don't get it Kix," Ty snarled. "For as long as I've been at Ivy Falls, I managed to avoid getting pranked during Saturn Week. I could see them coming from a mile away. Until now. My older brother made it through four years without getting pranked when he went here, and so did our dad and *his* dad. No one's ever gotten the best of us Cochran boys!"

"You're acting like they dumped pigs' blood on your head," Kix declared.

"I'd prefer pigs' blood compared to what happened!"

"Ty." Kix folded her arms across her chest, making a good impersonation of an exasperated mother. "You sat on a whoopee cushion."

"Just forget it!" Ty threw his hands up before turning to leave, clearly incapable of making Kix see his point of view.

Pinching the bridge of her nose with her gloved hand, she asked out loud: "*Why* did I have to get accepted by the only school in the country with a jester for a mascot?"

Because Ivy Falls State U has one of the best swim teams in the state, she reminded herself. *Because even though this place is like someone froze the 1990s in a bubble and everyone wears too much flannel, and sure, yeah someone was found dead in the pool, they've got an excellent faculty for sports medicine.*

But after three years of Saturn Week, seven whole days of something akin to April Fools' Day on steroids, Kix wondered if it was worth it. She didn't even have the energy to look forward to the upcoming "Feast of Fools" being held the next evening to signify the end of the festivities. Though she admitted until tonight, this year's Saturn Week was surprisingly tame. No one even saw—

"The Lord of Misrule!"

Damn it! Kix thought as she heard the familiar jingling of bells. She ran up to Ty, who was currently facing the living symbol of the Ivy Falls Jesters. Clad in an old-fashioned motley costume of green and silver (the college's colors), the fully masked Lord of Misrule gave an exaggerated bow and tip of his hat to the pair.

"Where the fuck were you hiding?" Ty demanded. "Wait, was that shit in the coffee shop because of you?!"

The Lord of Misrule dramatically placed his hands on his chest to pantomime *Who, ME?*

Every year, Saturn Week was kicked off by the Lord of Misrule. The person secretly selected to wear the costume by the highest ranked of the college's various teams (this year water polo got to choose) had the dubious honor of leading the light-hearted and well-intentioned mischief the college practically choked on every December. This year, though there were still your average practical jokers having their belly laughs, no one could directly attribute any of the hijinks to the Lord of Misrule.

"Ty, please," Kix begged. She turned to the jester and said "Look, Ty's already been pranked tonight so can we skip this please?"

The Lord of Misrule made a motion of rubbing at the eye holes on the mask, as though he were crying. Kix wondered who was wearing the costume this year. She heard offhand from her gal pal Bambi Mothersburgh it might've been Bambi's boyfriend Peter Dominique, but he hadn't been seen on campus for over a week. Maybe he had gone home for the holidays.

Come to think of it, Kix thought, *I haven't seen Bambi in a while either.*

Ty grabbed the jester and growled, "Listen you little—"

The Lord held up his index finger, then pulled out a bouquet of flowers from behind his back. Ty cried out and dropped the jester, who then got on one knee as he offered them in Kix's direction.

Kix found herself almost at a loss for words by the gesture. "I, I don't—?"

A stream of water shot out of the flowers. Kix dodged, meaning the spray hit Ty directly in the face.

"Oh come on!" Ty sputtered. "Jesus, what is this? It stinks! Ugh, it got in my mouth!"

The jester dropped the flowers and pretended to be shocked. He clapped his hands before pulling out a multicolored handkerchief from his sleeve. With a flourish he offered it to Ty.

"Ty no!" Kix shouted, sensing another prank. Too late. Ty pressed the handkerchief to his face to wipe off the foul-smelling substance. His groans of disgust became cries of confusion as he tried to pull the handkerchief off his face with no success. Kix shook her head. *You walked right into that one, Ty.*

"The hell?" His voice came out muffled as heTy yanked on the cloth. "The fucking thing won't come off!"

"Ty, don't pull on it!" Kix warned. She turned to the jester. "Joke's over, tell us how to get it off." The jester looked around before pointing to himself, as though Kix were speaking to someone else. "Seriously, this isn't funny!" She ran to Ty to assist him, but in his oblivious panic he knocked Kix to the ground. "Ty calm down!"

"It hurts!" Ty screamed. "Kix, it burns! I can't get it off! *Help me!*"

Kix tried to get up when the Lord of Misrule skipped over to Ty, the bells on his suit jingling with each step. He moved without a care in the world before he firmly placed his hands around Ty's wrists.

RRRRRRRIP!

Kix stood there, the sound akin to wet Velcro straps being torn apart.

Under the streetlamps, the Lord of Misrule took a step back from Ty to admire his handiwork.

Her boyfriend stood there in silence, wide-eyed, the handkerchief finally removed from his head—

—Along with most of his face.

She could make out a map of raw nerves and muscle where Ty's cheeks and lips had been, but the only expression she could recognize came directly from his eyes; a look of failed comprehension as he tried to determine what just occurred. The handkerchief fell from his hands not with a flutter, but a heavy wet *PLOP* on the snow. Kix's gaze wandered down to where the remnants of her boyfriend's face now lay on the ground.

Ty let out a wet gurgle, still numb from the shock, while blood dripped onto the snow.

The Lord of Misrule slowly turned his masked, grinning face towards Kix. He pulled from his other sleeve a baton topped with an identical jester head.

Anger and terror overriding common sense, she ran forward with her fist pulled back.

The Lord of Misrule pulled his arm back just as quickly.

WHACK!

Silver and green danced in Kix's eyes before the world vanished into black.

♠ ♠ ♠

TONIGHT—NOW

Kix groaned as the darkness was ripped away by a piercing light..She wanted to both shield her eyes from it and do something about the throbbing sensation on the side of her head, but for some reason, her hands wouldn't obey her commands.

"Kix?" A familiar voice weakly asked. "He got you too?"

Blinking, Kix turned towards the voice coming from her left side. She couldn't tell if she was awake or dreaming.

Is this what a concussion feels like?

"B-Bambi?" Kix groaned again. Seated next to her was her dear friend, who looked even worse than Kix felt. Bambi's eyes were red and bloodshot, her face stained with dry tears, her hair greasy and matted. The blonde woman's usually rosy complexion was sallow. Bags hung beneath her tired eyes. "Bambi, what…?"

"Welcome to the party, hon," a different voice announced. Kix strained to see beyond Bambi towards another woman, a redhead, seated next to her. She tried to lean forward to get a better view of their companion, and in the process discovered why her arms weren't listening. Looking down, she found her wrists bound to armrests with colorful ropes.

"The fuck?" Kix shouted, snapping to full awareness as she tried to pull her arms free.

"That's how we all felt," the redhead explained with sympathy. She looked just as exhausted as Bambi, but not quite as emotionally devastated. "Hi. I'm Honey Sheffield. Cooking major. You're Kix Victoria, right? Bambi's told us a lot about you."

We all? Kix wondered, before turning to her right. There were two others bound to seats, making five captives in total.

"Toni Butler, creative writing," the woman closest to Kix introduced herself.

"Chanel Dupree, fashion design," the woman to Toni's right revealed. "I wonder if you're here that means he's finally done or if he's 'invited' anyone else," Chanel said curtly.

"You mean the psycho who tore my boyfriend's face off?" Kix looked around. All five were bathed in light, but the rest of the

~220~

room was pitch dark. They were surrounded by vague shapes and outlines. Or maybe her head injury made it difficult to see; she probably did have a concussion. "Where are we?"

"We don't have a clue," Honey explained. "I was snatched after Bambi. We kept hoping the next arrival would be awake long enough to know where he took us. I'm guessing that bump on your head means you were not."

"Is it that bad?" Kix asked.

"Nothing some concealer won't fix," Chanel offered.

"What does he want with us?" Bambi asked in tears.

Toni rolled her eyes. "You know what he wants from us."

"What?" Kix asked.

"Obviously, he's gonna kill us," Toni the writer admitted bluntly..

Bambi started hyperventilating, earning groans of frustration from Chanel and Honey. Honey said, "Did you have to rile her up again, Toni?"

"When a man dresses like a clown and kidnaps five young women, I highly doubt he plans for those women to live!" Toni argued. "It's common sense!"

"If you're living in a bad horror movie!" Chanel screamed.

"Oh I'm sorry, and where have *you* been living for the past week?!" Toni nudged towards Kix, saying "She just said he killed her boyfriend! He probably killed ours, too!"

"It's alright Bambi, we're gonna make it out of this," Honey tried to comfort the panicking blonde, but Kix doubted Honey really believed her words.

That doubt intensified as the rest of the area was bathed in lights. The five captives cried out in surprise, seeing now they were confined inside an old theatre: in fact, they saw they were given front row seats.

Heavy red curtains were pulled apart to reveal a stage set like a Renaissance fair, a badly-painted backdrop of a medieval town with peasants and knights and nobles haphazardly crammed together to give an idea of the Middle Ages. Speakers built in the wings crackled to life, and the women heard a lute being plucked.

A body dropped down from the top of the stage, suspended from wires.

"Peter!" Bambi sobbed at the sight of her boyfriend's naked corpse. Peter Dominique's body was covered in rotting blisters and chemical burns, most of his skin having peeled away. Bambi's crying intensified as the wires wrapped around Peter's wrists and ankles jerked his body to-and-fro in a gross mockery of life.

Kix felt her stomach turn when a second body descended next to Peter to join the dance.

"Bobby? Bobby?!" Honey cried out at the sight of the bloated, bulging body hanging next to Peter. Her boyfriend's face was hideously distorted, an apple crammed in his mouth. The body jiggled haphazardly like some depraved balloon for a Thanksgiving parade hosted in Hell. "*You bastard! What did you do to him?! Bobby!*"

It was Chanel's turn to scream when the next body dropped. Kix could barely make out the name she shouted over Bambi's crying and Honey's pleading. The limbs rotated around and around, the head twisting in circles. They'd been chopped off and sewn back.

A blackened, smoldering skeleton fell in place next to Chanel's lover. Kix heard retching. She didn't need to guess that it was Toni who vomited. They could smell bits of charred flesh from their seats, and Kix was thankful she hadn't eaten anything tonight.

She didn't make a sound as Ty's faceless body completed the danse macabre. While she tried to break free of her bonds, she remained silent as her unwilling companions made their horror and despair vocally known.

"*Long, long ago,*" a voice on stage declared, "*Saturnalia was considered a time when society was flipped on its heads.*"

Kix's eyes widened. *I know that voice,* she thought.

"*It was the Romans who invented the holiday, in reverence towards the god of time. Medieval societies in Europe appropriated some of Saturnalia's tenants into their Feast of Fools, to the point where the two are sometimes viewed as the same thing. The Romans turned everything topsy-turvy, granting a feast to the slaves who usually catered to their every whim under threat of death. Such a thing was considered hilarious back then. A lowly peasant was given the honor of being the Lord of Misrule.*" The voice continued over the music and frightened hysteria of his captive audience. "*The royals and elites had to obey the Lord of Misrule if they valued their lives. The upper class experienced degradation and humiliation, just like the poor and downtrodden they'd humiliate daily. But for them, it was* fun. *No sense of shame. All a joke. You see—*"/

"Shut uuuuuuuuuuuuuup!"

The four captives stopped their screaming, their heads turned towards Kix in shock. Even the voice on stage momentarily stalled.

"*Uh,*" the voice tried to continue. "*You see the royals—*"

"Shut up!" Kix screamed again. "SHUT UP, SHUT UP, SHUT UP, *SHUT THE FUCK UP! You think this is funny?! You think this is scary, huh, you piece of shit?!* Oh yeah, you're fucking horrifying with your props and your pantomime bullshit or whatever the fuck you'd call that! You think you're so smart, so clever, you're full of shit! Hiding behind your fucking clown costume like a coward! Why don't you grow some balls, *Alex?!*"

"Alex?!" was the resounding chorus from the other four , their heads snapping back towards the stage. It was Bambi who said, "Alex Cresky?!"

The five heard the jingling of bells as a familiar figure emerged on stage.

"You couldn't let me have my moment, could you?!" The Lord of Misrule whined. "I had this whole thing planned for weeks and—"

"No one cares!" Kix screamed. "Alright? No one *FUCKING* cares, Alex!"

"I can't believe I was kidnapped by Alex Cresky," Honey moaned.

"No, no, there's no way that's him," Chanel shook her head.

"You better fucking believe it," the Lord of Misrule snarled as he ripped off his mask to reveal the sweaty, angular face of one Alex Cresky. Tossing the mask aside, he jumped off stage and got right up in Kix's face. "And you better watch your fucking mouth. In case you haven't noticed, all of you are at *my* mercy for once. Like all your precious little boy toys were. Thinking they're so great, strutting around—"

"Oh my God!" Kix cut him off once again. "We already get the picture, Alex! You and every other incel loser out there who decided to get even with the girls who wouldn't give them the time of day. Do you just love hearing your own voice? What part of 'no one cares' do you not—?!"

SMACK!

The four girls recoiled as Alex backhanded Kix in the face.

"And what part of 'at my mercy' do *you* not get?!" Alex screamed as he smacked Kix again. Bambi and the others screamed at him to stop as he brutalized her, but he ignored them. "Years of being pushed around! Being ignored by sanctimonious bitches and pinheads with no brains! Stepped on like I was nothing! Well *I'M* the king now! This is *MY* feast and you're all the main course! It's my turn to have the last laugh! All of you are just part of the fucking! *Punchline*!"

Kix spat blood in his direction. She felt one of her teeth come loose as he grabbed her face. His breath smelled surprisingly minty fresh as he leaned in to say "It's the fool's time to shine, sweetheart. It's my spotlight and I'm not sharing my chance to monologue with anyone. Now do us both a favor and gimme me a nice big smile before you make me *angry*."

Kix smiled.

WHUMP!

Alex screamed. He collapsed on the floor, moaning in agony. His hands grasped down at his nether regions from where Kix shoved her knee straight into his groin. Alex cried out again as brought her foot against his jaw.

Kix rubbed the bruises on her face. "You suck at tying knots."

The Lord of Misrule sobbed, huddled on the ground. As she stood up, Kix reached over and undid one of the ropes tying Bambi's hands down. Bambi quickly went to work freeing her other hand as Kix helped Honey, Toni, and Chanel while Alex tried to stand.

"You," he gasped as he tried to stand. "I'm—"

WHAM!

Kix socked him in the jaw, sending him down.

"You think you're fucking smart?!" Kix shouted as she punched him again. Alex stumbled towards a free Bambi, who delivered a punch of her own.

"You think you're funny?!" Bambi shrieked, her rage giving her a surge of energy despite how starved and exhausted she still felt.

"I-I'm sorry," Alex begged, all his sadistic bravado now gone as the five girls surrounded him at the base of the stage. "I-I didn't—please st—"

"Who the fuck do you think you are?!" Honey shouted as she shattered his nose. She didn't care about the pain in her hand as the skin on her knuckles tore open from the punch. Blood sprayed from his nostrils when Honey pushed him towards Chanel. Chanel swung his own jester's staff at Alex's head, shattering his cheekbone.

"Yeah, you're a real man, aren't you?!" Chanel screamed as Alex dropped like a sack of bricks. On his back, he feebly held his hands up as Toni stomped his stomach. Puke and blood emerged from his mouth.

"Who! Do you think! You're! Kidding! You! Fucking! *Monster!*"

All five pounced on the broken clown.

"Fuck you!"

"Fuck you!"

"*FUCK! YOU!*"

HOURS LATER

Heavily bandaged and tired of speaking with police officers, Kix dragged herself into her dorm room. She didn't care if they thought she should stay at the hospital; Kix wanted to crawl into her bed and never leave again. Thankfully her roommate Alice wasn't present to ask any questions she didn't feel like answering again.

After beating Alex Cresky to a pulp, the five had found a phone and called the cops. The other four were being treated for malnourishment; it was a miracle they found the ability to deliver that beating, but rage can give a person surprising strength.

In truth, she and the other girls had absolutely no idea what spurredCresky into his murderous rampage, and they didn't care. Whether or not he was treated as badly as he had ranted in the old theatre, even Saturn Week didn't give him the right to kill five people in cold blood and violate their bodies for his amusement. Kix was fine with never gaining any answers. All that mattered was that it was over and the festivities were done for another year.

She felt around in her mouth where her tooth was missing. As she sat on her bed, she wondered what her dental insurance—

PFFFFFFFFFFFFFT!!!!

Kix sat in silence for several minutes before she removed a whoopee cushion from beneath her blanket. Attached was a note: *GOTCHA! <3 Alice.*

"Heh. Heh heh. Ahaha. *Ahahaha! Ahahahahahahaha! Ahahaha AHAHAHAHAHA!!*"

Kix ripped apart the plastic cushion as she fell into hysterics, shredding the note attached to it like confetti.

Alice. Alice. Alice.

Tears streamed down her face as she laughed, thinking of how terrified she'd been only hours before. Seeing Ty with his face torn off. Those dead bodies suspended like puppets. The sheer hatred in Alex Cresky's voice and eyes as he hit her again, and again, and again.

The blood had flowed as the five girls pummeled Alex's body long after he'd been dead, leaving him an unrecognizable lump of torn flesh and broken bone amidst the corpses of their five lovers.

"It's my turn to have the last laugh!"

Though she had tried to be brave, tried to bluff the jester to get his guard down, as her laughter turned to sobs, Kix just couldn't fool herself any longer.

— FIN —

*With thanks to L.T. Williams
and to The Spice Girls.*

♣ ♣

"*A*nd that's *the way to do it!" says your host, the hand puppet taking his bows as the next-to-last mirror shatters behind you to your right. Then xer hand is only a hand again, the empty skin of the cruel little clown landing amongst the rest. The end is so near, your task so close to complete. You look straight ahead, past your host and the cat and the items piled on the table, to the final mirror, standing straight across from you on the other side of a ring which is a fraction of the size it was when you entered.*

The lion tamer in the sky cracks his whip once more, the strongest burst of thunder yet shaking the tent as you stare into the silvered sand in its ornate frame. In your head swim all of the things you've seen and felt and tasted and lived tonight—clowns wearing crowns, mermaids both counterfeit and real, things from beyond the stars and things from a home that is far too close for comfort; sharp teeth and dancing shadows, the living dead and the living pretending at death, chains broken and chains forged. "One tale remains," your host says. "One story left to live, and then you are free to go." You watch in hunger as the hat falls from xer head into xer hand one final time, as xe reaches inside to reveal...

"There you are!" your friend's voice says, their nails digging into your shoulders. "We need to get the fuck out of here, now."

You look over your shoulder, turn, see the wild, rolling fear in your friend's eyes, and then look back to the host. You try to protest, to throw them off and explain that this is far more important, but they wrench you to your feet. Didi hisses in displeasure, but your host merely watches, expression unreadable.

"I said now!" they command, pulling you towards the edge of the ring, away from the table, away from what you are so close to finishing... but whatever your friend has seen to fill them with such fear fills them with strength as well, and you find yourself compelled towards the curtains. "Come on!" You see the final mirror disappear, unbroken and unblemished, as you are wrestled back into velvet blackness, leaving the ring behind. Absurdly, you remember your lemonade still sits half-drunk on the table.

Your friend's hand grasps yours, tugging you through the maze of folded fabric, pressing heavy against you from every side, as if you are fighting your way out of the belly of some enormous stuffed beast. Surely, there had not been such a labyrinth when you had entered...?

A burst of staticky panic pops in your brain like the electric lights of the sign exploding, fear and terror at the consequences of leaving before you have completed your task, but then the voice of the storyteller breathes in your ear one final time.

"All part of the show..." the darkness whispers, and as you erupt out into the pounding rain, you understand the lesson: sometimes, the ride robs you of symmetry. Sometimes, the means deny an easy end. Sometimes, the odd trumps the even. This, you understand, is the last story—whatever waits beyond the gates, back out in the World.

The festival moves by in a blur as your friend darts around corners, dragging you through the alleys of the tent city, emptied of foot traffic by the rain. The mud splashes up against your shins as you run through a courtyard you had not seen before, a carousel at the center, turning and turning and turning despite the wind and the weather, sending twinkling calliope notes between the raindrops. You want to slow down, to watch its lonely ride, but then you are zipping through a door in the fence you had not noticed, stumbling together out onto the tarmac of the parking lot beyond.

NO REENTRY, *reads the plaque bolted to the bars.*

You keep running until you reach the overhang of the distant strip mall, the sudden lack of dark caramel and sizzling salt in the air tells you that you have left the land of fancy behind. You stop outside of an empty storefront, and now, finally, your friend slows, kneeling in the rain, laughing and shaking their head. Before you can ask, they look up at you with burning eyes, and you understand that whatever it is, they will not, or can not, tell. "What the fuck is wrong with you?" they spit. "I was looking for you everywhere. Who fuck was that freak with the cat?" They reach into their shirt and pull out their phone. "Dead!" they exclaim, swearing loudly. "Do you have any juice?"

You look up at the night sky as it splits open once again, looking through the rain and through the dark to the shimmering toyland you have left behind. The sound of breaking glass sparkles in your ears as you realize that the chime to which you had grown so accustomed is one you will never hear again, a moment of haunting melody which now is only memory. You wonder if the rest of the mirrors have already reset, waiting for the next seeker to wander into the tent, to trigger the series of unfortunate events which waited for them across the table. Your facepaint, disfigured by the rain, runs down your cheeks like tears.

"I asked if you can call an Uber," your friend says. "I need to get home, and I need a fucking beer, okay?" As they bury their face back in their hands, you're unable to tell if the noises they're making are whimpers of laughter or grief, and only now, on the other side, it occurs to you that the whole desperate exodus might have been a trick, that you had been robbed of your grande finale for nothing.

The rain has swallowed the tents completely now, turning the world beyond the fence to a glowing smudge behind the bars of falling water. The lightning licks once more and you see the shape of it a final time, stark like newspaper ink against the white sky. Like your host dipping into the hat, you reach into your jacket for your phone, but instead find only your printed paper ticket, safe and dry.

CAST BIOS

SAM LOGAN (he/him, "What's In a Clown Name?") emerged in 1984 from the depths of the Chesapeake Bay off the Maryland shore. He made it to Oregon where he is a university professor in kinesiology and teaches courses about punk and body horror. Sam lives with his partner, kiddo, and Dune the dog. He has stories in *Mouthfeel Fiction, Punk Noir Magazine, Divinations Magazine, Major 7th Magazine, Underbelly Press*, and *Wallstrait* (forthcoming).

KATHRYN HEALY ("The Lake Michigan Mermaid, & Other Freaks of Nature") is a horror author and narrative designer, as well as a writer for the "Tale Foundry" Youtube Channel. Her work has been featured in *Beyond and Within: Folk Horror* (Flame Tree Press), *December Tales II* (Curious Blue Press), and *Creepy Podcast*, among others. She can be found online at kathrynhealy.com, or in person wherever haunted antiques are sold.

TOSHIYA KAMEI (she/they, "On Gossamer Wings") takes inspiration from fairy tales, folklore, and mythology. They attempt to reimagine the past, present, and future while shifting between various perspectives and points of view. Many of their characters are outsiders living on the margins of society.

JOHN GREY ("A Clown Act") is an Australian poet, US resident, recently published in *New World Writing, North Dakota Quarterly* and *Lost Pilots*. John's latest books, *Between Two Fires, Covert* and *Memory Outside The Head* are available through Amazon, with work upcoming in *California Quarterly, Birmingham Arts Journal, La Presa* and *Shot Glass Journal*.

DIANE FUNSTON (she/hers, "Night") writes poetry of nature and human nature. She most recently has been the Yuba-Sutter Arts and Culture Poet-in-Residence for two years. It is in this role she created Poetry Square, a monthly online venue that featured poets from all over the world reading their work and discussing creative process. Diane has been published in *Synkronicity, California Quarterly, Whirlwind, San Diego Poetry Annual, Summation, Tule Review, Lake Affect*

Magazine, *F(r)iction*, and other literary journals. Her first chapbook, *Over the Falls* was published July 2022 from Foothills Publishing.

CATHY JOYCE LEE ("The Curtain") can be found forest bathing at night and paddling on the rivers by day. She enjoys exploring the unknown in the physical and creative worlds. Her professional job allows her to write health and wellness articles for daycare providers and offer professional training opportunities to the same audience. Her passion is writing poetry that reflects a connection to life, death and the unknown all of which can be subtle, beautiful, haunting and dark. This author has previously been published in *7th-Circle Pyrite, Young Ravens Literary Review, Pure Slush* and *Passager.*

FRITZ DRIES ("Last Night at the Circus") is a poet and laborer from Ontario. He has published three collections, Harvest Dogs, Four Seconds and Bury Your Teeth in the Yard.
—Twitter: @howlingmoth

DANIELLE DAVIS (she/her, "Quiksilver") is a liar, a cheater at cards, and a misrememberer of song lyrics: only two of these are true. Her horror and dark fantasy have appeared in *The Santa Barbara Literary Journal, Andromeda Spaceways Magazine,* and 45+ anthologies. She is also the author of *Bone on Bone: A Collection of Short Stories.* An active contributor to Writer Unboxed, she is also a member of Horror Writers of America (HWA). You can find her on most social media under the handle "LiteraryEllyMay" and at www.literaryellymay.com.

SERGIO "ENTE PER ENTE" PALUMBO ("House of the Dancing Shadow") is an Italian public servant who graduated from Law School working in the public real estate branch. He is also a co-editor, together with Mrs. Michele Dutcher, of the new steampunk anthology *Steam-Powered Dream Engines,* published in 2018 by Rogue Planet Press, an imprint of British Horrified Press, and of the new fantasy/sci-fi anthology *Fantastical Savannahs and Jungles,* published in march 2019 by the same publisher. The subsequent book edited by him, together with Mrs. Michele Dutcher, is the new sci-Fi anthology *Xenobiology – Stranger Creatures",* published in 2020 by Rogue Planet Press, an imprint of British Horrified Press. In 2021 he edited, along with Mrs. Michele Dutcher and Mr. Curtis Magnes as co-editor, the anthology *Bleakest Towers*, published by Rogue Planet Press. In 2022 he edited, along with Mr. Curtis Magnes as co-editor, the anthology *Of Poets, Spies and the Unearthliness - Otherworldly tales in the times of Shakespeare and Marlowe*, published by Rogue Planet Press, and, in 2023, the new horror/sci-Fi/fantasy Anthology titled *"Dickensian Steamfantasy — A Very Different 1800s"*, published by British Rogue Planet Press, along with a great many other publications in various other outlets and mediums. He is also a scale modeler who likes mostly science fiction and real space models, some of his little dioramas have been shown also in some Italian scale model magazines like *Soldatini, Model Time, TuttoSoldatini* and online on American site StarShipModeler, MechaModelComp, on the British SFM: UK site, and Italian SMF .

DIANE ARRELLE, ("The Queen") the pen name of South Jersey writer Dina Leacock, has sold more than 400 short stories and has three published books including *Just A Drop In The Cup*, a collection of short-short stories and her collection of horror stories, *Seasons On The Dark Side*. Retired from being director of a municipal senior citizen center, she is now co-owner of a small publishing company, Jersey Pines Ink LLC. She resides with her sane husband and her insane cat on the edge of the Pine Barrens (home of the Jersey Devil).
—www.arrellewrites.com
—FaceBook: Diane Arrelle

CORRIE HALDANE, ("Freaks", "Iron & Ink") has a number of online and print anthology publications. Most recently, her work can be found in the print anthologies *What We Talk About When We Talk About It Vol. 2* and *Branching Out*. Corrie lives in Holland Landing, Ontario, Canada with her husband and an assortment of their mostly-grown children. She finds inspiration in nature, bubble baths, and carefully curated playlists.

ALICIA HILTON ("Clowning Around Big Top: Where Wishes and Nightmares Come True") is an author, editor, attorney, professor, actor, and former FBI Special Agent. Her work has appeared in *Daily Science Fiction, Gamut, Mslexia, Strange Horizons, Vastarien, Year's Best Hardcore Horror Volumes 4, 5 & 6*, and elsewhere. She is a member of the Horror Writers Association, the Science Fiction and Fantasy Poetry Association, and the Science Fiction and Fantasy Writers Association. Her website is https://aliciahilton.com. Follow her on Twitter @aliciahilton01 and Bluesky @aliciahilton.bsky.social.

CORINNE POLLARD ("Flexible") is a disabled UK horror and dark fantasy writer, published in *Black Hare Press, Carnage House Publishing, Inky Bones Press, Three Cousins Publishing, The Ravens Quoth Press, Raven Tale Publishing, A Coup of Owls Press,* and *The Stygian Lepus.* Corinne writes reviews and the weekly newsletter for The Horror Tree. Also, Corinne is co-editor for the Yorkshire anthology *Aire Reflections* with her dark stories and poetry inside. Aside from writing, Corinne enjoys metal music, visiting graveyards, and shopping for books to read. Follow her dark world on Twitter, Threads, and Instagram: @CorinnePWriter

KERRY E.B. BLACK ("Circus Tent") has authored two YA novels, a novella, a book of poetry, a pseudo-historical novella, and four collections of short stories, and many of her short works have crept into anthologies, magazines, and online journals. When not writing, Kerry sings songs with seniors, advocates for the disabled, and reads (and reviews) everything she can. She's a member of the HWA, Wily Writers, Nomadic Wordsters, and is a Rough Writer at Carrot Ranch. Find more fun facts at www.KerryEBBlack.com

TREVOR WRIGHT ("Of Beast & Blood", "Shattered Self", "The Last Toss") is a poet from Central Illinois who weaves resilience, loss, and the supernatural into his work. His writing dances between the real and the fantastical, inviting readers into worlds full of wonder. After the loss of his mother, he turned to poetry as a way to heal. He lives with his wife and two daughters, finding magic in the everyday. He invites you to follow his creative journey on Instagram @wrightspoetry.

KEVIN HOPSON'S ("The Living Corpse") work has appeared in a variety of anthologies, magazines, and e-zines, and he enjoys writing in multiple genres. You can learn more about Kevin by visiting his website at http://www.kmhopson.com.

WARREN BENEDETTO ("Dragonsbreath") writes dark fiction about horrible people, horrible places, and horrible things. He is an award-winning author who has published over 250 stories, appearing in publications such as *Dark Matter Magazine, Fantasy Magazine, and The Dread Machine*; on podcasts such as *The NoSleep Podcast, Tales to Terrify, and Chilling Tales For Dark Nights*; and in anthologies from Apex Magazine, Tenebrous Press, Scare Street, and many more. He also works in the video game industry, where he holds 50+ patents for various types of gaming technology. For more information, visit warrenbenedetto.com and follow @warrenbenedetto on Twitter and Instagram.

GLEN HELD ("The Takeover") is doing okay as a writer. He's just had a new pulp adventure novel (*The Devil You Know*) published by Airship 27, a similar style book coming out later this year by Pro Se Press as well as short stories published (or about to be published) in issues of *Doc Talos Magazine, Mystic Mind Magazine and Atomic Stories*. Glen is recently retired—for good this time —and lives on Long Island in New York with his wife and the fabulous Eddie the dog. He has recently started to eat salads for lunch and doesn't hate it as much as he thought he would. Visit him on Facebook or Instagram.

KAY HANIFEN ("Carnival Imaginarium Presents: The Siren from the Deep") was born on a Friday the 13th and once lived for three months in a haunted castle. So, obviously, she had to become a horror writer. Her work has appeared in over forty anthologies and magazines. When she's not consuming pop culture with the voraciousness of a vampire at a 24-hour blood bank, you can usually find her with her black cats or at kayhanifenauthor.wordpress.com.
—Twitter: https://twitter.com/TheUnicornComi1
—Instagram: https://www.instagram.com/katharinehanifen/

JUDE DELUCA ("You Ain't Fooling Nobody") can be found on Twitter at @judedeluca1990, and on Bluesky, Tumblr, and Instagram at @judedeluca.

V.F. THOMPSON (editor) is both compost in training and a card-carrying member of the World Clown Association.
—Twitter: @VF_Thompson
—Instagram: @v.f.thompson

Acknowledgements

This book would not be possible without those who supported this book on Indiegogo, as well as our previous Halloween anthology, *Trans Rites: An Anthology of Genderfucked Horror*, and those who have held space for our events, supported us on Patreon, or in other forms over these first few years of development.

Ellie Wright, Simon K, Walter Andrew Simpson, Poppet, Charlotte Gremel, Antoinette Del Rae, Tricia Flowers, Alex Riley, jessica gilbert, Makarenna Binimelis, Ju Collins, Lexx Ambrose, Heidi Luby, Heather Green, Carter Cesareo, charlearning, kungfuturtle, Mal Harrigan, Heather Tobin, blaneyma1, Vanessa Hillier, Emily Brent, Dion Power, Alison Power, kpuddister3, Ally Thoden, Kellan McCormick, Leilani Roser, Kirsten Craig, Courtney Bennett, Lisa Campbell, Bridgit Shebib, Emily Shebib, Solaris O'Dell, Christina White, Oma Meade, Soundararajan Varathappan, Mitchell Noel, Kayla Dober, Josh Søn Af Mørten, Stephen Maley, Amanda Hickman, Meagan Thompson, Kel Craghead, Katelyn Hayden, Vivek Subramanian, Nikki Kumar, Karan Kaul, Beth Stephens, Beth Stephens, Dan S, Kat Jepson, Rowan Wright, kale woods, Mathias Lobban, Wendy Boden, Krista Lindemann, Amanda Keith, dasue123, Rebecca Mead, Sy Mander, skandarks, Ria Doolan, Shanmugam Krishnasamy, Sephi Coleman-Tunney, Jay J, Asherah Sussmeine, Kelly Thompson, Books & Mortar, The First Congregational Church of Kalamazoo, Sandra Jatkowski, Jennifer Fargo, Dean & Michigan News Agency, Juniper Books, Alexander Gray and the WMU Student Center staff, the Kalamazoo Nature Center, the Matt Hybels & the Hellhole, Mahtay Cafe & Lounge, Montie House Cooperative, and the WMU Office for Sustainability!

In addition, we would like to thank the **Dormouse Theater** in Kalamazoo for giving us a place to hold the release party for this book, the 2nd Annual From Above, From Below Ball and **Sophie Bonnen** for her patronage of the project.

Enjoy this book? Consider subscribing to future issues
and other Dionysian Public Library projects at
patreon.com/dionysianpubliclibrary.

Don't want to subscribe, but want to be kept in the loop?
Visit us at dionysianpubliclibrary.com or follow us at

Twitter: @DPublicLibrary
Facebook: DioPublicLibrary
Tumblr: dionysianpubliclibrary
Insta: @dionysianpubliclibrary

You can also find our editors on Twitter at and @VF_Thompson
and on Insta at and.

Interested in contributing to future projects?
Take a gander at dionysianpubliclibrary.com/submissions